☑ W9-BWU-857

F
PET
Peters, Elizabeth 19,139

Summer of the dragon

		DATE	
JUN 30	OCT 13	FEB 6	AUG 11
JUN 30	OCT 23	FEB 14	FEB 7
JUL 14	OCT 23	FEB 21	JUN 19
	Nov 6	MAR 15	
	DEC 14	APR 23	JUL 27
AUG 20		MAY 15	
AUG 30	JAN 10	JUN 2	SEP 28
AUG 31		JUN 8	DEC 15
SEP 20	JAN 28		
		JUN 11	FEB 12
SEP 27	FEB 6	JUL 16	MAY 3
			JUN 2

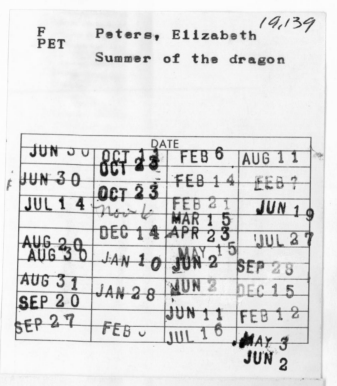

AUSTIN MEMORIAL LIBRARY
220 S. Bonham
Cleveland, Texas 77327

106970

© THE BAKER & TAYLOR CO.

Summer of the Dragon

ALSO BY ELIZABETH PETERS

Summer of the Dragon

ELIZABETH PETERS

Dodd, Mead & Company New York

Copyright © 1979 by Elizabeth Peters
All rights reserved
No part of this book may be reproduced in any form
without permission in writing from the publisher
Printed in the United States of America

1   2   3   4   5   6   7   8   9   10

Library of Congress Cataloging in Publication Data

Peters, Elizabeth.
    Summer of the dragon.

    I. Title.
PZ4.M577Su [PS3563.E747]   813'.5'4   79–9782
ISBN 0–396–07689–0

For Beth and Brian—*the* anthropologists

Summer of the Dragon

Chapter One

I went to Arizona that summer for my health. Talk about irony. . . .

No, I don't have asthma, or anything like that. What I had—and still have, for that matter—was a bad case of parents. Two of them.

Mind you, they are marvelous. I love them. Separately they are unnerving but endurable. Together . . . disaster, sheer disaster. Ulcer-making. Productive of high blood pressure, nervous tension, hives, indigestion, and other psychosomatic disorders.

1

I had not meant to mention my parents. I don't want to hurt their feelings. However, there is no way of accounting for my presence at Hank Hunnicutt's ranch that summer unless I make unkind remarks about Mother and Dad. Pride prevents me from allowing anyone to suppose I went there of my own free will. Oh, well. It's unlikely that they would read a book like this. Mother only reads cookbooks and Barbara Cartland; Dad has never been discovered with any volume less esoteric than the *Journal of Hellenic Studies.*

I am not knocking my mother's literary tastes. She is probably the best cook in the entire Western world, and if, after a life which has included economic depression, World War II, and assorted personal tragedies, she can still believe in Barbara Cartland, then more power to her. I wouldn't mind her believing in *Ro-*mance, with the accent on the first syllable, if she didn't try to foist her opinions on me.

Mother thinks every nice girl ought to get married, read cookbooks, and have lots of children so *she* can be a grandmother. I don't know why she expects me to produce the grandchildren. I have four brothers and sisters. But I'm the oldest, and Mother's grandmotherly instincts began to burgeon when I hit puberty.

Dad thinks that every nice girl, and every nice boy, and all the boys and girls who aren't nice, should be archaeologists. He can't really understand why anyone would want to do anything else. He feels that there are too many people in the world anyway, so if they would just stop perpetuating themselves, then they could all live in the houses that have already been built, and grow just enough food to give themselves the strength to perform mankind's most vital endeavor—digging things up.

2

If he had left me alone, I might have turned out to be a classical archaeologist. It was a case of overkill. The first toy I can remember playing with was not a doll, or a toy train, or a stuffed kitty. It was a Greek stater. (That's an ancient silver coin.) The reason why I remember it is because I swallowed it, and the ensuing hullaballoo left a deep impression on my infant mind.

My room, during my formative years, was a horrible mixture of my parents' tastes. Mother contributed dolls that wet their diapers and threw up. Dad sneaked in copies of antique statues. The walls were hung with drawings of Winnie the Pooh and photographs of the Parthenon. When I outgrew my crib, Mother bought me a canopied bed with ruffles dripping from the top. And Dad found, God knows where, a bedspread with heads of Roman emperors printed on it.

So it went, all the way along: cooking lessons from Mother, visits to museums with Dad. It's no wonder that when I went to college I promptly flunked the introductory Greek course.

At the time I was absolutely crushed. I studied for that course. My God, how I studied! Six hours a day. I'd go in for an exam, smugly sure that I had memorized every ending of every declension, and then my mind would go totally blank. I can see now why it happened, but five years ago, when I was eighteen, I could only conclude that I was hopelessly stupid. I contemplated slashing my wrists. I mean, one takes things so seriously at that age. The day my adviser called me in, to tell me as kindly as possible that I had better drop Greek before it dropped me, I got sick to my stomach at the very idea of calling Dad to tell him I was a failure. I even got out a bottle of aspirin—it was the deadliest drug I owned—and sat contemplating it for about two and a half minutes. Then I remembered that poem of Dorothy Parker's:

Guns aren't lawful;
Nooses give;
Gas smells awful;
You might as well live.

It made better sense than anything I had heard in Greek class. So I went out and had a double hot-fudge banana split and, thus fortified, called Dad.

He didn't yell at me. I knew he wouldn't. He was just sweet and pitying and encouraging, which is lots worse than being yelled at. He's felt sorry for me ever since. Poor girl, she will never be able to read Homer in the original ..

I slid into anthropology through the back door. It was the closest thing I could find to archaeology that didn't require any dead languages. If I ever get to my Ph.D., I'll have to pass an exam in German or French or something, but I do all right with spoken languages; and everybody knows how ridiculous those graduate language exams are.

Anthropology had another advantage. It disappointed both my parents. I mean, living with those two required a delicate balance. International diplomacy is nothing compared to the skill and wit involved in keeping Mother and Dad more or less even in their fond disapproval of my activities. If I pleased one of them, the other fell into a deep depression, while the favored parent gloated offensively. No, the only way to handle them was to keep them both in a gentle sweat of frustration.

I needn't mention what Mother's idea of a suitable college major was, do I? Right. Domestic science, or whatever they call it these days. I wouldn't know. I never got near that part of the university, if there was such a part. I took pains not to find out.

I seem to be wandering off the track here. I was going to get right into the mainstream of the symposium, as one of my duller professors used to say, and explain how I got to Arizona. But you can't possibly understand why I did what I did without some background. I'm almost through with that, but there is one more thing I've got to explain.

My name. I sign all my papers D.J. Abbott. My friends call me D.J. They call me that or they don't stay friends with me. That includes even my childhood friends, who know my real names; I'd have kept the horrible truth from them if I could have, but there was no way of concealing it with Mother bellowing my first name out the front door every afternoon at supper time, and Dad greeting me by my middle name whenever we happened to meet. They couldn't agree on a name any more than they could agree on any other vital subject, so my first name is Mother's contribution and my middle name is Dad's. They reflect the personalities. . . . I'm stalling. I still hate to write it.

Deanna Jowett Abbott is my name, and humble is my station; Cleveland is my dwelling place—but I doubt that heaven is my destination. There, that's done. Every female over fifty who reads this will know where Mother got Deanna. "She had such a bee-yootiful voice," Mother would murmur. "And you look like her, too." They don't rerun Deanna's movies very often, but I caught her once, on the Late Late Show, and I do look a little like her; not as much as Mother thinks, but I've got longish dark hair and one of those round, dimpled faces. Too round, alas, and too dimpled; I don't resort to hot-fudge sundaes only when I'm disturbed. I eat them when I am happy, or working hard, or relaxing, or celebrating, or. . . . That's

5

right, most of the time. I also like pizza and potato chips and cheeseburgers and anything else that is heavier in calories than in food value.

There I go again, getting off the track. Writing a book isn't as easy as I thought, not if you have a disorganized mind.

But before I go into the subject of my disorganized mind I had better finish explaining about my name. Jowett is not a family name. It is the name of a famous English scholar whose translations of Thucydides, Plato, and that crowd, are classics. Can you imagine a man greeting his five-year-old daughter with "Good afternoon, Jowett"? That tells you all you need to know about my father. I needn't have bothered to say anything else.

You may be mildly curious about the names of my brothers and sisters. Ready? Mickey Grote *(History of Greece)* Abbott; Judy Meyer *(Geschichte des Altertums)* Abbott; Shirley Zimmern *(The Greek Commonwealth)* Abbott, and the baby, little Donald Büchsenschütz *(Die Hauptstätten des Gewerbfleisses im klassischen Alterthume)* Abbott. You will not be surprised to learn that Don will turn and run rather than meet Dad out on the street.

So now you know why I insist on being called D.J. I used to sign myself Deejay, when I was a kid. But that's a little too cute for a graduate student.

Surprisingly enough, I did fairly well in anthro. Or perhaps it is not so surprising, since the field probably offers more diversity than almost anything else a person can study. Everybody specializes these days; you can't just be a lawyer, you have to major in criminal law or commercial law or torts—whatever they are. But the specialties in other fields are much more closely related than

6

the hodgepodge of subjects lumped together under the name of anthropology. The word means "the study of man." That's a broad field.

One problem about anthro is that you can't dabble. You have to decide fairly early in the game whether you are going to major in cultural anthropology—the social habits of modern man—or physical anthropology—the physical characteristics of persons living and dead. Each of these subdivisions has *its* subdivisions. Cultural anthropologists study everything from the dating habits of American teenagers (an exotic subspecies if ever there was one) to the nuances of cannibalism. Physical anthropologists can specialize in fossils—the various petrified ancestors of man—or in the characteristics of living populations. I'm trying to keep this simple, but it isn't easy, because the topic is complicated, and it slides over into other disciplines, such as geology, biology, paleontology, and so on.

Then there's archaeology. For a number of reasons, none of which would interest you, New World archaeology is generally considered a subdivision of anthropology, instead of a separate discipline like classical archaeology or Egyptology. Not that anthropologists have refrained from dabbling in Old World archaeology; they get their sticky little fingers into almost everything sooner or later. Look at Margaret Mead. But none of the Near Eastern civilizations influenced the cultures of the Western hemisphere until the descendants of Socrates and Khufu met the Aztecs and did their damnedest to exterminate them. So much for civilization.

Sorry. I'm off the track again. What I'm trying to explain, in my fuzzy way, is that an anthropologist can be an expert in anything from fossil bones to Pueblo Indian

7

pottery, from Eskimo sexual habits to African music. But he (she) has to specialize. I had to specialize.

I had no strong leanings toward any of the subdivisions of the field, which is not surprising when you consider that I took it up out of spite. I ended up specializing in fossil man, more or less by accident. I had taken a course my junior year and found it fairly interesting. Then our local museum came up with a grant for a summer job. They had gotten lots of money from one of the foundations and had decided to begin by excavating their storerooms. They found all kinds of things they had forgotten they owned, including bones—not only originals, but plaster casts of well-known skulls. So they decided to set up an exhibit: "Who Was Who Among Fossil Man." The job was one of the few things Mother and Dad ever agreed on. Mother thought it would be nice if I stayed home that summer, and Dad was more or less on speaking terms with the curator of the museum. They used to sit around and drink beer and sneer at one another's fields.

So I spent the summer classifying and cleaning and preserving bones. I worked about twelve hours a day, six days a week, and acquired an enviable reputation for diligence, which was undeserved, because the only reason I spent so much time at the museum was because I didn't want to go home. I went off to grad school with these unmerited laurels wreathing my brow, and with an amorphous feeling that I never wanted to see another skull. But, being basically a drifter by nature, I slid along through the year, and somehow or other it got to be April. Not until I heard my fellow students discussing their summer plans did I realize that I had none.

Bunny threw a wine-and-cheese party to celebrate

Frank's grant. The International Council on Giving Away People's Money had just awarded him umpteen-thousand dollars to investigate cooperation and conflict as modes of social integration among the Ubangi. We all pretended to be unselfishly delighted when an associate got a deal like this. In reality we were all green with envy, and some of us let it show.

"Strange that they took so long to let you know," said Bunny, twirling her wineglass. What she meant to imply was that all the other applicants must have died or come down with leprosy, otherwise Frank would never have gotten the grant.

"Well, the bigger the grant, the longer it takes to hear," Frank answered, implying that miserable little grants like Bunny's five hundred dollars (to correlate statistical data on the anthropometry of Tenetehara Indians) were just handed out to any idiot who bothered to apply.

They went on sniping at each other, with other "friends" tossing in rude comments. I didn't say anything. I had eaten all the cheese. There wasn't much. Bunny is awfully cheap. She's the only one of the crowd who has an independent income—child support, from a rich, guilty ex-husband who had run off with her best friend —and you'd think she could at least supply enough supermarket cheddar.

Eventually one of the gang turned to me.

"What are you doing this summer, D.J.?"

"I haven't made up my mind yet," I said. "Is there any more cheese?"

"No," Bunny said.

Next morning I went to see my adviser. I had been thinking about the problem all night (except for nine long, dreamless hours of sleep—I'm as good a sleeper as

I am an eater), and by the time I faced Dr. Bancroft across his littered desk I was feeling pretty panicky.

"I tell you, I've got to get a grant for this summer," I said, summing up a long, passionate statement.

"You should have thought of that six months ago," said Bancroft heartlessly.

"It's not six months ago, it's now," I pointed out. "Let us deal with the situation as it exists, not as it might have been."

"The situation is that it's too late to apply for aid," said Bancroft, shoving his flints around.

He does that when he's nervous or bored. In this case I assumed it was the latter, since I, not he, was the nervous one. Flints—arrowheads, lance points, scrapers, you name it—compose most of the litter on his desk, though it also includes unanswered letters, rough drafts of articles he'll never finish, and the scraps of his last few lunches. Flints are his passion. He knows more about Folsom points than anybody in North America. Isn't that impressive? He carries flints around in his pockets, and rumor has it that he takes a few to bed with him. You can imagine the commentary on that, when his students have had a few drinks —and even when they haven't. Anyway, he plays with the darned things all the time. As one of the women said, better them than me. He looks like one of the less comely Neanderthal reconstructions, and there are black hairs on the backs of his fingers.

He arranged his arrowheads in a circle, with the points toward the center, before continuing.

"You kids are too damned spoiled. In my day there wasn't all this research money available. We had to work, by God. I earned my way by scrubbing pots in a greasy spoon. . . ."

10

I had heard this before, so I let my mind wander to what I was going to wear Friday night for my date with Bob, until Bancroft ran down.

"You were brave and noble and brilliant," I said politely. "I'm not. I am a member of the spoiled, effete younger generation, and I need a summer job. I will wash pots if necessary, so long as they are old Indian pots, or old colonial pots, or anything distantly related to my so-called field, and so long as the washing of pots takes place at least six hundred miles from Cleveland, Ohio."

The figure caught his attention. He stopped in the middle of a snake design, flints overlapping like scales, and looked up interestedly.

"Why six hundred?"

"Because my father won't drive, and he only takes planes when some convention of Hellenists is meeting. My mother will drive no farther from Cleveland than five hundred miles."

"That's ridiculous," Bancroft said, finishing the snake. "Unfilial, too," he added. "Why do you hate your parents?"

"I don't. I love them. But I can't live with them. Look, it isn't just Mother and Dad; I don't mind spending the day cooking with Mother and the evening listening to Dad read aloud from the *Journal of Hellenic Studies.* But my brothers and sisters are too much. Do you have teenage children?"

A shudder ran through Bancroft. His fingers trembled so that he almost dropped a Folsom point.

"Then you know what I mean. I have four brothers and sisters, ranging from thirteen to nineteen. They each own a stereo. One of them is an early riser. He starts playing Kiss records at seven A.M. Another is a night owl. He plays

11

Elton John records until four A.M. Dr. Bancroft, forget what I said before. I retract all my conditions except one. I will wash pots or scrub floors or do anything, so long as it is at least six hundred miles from Cleveland, Ohio."

I could see Bancroft was moved. He arranged the points into the shape of a heart, with one long lance blade piercing it.

"I don't know what you can do," he mumbled. "Damn it, D.J., I seem to remember telling you last November. . . . Wait. Wait just a minute."

His fumbling at the litter had dislodged a sheet of paper. He picked it up and stared at it. You could almost hear the little wheels going around in his mind. Then he looked at me and there was a glint in his eyes that made me very, very suspicious.

"You mean that?" he asked. "Anything?"

"Well, almost anything," I said.

He started to speak, and changed his mind. Instead he handed me the piece of paper.

As this narrative proceeds you will understand why the document made such a profound impression on me. I can't reproduce it verbatim, but this is the gist.

"Dear Phuddy-Duddy," it began. "How are tricks? Terrible, I hope. I read your last article in *The American Anthropologist.* It was rotten. You're still on the wrong track about everything.

"Never mind, I know it's useless to try to penetrate the fossilized skulls of scholars like you. I'm hoping you have a student who is not quite petrified in the brain yet. I've found something, something sensational. No, I won't tell you what it is; that would give you a chance to marshal all your stupid, ignorant, boneheaded prejudices. Send me

12

a student. I'll show him and let him convince you and all the other Phuds. Your old friend, H.H."

There was a P.S. that caught my attention. "I'll pay all expenses, of course, and a thousand a month—if I approve your choice."

"A thousand a month!" I gasped. "I accept."

"That's your trouble, Abbott," Bancroft said. "You don't think at all for weeks at a time, and then you jump to conclusions. Don't you want to know who this person is, and what he wants you to do for a thousand a month?"

"I don't care what he wants me to do," I said honestly. "And I don't care who. . . . Wait a minute. No, it can't be him."

There was a brief pause. Bancroft sat glowering at me from under his Neanderthal ridges, and I thought.

"Actually," I said, after a time, "there are only two things I can think of that I wouldn't do for a thousand a month. And I might consider one of them if the working conditions were right. However, a nasty doubt has crept into my feeble brain. Why hasn't this deal been snapped up?"

"Ah, I was wondering if that question would occur to you," Bancroft said. "I do like to see traces of rudimentary intelligence in my students. . . . The reason why it has not been snapped up is that H.H. is Hank Hunnicutt."

"Who's he?"

Bancroft slammed his fist down on the desk. Flints bounced and he grabbed at them, crooning apologies—to the flints, not to me.

"I don't know why the hell I gave you an A minus in that course last semester," he snarled. "Did you hire someone to write the paper for you? You've never heard of Hunnicutt? Have you heard of Velikovsky? Have you heard of Donnelly and Heyerdahl, Lost Atlantis, and Lemuria, and little green men from outer space, and UFOs, and—"

"Oh," I said. "That Hunnicutt."

Some of the names on Bancroft's list may be familiar to you, some probably are not. The list was a list of crackpots who called themselves scientists, and whose books, expounding their weird theories, inevitably hit the bestseller lists. The screwballs claim that's one of the reasons why scientists hate them, because they are so successful. And it is true, if perhaps irrelevant, that Dr. Bancroft's book, which has the enticing title *The Ethnoarchaeology of Central America,* had sold a grand total of 657 copies.

Despite their sneers, scholars read these books. Some of them do it out of sheer masochism. Others do it because they feel obliged to combat error; they write long, learned refutations which never get published. Then there are the professors who force their students to read the stuff and pick out the errors. That was why I was familiar with some of the authors Bancroft had mentioned. He made us read parts of Velikovsky, though he used to get so red in the face when he discussed the book I honestly worried about him having a stroke right there at the blackboard. I had read another little gem, something about Ancient Mysteries, or the Golden Gods, or some such title, out of idle curiosity. It was all over the bookstands at the local drugstore.

Hank Hunnicutt came to my notice in another way. He was always in the newspapers. One month he had seen a UFO, big as a barn, with red and green lights on it spelling out BAN THE ATOM BOMB OR WE WILL DESTROY EARTH. Another month he got into print by giving six million dollars to the Brothers of the Golden Circle of Reincarnation. He was not a millionaire, he was a multi-multi-billionaire, one of the richest men in the whole world, and he was crazy. He believed in every far-out theory that had ever been proposed. I hadn't connected him with the letter because I couldn't imagine a man like that offering money to a regular university.

I looked at the letter again.

"Phuddy-duddy?" I said questioningly.

"From Ph.D.," Bancroft said coldly. "It's a term of abuse coined by an early crackpot and applied to any scholar who ventures to question any insane theory." Then his face relaxed, just a little. "Hank isn't a bad guy," he admitted reluctantly. "He is totally uncritical, of course . . . but he's damned good company. That ranch of his, in northern Arizona. . . . You'd be staying there, I presume, since his great discovery is located nearby. He wrote me again last week, giving me that much information, but I seem to have lost the letter. Anyhow, you can imagine what room and board at that establishment are like. You'll get fat, Abbott."

"I certainly will not," I said coolly. I do not like references to my weight. "It sounds like a good deal. I'll take it."

If Bancroft had been a nice fatherly type, he would have patted me on the head and told me to go home and think about it for a few days. Instead he grinned nastily.

"Okay. I'll write Hank and give him your credentials. He may not approve them, though I doubt if you will be that lucky. You know, of course, that this summer could put the kiss of death on your scholarly ambitions, if any. Hunnicutt's reputation is so bad that being associated with him damns a researcher."

15

I leaned back in my chair and looked at him askance. "Come off it, Spike," I said.

He hates being called Spike, but he couldn't do anything about it because he is one of those fake liberals who likes to pretend he is a buddy to his students. Also, the man does have a rudimentary sense of humor. He managed a sickly smile.

"You're right. We talk high and mighty, but we'll take money from any source whatever. The truth is I've sent him several names. He turned them all down."

"Why?"

"He wouldn't say why. Maybe he's just hassling me. We were undergraduates together, and there were a few incidents. . . ." Bancroft coughed and looked coy.

I knew now why Frank had been late in applying for his grant. Hunnicutt must have turned him down. I filed the information away in case Frank ever got snotty with me.

"I'll take my chances," I said.

I meant chances with my reputation. I didn't mean chances with my life.

Chapter Two

The stewardess asked me if I'd like a little more champagne. I managed to nod casually, though my first impulse was to grab the bottle, in case she changed her mind.

I was flying first class on a great big superjet. First class! Not only had I never flown first class, I had never known anybody who had. It's nice up there in the front cabin. More space, free booze, and that indefinable feeling of being superior to the hoi polloi. When Hank Hunnicutt said "expenses," he meant it. He had apologized for not sending his private plane to pick me up.

The second glass of champagne made me feel very mellow about good old Hank, and that was just as well, because I had begun to wonder whether I was making a serious mistake. Hunnicutt had accepted my credentials with flattering promptness. At least it would have been flattering if I hadn't been fairly sure he was getting desperate. Then came the first-class ticket, with an advance on my "salary," in case I needed to buy anything for the trip. . . . All that was fine. I'd have had only kindly thoughts about my benefactor if I had not spent some time reading up on the crazy theories he had endorsed.

After the acceptance letter arrived I went straight to the library. Not the university library; I knew they wouldn't carry the kind of trashy books I wanted. The public library in town had most of the ones on my list. I found a copy of *Atlantis: The Antediluvian World* in a secondhand bookstore and discovered, with astonishment, that some paperback company had recently seen fit to reprint Churchward's illiterate essays on the lost continent of Mu. Then I went back to my one-room apartment and baked a double batch of chocolate-chip cookies, and I took them and the eight-pack of Coke I had picked up on the way home and settled down for an orgy—of research, that is.

At first I enjoyed it. I started with the skeptics, like Martin Gardner and Sprague de Camp—men who knew how to write and who did their debunking with humor and devastating sarcasm. They gave good summaries of the crazier cults, from Symmes' Hollow Earth theory to Velikovsky's naive belief that the miracles of the Old Testament were caused by comets whizzing back and forth around the earth at convenient intervals. Some of the ideas were so wild they were funny. I loved Le Plongeon, one of the nineteenth-century explorers of Yucatán, who believed that the Mayans had carried civilization to Egypt, Sumer, and elsewhere eleven thousand years ago. I particularly adored Queen Moo (pronounced "moo," as in cow) a prehistoric (and purely fictitious) Mayan queen whose brother Aac murdered her husband Coh, so Moo fled to Atlantis (Le Plongeon believed in Atlantis too), and then sailed on to Egypt. She had another brother named Cay. Aac, Moo, Coh and Cay. . . . It suggests a nice vulgar limerick, doesn't it?

One of Le Plongeon's "proofs" that Near Eastern culture and language were derived from the Mayas was his translation of the words Christ said on the cross. I bet you didn't know that *Eli, eli, lama sabachthani* doesn't really mean "My God, my God, why hast thou forsaken me?" No, what He really said was—in Mayan—"Now, now, sinking, black ink over nose."

I'm serious. At least Le Plongeon was, poor man.

Le Plongeon was fun. So was George F. Riffert, who wrote a book called *The Great Pyramid, Proof of God.* He and some other Pyramid Mystics thought that one of the bumps on the Great Pyramid of Giza represented the vital date of September 16, 1936. The only trouble was, forty years later he still hadn't figured out what had happened that day, unless it was that the King of England told the Prime Minister he was going to marry Mrs. Simpson. Those ancient Egyptians really did have insight into world history.

Charles Russell, the founder of Jehovah's Witnesses, also believed that the cracks and bumps in the Great Pyramid foretold what was going to happen in history. According to his calculations, the Second Coming of Christ had taken place in 1874—invisibly. He and a few other selected saints were the only ones who had noticed.

After a while, though, I stopped laughing and started to feel a little sick. (No, it wasn't the cookies. I can eat incredible amounts of chocolate-chip cookies.) The crackpots varied in intelligence, from the plausibly pseudo-scientific to the out-and-out moronic, but they had several disturbing qualities in common. The most conspicuous of these was an immense persecution complex. Each and every one of them believed he was a genius, and that everybody else in the whole world was *wrong*. They were martyrs, everybody hated them and despised them and refused to listen to them. They were all also incredibly dull. I remembered what a hard time I had had plowing through Velikovsky; he was far more boring than any of my textbooks, and they weren't *Gone With the Wind*.

As I read on—and on, and on—I realized that all these people shared a humorless, frightening paranoia. Buried somewhere in most of the books was a need to justify some fundamentalist religious code. Velikovsky started with the assumption that the books of the Old Testament describe events that actually happened. God knows—at least I hope He does—that I don't want to poke fun at anybody's religious beliefs, but if you start with the idea of proving Holy Writ, it's hard to know where to stop. And biblical fundamentalists—Catholic, Protestant, Jewish or other—tend to be equally dogmatic about other issues, such as the superiority of the descendants of one or the other of Noah's sons.

Racism kept rearing its ugly head among the luxuriant vegetation of these imaginary worlds. The superior-civilization-bearing citizens of lost Atlantis were almost always tall, blond, blue-eyed Aryans. The Spanish monks who were the first ones to push the idea that the American

Indians were descended from the Lost Tribes of Israel pointed out that the Indians, like the Jews, were ungrateful for the many blessings God had bestowed upon them —such as slavery and the Inquisition, I suppose. And Heyerdahl, three hundred years later, concluded that only Indians showing Caucasoid—ie., "white"—traits were intelligent enough to make the trek across the Pacific to Polynesia. The Negroid types there had been brought as slaves.

It wasn't hard to figure out why so many of these people were fascists, open or covert. They were arrogant snobs who thought they were superior to everybody else. They couldn't endure the slightest criticism of their ideas. Racists are arrogant people too.

It left a very bad taste in my mouth, and by the time I was through reading I was prepared to dislike Hank Hunnicutt very much. Not that I decided to give up the grant. Oh, no. I am noble, but I am not that noble. Besides, I figured I could get in some missionary work. Hank seemed to be susceptible to any crazy idea; why not to mine?

Full of champagne and other munchies, I was feeling no pain by the time the plane began its descent over the tortured bare rocks of the northern plateau of Arizona. I knew I might be in for some trouble, though. I could sit and smile and nod while Hank explained to me about colonists from Lemuria, and Martians digging the Grand Canyon; a man is entitled to his fantasies. But if he started spouting any of the Anglo-Saxon superiority stuff, I wouldn't be able to keep quiet. It's not a matter of conviction, it's pure reflex. I can't stand that garbage. Oh, well, I thought; if we fight, he can fire me. At least I've had a nice trip.

Since my mother will not drive more than five hundred miles from home, and since classical scholars do not make enough money for expensive vacations, I had never been west of the Mississippi before. I gawked out the window with unashamed appreciation and curiosity as the plane came in to Phoenix. The terrain was utterly different from anything I had seen. Phoenix is a big, sprawling city; there are a few modest skyscrapers downtown, but most of it is low and spread out and surrounded by isolated local mountains. The stewardess pointed out Camelback which, I guess, is a well-known landmark. It didn't look like a camel from where I was sitting, but it was an excellent mountain. It was so bare. All the mountains I had ever seen had trees on them, all the way to the top.

I have forgotten whether I mentioned that the month was June. (Most colleges get out earlier than that, but mine ran on the trimester system; we get a long vacation from Thanksgiving to New Year's, and run longer in the summer.) June isn't the height of the summer in Arizona. It gets a lot hotter in August. The temperature was a mere ninety-eight in the shade when I emerged from the terminal.

By that time I was mad at Hank again. He had said someone would meet me, but there was nobody at the gate, nobody at the baggage pickup, though I waited till the last suitcase rolled through, and everybody else had left.

Normally I can get everything essential to my happiness (well, almost everything) into a backpack, but this time Mother had insisted on helping me pack. I'd slipped half the items she gave me under the bed when she wasn't looking. Even so, I had ended up with a good-sized suitcase in addition to my pack.

I dragged this load back to the information desk. There was no message for D.J. Abbott.

The terminal building in Phoenix is really pretty. There's a big exotic mural of the fictitious bird which the city is named after, and a stand loaded with flowers, and the usual little shops. I investigated them all. The merchandise was tourist stuff, but it was fun; with Hank Hunnicutt's advance burning a hole in my pocket I was feeling affluent, so I blew thirty bucks on a silver ring labeled "genuine Indian made." The bezel was in the shape of an owl made out of pieces of shell, with one little bit of turquoise for a tail.

I had a cup of coffee and then I went back to the information counter. Still no message. Then I got mad. I grabbed my bags and marched toward the exit and reeled, literally, as the heat hit me like a fist in the face. I reeled forward, into the fender of a car that was parked in front of the door, in flagrant violation of the signs.

It was a Rolls Royce. I didn't recognize it, of course; I don't have much to do with cars like that. I found out what it was later. All I noticed then was that it was black, with a silver hood ornament and door handles and the like. I don't mean silver-colored, I mean silver. I didn't know that at first either.

I didn't pay much attention to the car. Leaning against the back fender—I had staggered into the front fender, several miles away—was the handsomest male I had seen since *Butch Cassidy and the Sundance Kid.*

This person was dark: black hair and eyes, skin so bronzed he might have been part Indian. The coppery shade was not restricted to his hands and face. His shirt was open all the way to his belt, displaying beautiful ripply muscles. His arms were folded. His ankles were crossed. He looked completely relaxed, except for his face, which was set in an expression of freezing disapproval. He had a handsome drooping black mustache that made him look like a Spanish pirate. He was gorgeous.

I will always be a peasant at heart. It never occurred to me that the car and the beautiful man might be mine, if only temporarily. I collected my bags and my wits and started to walk away.

"Hold it," said the apparition of male loveliness.

I held it.

"Your name Abbott?"

I nodded.

Without uncrossing his ankles the man extended one arm and opened the back door of the car.

"Toss your stuff in here."

I am ashamed to say that I started to do it. Forgive me, Betty Friedan. I'm just a pushover for a handsome face.

"Hold it," I repeated, as much to myself as to him. "Your name?"

"Tom De Karsky."

"Ah." I dropped my suitcase, folded my arms, and smiled. "Mr. Hunnicutt's chauffeur, I presume? May I ask why the Hades you didn't meet me inside—or at least leave a message?"

"I did leave a message. I presume the fools lost it, they usually do. What are you standing there for? If you're waiting for me to take your bags, I don't carry things for liberated females."

"I wouldn't dream of asking you to tire yourself," I said. I heaved my things into the car, letting them fall where gravity demanded and noting, in passing, that the upholstery was a pale-gray velvet. De Karsky watched me expressionlessly. I slammed the door.

24

"I'll sit up front," I said.

"Suit yourself."

He pried himself off the fender and sauntered toward the driver's side, leaving me to open my own door.

The reason why I decided to sit in front was partly because I had a lot of questions and partly because I wanted to annoy Mr. De Karsky, who obviously wanted to stay as far away from me as possible. I was distracted from this latter aim by purely material considerations. That was an amazing car. The dashboard looked like the control panel of a flying saucer. It was basically rosewood or mahogany or something of that ilk, but the wood was almost hidden by dozens of buttons and accoutrements, such as a miniature TV screen. I punched a button experimentally, and jumped back as a tray slid out from under the dash and hit me in the diaphragm. Simultaneously a door on top popped open and ejected a tall glass filled with ice cubes and a pale-amber liquid.

"Hey," I said appreciatively.

De Karsky started the engine. At least I guess he did, because we started to move. I didn't hear anything as vulgar as an engine.

"Cut that out," he snarled, as I reached for another button.

"Why should I?" The television screen flickered and presented me with the grinning face of a game-show host. I don't care for game shows—I never know the answers —so I turned it off and tried another button. A plate of cheese and fancy hors d'oevres landed on the tray.

"Look," said De Karsky, in a muted roar, "at least wait till we get out of town, will you? It distracts me, having all that junk jumping back and forth. The traffic here is wild; all these little eighty-year-old grandmas trying to drive."

It was the first halfway reasonable remark he had made, so I decided to humor him.

"Why grandmas?" I asked, sipping the liquid in the glass. It was Scotch, but a lot smoother than any variety I had ever sampled. The cheese was good too.

"Arizona is a retirement state, like Florida," De Karsky explained, sliding through the stop sign at the exit from the airport. "There is no more vicious driver than a little old lady."

"Male chauvinist," I said reflexively. De Karsky didn't answer. He hunched over the wheel, clutching it with both hands and glaring wildly at the other cars as if he really believed his paranoid fantasies.

For a while I was too engrossed by the scenery to hassle him. There were palm trees, growing in people's yards like elms and maples. Cactus, too. After we left the airport, the first part of the drive was fairly dull, just streets of shops and garish signs, like the approaches to most airports; but the low profiles of the buildings and the wide, dusty street suggested those old Western towns you see in the movies.

After a time we got into a residential neighborhood. That was where I saw the palm trees and the cactus. Some people had given up the effort to keep grass green, and had converted their yards into miniature, landscaped deserts. The effect was austere and rather attractive, like Japanese gardens. Some of the cacti were elongated poles, ten or twenty feet high, with branching arms. I learned later that they were saguaro, and that it took them eighty years to grow a single branch. The little fat cholla, glistening like ice-encrusted bushes, were deadly things; the icicles were thorns, and the old-timers claimed that the thorns didn't just stick you when you brushed them, they jumped out at you.

The neighborhood became fancier as we proceeded and the lawns got more elaborate. I was trying to appear cool and sophisticated in front of De Karsky, but when I saw my first orange trees I let out a juvenile-sounding squeal. They grew in people's front yards. They really did. They were pretty, low trees, with vivid emerald leaves and white-painted trunks. The fruit hung like golden-orangy Christmas balls. Many of the houses were hidden behind walls and oleander hedges, but from what I could see of them they favored the Southwest-Spanish style of architecture, with buff adobe walls and red-tiled roofs.

I was beginning to wonder where De Karsky was going. We were supposed to head straight north, to Hunnicutt's ranch, and most big cities these days have circumferential roads so you don't have to go through town to get from one side of the city to the other. Then De Karsky made a quick, neat turn into a driveway, and stopped the car.

The house was almost big enough to be called a villa. I couldn't see much of it, or of the grounds, because of the wall; the drive was blocked by high wrought-iron gates.

"Got to run an errand," De Karsky explained. "Wait here. I won't be long." He gestured at the instrument panel—I mean the dashboard. "Amuse yourself."

It was perfectly reasonable that he should stop to do an errand. I wouldn't have thought twice about it except for one thing. He walked up to the gates, pushed one open enough to slip through, and proceeded along the curving drive.

It was the first time I had seen him walk. The process was worth watching. I mean, if men think they are the only ones who like to study the movements of a well-constructed body, then they are kidding themselves, poor lambs. De Karsky had lean hips and broad shoulders and he walked with the slow, cocky swagger affected by heroes of old Westerns—you know, when they saunter into the saloon filled with bad guys.

However, animal lust did not distract me to the point where I failed to notice that small anomaly. If the gates were unlocked, why didn't he drive straight on up to the house? It was some distance away, and the temperature was pushing a hundred degrees.

He wasn't gone more than five minutes. I occupied myself as he had suggested, locating a stereo tape deck and a miniature movie projector before he came back, carrying a brown paper bag.

It could have been his lunch—a late lunch. It could have been a head of lettuce, or a loaf of bread. Admittedly, I think about food a lot, but most people would have gotten the same mental image. Brown paper bags suggest grocery stores. Only he had not been to a grocery store.

Even before he reached the car my brain, working with its usual lightning speed (I jest, of course), had arrived at a brilliant deduction. This errand was his own personal business, not something he was doing for his employer. I simply could not picture Hank Hunnicutt collecting anything that came in brown paper bags. Leather brief-cases, yes; dispatch boxes wound around with red tape, no doubt; crumbling antique trunks with rusted padlocks, containing the secrets of the Lemurians, undoubtedly. Brown paper bags, no.

De Karsky didn't want his boss to know about his errand. That was why he had left me, and the car, outside the gate, so I would be unable to describe the house in case I happened to mention the unscheduled stop. But why the devil should it matter? Was Hunnicutt such an ogre that he would object to an employee's taking a few minutes off to run a personal errand?

I watched closely as De Karsky opened the car door and stowed the paper bag out of sight under the seat. I could tell from the way he held it that the contents were heavy. The contents were not—was not—I never can get that point of grammar straight. . . . It wasn't lettuce. But the bag had once held something of that nature, something wet. Damp had weakened the paper; and as De Karsky shoved it out of sight, a corner tore. I caught only a glimpse of a dark, dully gleaming surface, but I saw enough to rouse my worst suspicions.

The car purred smoothly off down the street, with De Karsky peering intently out the front window like Luke Skywalker getting ready to bomb the Death Star. I had the idea that he was trying to avoid conversation—and also that he was worried about something.

I had a few worries of my own. The object in the brown paper bag was a gun, I was almost certain of it. If he hadn't made such a production of hiding it I wouldn't have wondered about it. Like most ignorant easterners, I assumed the Arizona deserts were full of dangers—rattlesnakes, pesky redskins, renegade white men, coyotes. . . . So why hide the gun? Why not toss it into the back seat and say something like, "Them coyotes have been pesky lately"? I was forced to the conclusion that Mr. De Karsky had borrowed a firearm from a friend, thus acquiring a weapon which could not be traced to him.

A nice way to start a vacation, I must say.

II

When I emerged from my profound reverie concerning guns and such things, we were on a wide highway with nothing around but sky and cactus. The sky was bright blue and the cactus was greenish brown. The air shimmered with heat, though the car was pleasantly cool.

I sighed.

"Welcome back," De Karsky said.

"Huh?" I turned my head and stared at him.

"Talk about brown studies. What were you thinking about?"

I decided not to tell him what I had been thinking about.

I started to reach for the dashboard and then had second thoughts. I didn't want to irritate him, not just then.

"Does anything else to eat come out of here?" I asked.

De Karsky let out a muffled sound that might have been a laugh if it had lived to grow up.

"Third button from the right, second row."

This time it was chocolates—the kind they sell only in the most exclusive stores, five creams in a box trimmed with red velvet roses.

"Want one?" I asked, waving a plump dark one with a candied violet on top under De Karsky's nose. He made a hideous face.

"No, thanks."

"This is a fabulous car," I said.

"It belonged to some oil sheikh," De Karsky said.

"You mean this is a used car? How degrading. I'd have thought Mr. Hunnicutt could afford a brand-new one."

"You'd better call him Hank, everybody else does. He is a funny mixture of extravagance and thrift. He'll spend any sum on other people, or on his wild theories, but like

30

most millionaires he is naively pleased when he can acquire a bargain."

"Have you been acquainted with many millionaires?" I inquired.

"Not yet. But I've made a study of their habits."

"Ethnologically speaking?"

"Precisely."

"What are you, a sociologist?" I asked, half kidding—but only half. He was no illiterate handyman.

"I have a degree in archaeology," De Karsky said, with a thin unpleasant smile. "We are colleagues, Ms. Abbott."

"Call me D.J."

"I consider the use of initials affected."

"Then you can stick to Ms. Abbott. That's Ms., M.S."

There was a brief hostile silence. I didn't seem to be doing too well in my attempts to ingratiate myself. I wondered why he was so antagonistic. A possible explanation presented itself. I approached it with my usual tact.

"Look, if you are Mr.—I mean Hank's—anthropologist in residence, I've no intention of trying to take your job. I'll be going back to school in the fall; I just came out here because—"

"I don't care why you came, and I don't feel at all threatened, thank you."

"Why not?"

"Oh, dear me, I have offended the poor little feminist. I'm not questioning your brains, Abbott, for the simple reason that I don't know whether you have any. You may be the brightest thing to come down the pike since Margaret Mead, but you can't challenge me. I've made a profound study of what Hank wants and I can supply it better than anybody else."

"What does he want?"

De Karsky made another of those unmirthful laughing noises.

"There, that's what I mean. You're about as subtle as a bulldozer, aren't you? I have no objection to giving away my technique, because you'd never be able to emulate it. You're traditionally trained, and you've got a big mouth. You'll never be able to listen to Hank's ideas in silence, much less agree with them."

"Is that what he wants—somebody to support his wild theories?"

"That should have been obvious."

"But he must have plenty of other sycophants," I said rudely. "Hangers-on, spongers, hypocrites who will say anything to keep a soft berth."

"Yes, he does. The ranch is crawling with weirdos. But I, my dear, am no weirdo. I have a good degree from a reputable institution of learning. Summa cum laude, in fact. Hank is naive, but he's no fool. When Professor Screwball and Madame Charlatan tell him he is right, he knows they are speaking from ignorance. When I tell him he is right. . . ."

"I see. And of course you tell him he is right?"

"Most of the time. An occasional outburst of skepticism is necessary in order to maintain my scholarly image. The outbursts have to be well timed, however. That takes practice."

"Now wait a minute," I said, mostly to myself. "Maybe I'm being encouraged to misjudge you. Maybe the theories aren't as crazy as everybody thinks. Which one are you supporting at present?"

"The last one was reincarnation," De Karsky answered readily. "Madame Charlatan's real name is Karenina—"

"Oh, come on."

32

"It's possible. There must be other Kareninas besides Anna. However, I am inclined to agree with you that the lady's name is as fictitious as her title. She's a graduate of the Edgar Cayce Association for Research and Enlightenment, Inc. Cayce started out as a psychic diagnostician; people would write him letters describing their aches and pains, and then he'd go into a trance and write back telling them what was wrong with them. It was usually spinal lesions. He had worked for an osteopath as a young man—"

"I know about Cayce," I interrupted.

"You do?" He shot me a quick, suspicious glance. I responded with a sweet smile. That worried him. "Well," he went on, slowly, "then you know Cayce eventually turned to the occult and claimed he could give people details of their past lives. That's what Madame is doing for Hank."

"Like Bridie Murphy," I said. "Who was Hank?"

"Who was . . . ?"

"In his past lives. Pirate, gambler, prince of lost Atlantis?"

"All of them." A faint but genuine smile curved the well-cut corners of De Karsky's mouth, and my liberated glands released a flood of appreciative symptoms. "Not simultaneously, of course; one after the other. The life they were concentrating on was the one in which Hank was a chief of the Anasazi, the Indians who lived in northeastern Arizona in prehistoric times."

"I also know who the Anasazi were. There's a certain consistency in Hank's mania, isn't there? American prehistory seems to be a recurrent motif in his fantasies."

De Karsky gave me another of those hard looks and did not reply.

"I told you you don't need to worry about your precious job," I snapped. "The chances are I won't last a week."

"You're going to tell him his theories are full of—"

"Probably. You said reincarnation was the last kick. What's he on now?"

De Karsky's scowl faded. When he answered, his voice was without rancor. He sounded genuinely puzzled.

"I don't know. Nobody knows. He's been very mysterious about this latest deal, which is unlike him. All I know is, he went off on one of his safaris into the mountains a few months ago, and came back all lit up."

"You don't know where he went or what he found?"

"I tried to follow him," De Karsky admitted. "But it's wild country, and Hank is an experienced desert rat. He goes off on his own every so often."

"Isn't that dangerous?"

"It can be, if you don't know what you're doing. You can die of dehydration out there pretty fast. We lose a few poor damn-fool tourists every year that way. Some of them were only half a mile from a highway, wandering around in circles, when they died. But Hank knows his way around."

"Well," I said optimistically, "maybe this theory won't be as crazy as the last one."

"And if it is?"

"Then I'll tell him so."

"Then you won't even last a week."

"That's okay with me. I told you I wouldn't have your job. I think it's contemptible."

"The job is contemptible?"

"You are, too."

"Well." De Karsky moved his hands on the wheel as if

he were squeezing something soft, like a throat. "Well. We've got that straight, haven't we?"

"Right."

"Right. I suppose if I were to tell you at this point that I had hoped to talk you into going home as soon as possible you'd suspect my motives."

"Right again."

"Then I won't try. You'll have to take your lumps."

"What lumps?"

"Never mind. You wouldn't believe me." He was silent for a moment, staring straight ahead with the same puzzled frown he had worn when he spoke of Hank's latest enthusiasm. "Maybe I'm wrong," he said, as if to himself. "I hope to God I am."

Chapter Three

De Karsky's final comment—not one of the most encouraging remarks I have ever heard—was his last conversational effort for the remainder of the trip. He didn't even snarl when I started playing with the buttons again, so I gave that up.

There was plenty to occupy my eyes and my brain. The country wasn't real desert, with great rolling sand dunes. It had enough water to support some plant life: cacti of all shapes and sizes, including the striking monumental saguaro, plus low brownish scrubby plants that suggested

36

sagebrush to my movie-fed mind. The road climbed slowly but steadily, and hills began to close in around us. Finally they opened up, with spectacular effect, presenting a view of a beautiful green valley with a glittering river winding through it. We descended into the valley in a series of swooping loops. I bit my lip and did not comment on De Karsky's driving.

While my eyes took in the scenery, my mind worried at the problems De Karsky had suggested. I saw no reason to alter my appraisal of him. He was a cynical, self-seeking hypocrite, and a traitor to his training—and to common sense—if he encouraged Hank Hunnicutt's delusions.

Naturally I dismissed De Karsky's vague hints as part of a plan to scare me into leaving. Whether I meant to or not, I did threaten his comfortable job. Hank might take a fancy to me. He sounded like a man of quick, irrational fancies. If he did, De Karsky would find himself out in the cold. The gun—if it was a gun, and not some other similarly finished tool—could be part of the same plan. De Karsky had probably envisioned me as a timid eastern female. Wave a gun in front of the girl, mutter ominously, and she'll run.

All it did was make me more determined to stay. Another unexpected corollary—unexpected even to me— was that I began to feel sorry for Hank Hunnicutt. De Karsky was no different from Madame Karenina and the other "weirdos" he had mentioned; they were all intellectual vampires, making a good living out of Hank's innocence.

We turned off the highway and the country got really wild. Centuries of wind and water had carved the surrounding rocks into fantastic towers and spires. The road deteriorated as it began to climb again until finally we were bumping along an unpaved track enclosed by low walls of stone. The sun was a dull red ball, its brilliance dulled by blowing sand, balanced on the top of cliffs that loomed up to the north.

There were strands of barbed wire on either side of the road now, though what they fenced in I could not imagine; I couldn't see any cows, or any pasture, only more of the rocky high desert with its brownish bushes. De Karsky stopped the car and got out, leaving the door open. I winced back, expecting a blast of furnace-hot air. It was warm, certainly, but there was a hint of coolness approaching, a rarefied clarity that struck welcomingly on my skin after hours of stuffy air conditioning.

De Karsky had gone to open a gate. Set between high columns of randomly piled rocks, it was no fancy wrought-iron creation but a prosaic iron gate like the ones on farms in Ohio. We drove through; De Karsky closed the gate, and we went on. The surface of the road was so dusty it could hardly be distinguished from the surrounding dirt, but it was surprisingly smooth under the wheels. Ahead, on the horizon, was a dark blotch. As we swept toward it, it took on shape: trees, their rich green soothing to eyes weary of dust and sun.

I had expected trees. You can't have a ranch without water. But I was not prepared for the luxuriant vegetation that adorned the grounds. We passed through another gate and into a long avenue lined with green. Through the tree trunks I caught an occasional glimpse of a velvety lawn set with shrubs and flower beds, but most of the parklike area had been left as nature designed it. It teemed with wildlife. De Karsky had slowed to a crawl; I wondered why, until we turned a corner and saw a deer standing in the middle of the road. It glanced casually at us before it ambled off into the trees. I located the button that opened the window and inhaled a long, deep breath of fresh air. Birds swooped and sang among the trees, and a rabbit hopped along beside the car for a while, as if trying to race.

"It's gorgeous," I said.

"Underground streams and springs," De Karsky said. "A real-estate developer would give him a couple of million for this land."

I ignored this tasteless comment.

"It must be nice to have lots and lots of money," I said. "I could get used to living like this."

"Why don't you marry Hank, then? He's a widower; has been for thirty years. He ought to be ripe for a fresh young thing like you."

I hadn't thought about Hank's marital status. I had assumed that, like the millionaires whose antics filled the gossip columns, he had had the usual succession of wives. I was about to pursue the subject—Hank's marital history in general, not my prospects of marrying him—when we came out of the trees and saw the house.

It appeared fairly unpretentious until you realized how big it was—a low, sprawling hacienda-type building, with arched windows and tiled roofs and a lot of intricate wrought iron on balconies and window grilles. We drove through an open gate into a courtyard whose other walls were formed by wings of the house. Roofed loggias supporting balconies ran along the house walls; red-brown pottery jars between the thick white columns overflowed with vines and flowers.

I got out, only mildly disconcerted to find that there was a chocolate stain on my slacks.

"One of the housemen will get your luggage," De Karsky said.

"One of the housemen. . . . Of course. I should have known you wouldn't take up with a millionaire unless he had a couple of dozen housemen."

"Don't just stand there, go on in. Hank will be waiting."

"Isn't one of the housemen going to drive the car to the garage?" I inquired.

"Yes, as a matter of fact."

"Then do join me. I don't believe in these outmoded class distinctions. You don't even have to walk a pace or two behind me."

De Karsky glared at me and stalked toward the house. I followed him toward a door in the opposite wall. Before we reached it, it opened, and a man came out.

If De Karsky hadn't greeted him by name I wouldn't have known who he was. He didn't look anything like what I had expected; tall and lean and weatherbeaten, he looked like John Wayne and Gary Cooper and Tom Mix—all the old cowboy heroes rolled into one. His clothes suited the image—well-worn boots, jeans, and a shirt of faded blue-and-white-checked cotton. I was amazed that he didn't have a star pinned on his chest and twin holsters dangling low on his hips. The only incongruous note in the costume was his belt, a row of silver medallions the size of saucers, set with huge chunks of unpolished turquoise. His eyes were the same shade as the turquoise. They squinted at me from under thick sandy eyebrows. I would not have been surprised to hear him address me as "little gal," and crush my hand in his.

His handshake was firm and not at all crushing.

40

"How do you do, Ms. Abbott," he said. "I'm grateful to you for coming."

"It's a pleasure to be here." I hesitated. Then I said in a rush, "I ate all the chocolates. And the cheese. It was divine, thank you. I mean, all of it was divine, but I especially liked the cheese."

His tentative smile opened up into a wide grin.

"Spike told me you were a good eater. I was glad to hear it. Can't stand these women who are always on a diet. Most of them are too thin anyway."

I promised myself I would get back at Spike Bancroft for that crack about my eating habits. But I couldn't hate him too much, since Hank obviously meant what he said. His eyes were going over my curves (I have plenty of curves, most in the wrong places) with candid but inoffensive appreciation.

"Come on in," he continued, turning toward the house. "You must be tired and hot."

"I feel great."

"Those crumbs of cheese didn't spoil your appetite, I hope. Dinner will be served in about an hour."

"I can always eat," I admitted.

He beamed at me approvingly, and then turned to De Karsky, who was leaning against one of the columns watching.

"No problems, Tom?"

"No problems."

"Good."

The main door might have been stolen from an ancient Spanish mission. It was black with age, and carved with strangely effective patterns of primitive saints and sinners.

I could go on describing that house, but you would get

tired of adjectives after a while. Everything was spacious, beautiful, old, rare, expensive. Just put one or more of those words in front of every object in the place and you've got it. Yet the overall effect was restful and deceptively simple. The Spanish-Indian style suited the climate and the terrain; it even looked cool, with its contrasting white walls and dark beams, its shining tile floors and large, uncluttered spaces.

A slim, dark-skinned little maid led me up a broad curving staircase onto a second-floor gallery, and showed me to my room. I am sure I need not say it was the most elegant room I had ever occupied. At home I always had to share with Judy or Shirley, or, when company came, with both. This room was bigger than our living room. Dark beams crossed the ceiling; the walls were white, hung with brilliantly patterned Indian rugs and a few paintings. There were two balconies, one overlooking the courtyard and the other opening onto a dazzling view of carved red cliffs and deepening sky. There were a private bath and a dressing room whose amenities included a refrigerator tucked in under a counter. It was stocked with a mouth-watering assortment of goodies, including several tall bottles.

The maid displayed all these things in silence, smiling; I smiled back and made appropriate noises. I was trying to be cool, but not blasé. The process took some time, there was so much to see. Before it was over, there was a knock at the door, and an elderly man came in, carrying my stuff. Like the maid, he appeared to be pure-blooded Indian. His face was a mass of wrinkles and his hair was white. Before I thought, I jumped to help him. The look he gave me stopped me in my tracks. He was as strong as he was wrinkled, and I realized I had deeply offended him.

He went out shaking his head and mumbling to himself, after depositing my bags on a luggage rack.

"I guess I hurt his feelings," I said.

"They're all very macho," the maid said calmly. "You've got to expect it of their generation. Want me to unpack for you?"

"Thanks, I can manage. I've only got three pair of jeans and two shirts."

"Okay. That strip of fabric over there is a bell pull, believe it or not. If you want me, use it."

"I probably won't," I said.

"I don't suppose you will, but feel free. My name's Debbie."

"Is it really?"

"Well, I've got an Indian name too. Ken-tee. My grandfather calls me that. So do some of Hank's guests. They think it's quaint. But I prefer Debbie."

"I know what you mean. I refuse to tell anybody what names my folks saddled me with. You can call me D.J."

"Parents are a trial," she agreed, and we both laughed. "Well, if there's nothing else. . . . Go on down to the living room when you're ready; cocktails in half an hour."

"Wait a minute," I said, as she started for the door. "Do they dress for dinner or anything like that? I haven't got—"

"You could come down stark naked and nobody would notice," she said cryptically.

After wallowing in the sunken tub and refreshing the inner woman from the contents of the refrigerator, I investigated my wardrobe, trying to decide what to wear. In spite of Mother's efforts I didn't have much choice; I had kicked under the bed most of the "evening dresses" and "cocktail frocks" she had tried to urge on me. From what I had seen and heard I didn't think evening dress was de rigueur, but I decided to wear a long skirt anyhow. Mother put it into the suitcase with her own hands and I never had a chance to take it out. She had made it herself. If I hadn't been automatically turned off by her domestic efforts I'd have liked the skirt; she's a superb needlewoman, of course, and she had embroidered flowers and leaves all around the hem and on the patch pockets, turning a cheap green-and-white cotton print into something quite lovely. Now that I was away from her I realized that I kind of missed her. I snuffled a little, enjoying the faint spasm of homesickness, as I put on the skirt and a simple white sleeveless top.

I cured the homesickness with a couple of pieces of cheese (I really do adore cheese) and went looking for the living room. It was easy to find. As soon as I stepped onto the gallery I could hear the noise. The closer I got, the more outrageous it became, and I started to feel right at home. The shrieks and shouts and voices raised in loud argument reminded me of the last professional society meeting I had attended.

The room was big, forty or fifty feet long. The far wall was entirely of glass. It faced west.

That was the only decoration the room needed. Fine particles of dust and sand give desert sunsets a spectacular glory other climates never see, and this was a particularly good one. The sky looked like the palette of a demented, color-mad painter. Outlined against the flaming gold and crimson clouds were grotesquely shaped mountain peaks, erratic in outline, as if someone had spilled ink and let it run.

The room seemed crowded, for all its size. There weren't all that many people present, but each of them was making enough noise for three or four. I never did get to know all of them. The population was transient; people came and went as in a hotel, and I got the impression that Hank never knew or cared how many mouths he would be feeding on any given night. But there was a hard core, so to speak: legitimate members of the household and illegitimate crooks who had found a good deal and were holding on to it. If I don't mention the legitimate members, such as Hank's gray-haired housekeeper, it's because they ran the place with self-effacing efficiency. The crooks were much more conspicuous.

The group nearest me consisted of a fat little woman in a long, flowing robe and a preposterous turban of molting feathers. Rings flashed on her plump hands as she waved them in animated debate with another turbaned personage, a tall, brown-faced man wearing evening dress with a red ribbon across his chest. His turban was red too. The third person in the group was a short man whose little round belly hung out over his loud plaid pants. His black eyes darted from the lady in the turban to the man in the turban as they exchanged comments like duelists swapping blows.

Before I could spot any more interesting characters, Hank came loping over to greet me.

"Hi, there. No problems?"

I hesitated, wondering what he meant. Then I realized this must be his conventional way of greeting people. I had a feeling that if you told him there was a problem, he would do something about it.

"No problems," I said.

"Good. Come and have a drink."

The person at the bar was presumably a houseman. Dressed in a neat white jacket and a black string tie, he

45

might have been Debbie's brother. He had the same round brown face and cheerful smile.

Hank hovered till I got my hands on the glass and then took my elbow.

"Come and meet some people. You'll have a lot in common. Er—do you prefer Ms., or Miss?"

"Just make it D.J.," I said, hoping we wouldn't have to go through one of those agonizing explanations as to why I preferred initials. I might have known Hank wouldn't care. He'd have introduced me as Muhammad Ali if I had requested him to.

I saw two faces I recognized as we crossed the room. One was that of a young quarterback who had led his team to the Super Bowl the previous January. The other was the pug-nosed profile of a well-known Italian coloratura. Hank paid no attention to either; instead, he led me up to a tall, gray-haired man who looked like a French diplomat.

"This is Marcus Featherstonehaugh," he said, adding proudly, "Dr. Featherstonehaugh, that is. Marcus, meet D.J. Abbott, the anthropologist."

I cannot keep typing that name over and over, so I will refer to the gentleman as Marcus, though I certainly did not ever learn to think of him in such friendly terms. He eyed me as warily as I eyed him, and I couldn't entirely blame him. *The* anthropologist, indeed! There *were* others.

A woman swathed in flowing chiffon tugged at Hank's elbow, shrieking unintelligible demands, and he turned away. Over his shoulder he said, "You two will have a lot to talk about. The Mayans . . . Atlantis. . . ."

"Oh, no," I said involuntarily.

Marcus's well-bred, bony face stiffened. In a fairly good imitation of an English accent he said coldly, "We need not talk at all, young woman, if your attitude is that of the majority of scholars. I am only too familiar with the criminal narrow-mindedness of the anthropological profession. I have suffered from it all my life."

"Ah, the common denominator," I said. "Delusions of persecution."

Marcus passed over the implicit insult and pounded unerringly on the key word.

"Persecution is not too exaggerated a term. When I submitted my last paper—"

"Never mind," I interrupted. "What is it you believe, Doc—I mean, Marcus?"

It was the same old stuff Le Plongeon and his cohorts had been pushing—the idea that the brilliant, advanced citizens of Atlantis seeded the ancient civilizations of both hemispheres before their country sank under the sea. Marcus had jazzed it up a little by making the Atlanteans visitors from another galaxy. He wasn't specific about which galaxy. Even that touch wasn't new. None of the crazy theories are.

The thing was, he really believed it. As he talked, spots of febrile color flared up on his thin cheeks, and his eyes shone with a wild light. Somehow I hadn't really accepted that before—that the crackpots honestly believed their own theories. Now I realized that if I wanted to straighten Hank out, I would have to combat not only the professional con men, but the honest fanatics as well. I had a feeling the latter group would be the hardest to fight.

Despite what some people have claimed, I am not an argumentative person. Fighting, physical or verbal, is hard work. I only expend energy when there's something to be gained by it, and there was no point in debating with

Marcus; better men (I use the word "men" in the generic sense) than I had undoubtedly tried. That's a point the screwballs never acknowledge—that they do get a fair hearing. Even Spike Bancroft, who is not one of the nicest people in the world, spends hours listening patiently to idiots who wander into his office.

Marcus was in the middle of a long explanation of how he had deciphered the Mayan hieroglyphs when somebody tapped me on the shoulder.

"May I interrupt?" he asked, giving me a big white smile.

"You certainly may," I said.

One thing about Hank—he collected good-looking young men. This one was on the short side, stockily built, with arms and shoulders that bulged with muscle. Like Tom, he was dark as a Spaniard; unlike Tom, he was clean-shaven and pleasant looking. His smile wasn't a contortion of the lips; it showed all his teeth and warmed his brown eyes. They were nice eyes, and there was nothing wrong with the rest of him, either.

"My name is Jesse Franklin," he said.

"D.J. Abbott. Call me D.J."

"Gladly. Hello, Marcus; do go on with what you were saying."

"No one was listening anyhow," Marcus said bitterly. He turned and marched away, straight toward the bar.

"I figured you might need rescuing," Jesse said.

"I cannot tell a lie," I said, wondering if he wore his shirt sleeves rolled up clear to the shoulder on purpose to display his muscles. Whatever his reason, it was an excellent idea. "I don't need rescuing from people like that. I could have walked away clean anytime. I was just trying to get the flavor of the meeting."

"If that's what you were after, Marcus is a representative sample."

"I was warned that Hank is afflicted with screwballs."

"Right." He flashed me another wide white smile. "Since we're being honest with one another, I may as well admit that I'm one of the screwballs."

I didn't say "oh, no" out loud this time, but I thought it. With some trepidation I asked, "What's your bag?"

"Well, I like to think I'm not quite as crazy as some of the others. I'm a buried treasure freak."

"That's a new one to me," I said. "Uh—you don't believe in Martian buried treasure, do you, or in—"

"The lost crown jewels of Atlantis?" He laughed. "No. What I'm after is a good deal more recent, and more real. You've heard of the Lost Dutchman Mine, haven't you?"

"The name sounds familiar."

"It all started with Coronado, of course. When the Spaniards first explored this area, they were looking for gold. They hoped to find another Mexican empire, rich with treasure, and they were lured on by the legends of the Seven Cities of Cibola. They never found any empires, only Indian villages. But they did find gold. According to Coronado's Apache informants, one of the richest of all lodes, a vein of almost pure gold, was located in the slopes of the mountain where their Thunder God lived. They told Coronado about it, but such was their fear of the god that not even torture could force them to lead him to the spot. Coronado had to give up. He called the peak Superstition Mountain because of the Indians' terror of it."

He spoke with the fluency of someone who has repeated the story over and over, to himself as well as to others. His brown eyes had gone all soft and dreamy. I thought what a pity it was he didn't look at *me* that way.

"It's a good yarn," I said. "But if you are looking for gold on the basis of evidence like that—"

"Wait, that's just the beginning. I told you I wasn't as crazy as Hank's other associates, didn't I? Why do you suppose it's called the Lost Dutchman Mine?"

"I don't know, but I expect you are going to tell me. No, please do. It's interesting."

"I need very little urging. Okay; the next act of the play begins three hundred years later, in 1845, when a Mexican rancher named Don Miguel Peralta found gold on Superstition Mountain. Yes, my little skeptic, he really did! In succeeding years he shipped millions of pesos' worth of gold concentrate back to Mexico from the mine he had called Sombrero Mine, after a peculiarly shaped mountain nearby. But to the Apaches the mountain was still the abode of the Thunder God, and they were determined to wipe out the man who had defiled his sanctuary. The name Cochise may be vaguely familiar to you too. Cochise and his fellow chieftain Coloradas led the Apache forces that ambushed the Mexican column as it was heading home with burros loaded with gold. The place where it happened is known as Massacre Ground.

"Peralta had received warning of the Apache plan, and he took as many precautions as he could. One was to conceal the location of the mine, to prevent other people from working it before he could return, as he hoped to do. Not only did he hide the entrance, but he moved his men and equipment to a camp some distance away. He never did return. He and all his men were killed.

"The Apaches weren't interested in the gold. They dumped the ore-laden saddlebags out on the ground and ate the burros, which they considered great delicacies. But

50

some of the burros got away during the fight. Still loaded with incredible wealth, they wandered the arroyos and canyons till they died of accident or starvation or old age."

I felt like the Wedding Guest in the hypnotic spell of the Ancient Mariner. Well, it was a good story. Even the most skeptical of us is susceptible to the lure of buried treasure.

"Is it really true?" I asked eagerly.

"It is really true. A few years after the massacre, a U.S. Army troop came on the scene and buried the remains of the bodies. They never found Peralta's. Possibly the Indians carried it off as a trophy. Anyhow, in the early 1850's a couple of Irish prospectors found the skeleton of a burro and a rotting packsaddle filled with gold ore. They knew the Peralta story; everybody in the area did. They searched for more burro carcasses, and found them. When they finally carried their find back to California, they had almost forty thousand dollars' worth of gold. The word spread, naturally, and everybody rushed out to look for burro skeletons. Pickings got leaner and more dangerous; men like that thought nothing of shooting a buddy in the back in order to steal his loot. The last person to find one of Peralta's burros was named Silverlocke—appropriately enough. In 1914 he appeared in Phoenix with some scraps of rotted leather and eighteen thousand dollars' worth of gold concentrate."

"You still haven't gotten to the Dutchman," I said.

"He wasn't Dutch; he was German, as in 'Pennsylvania Dutch.' His name was Jacob Walz.

"During the period when people were looking for Peralta's burros, they were also searching for the mine. The only ones who knew the location were the Apaches,

51

who guarded the knowledge as a sacred secret. Walz had an Apache girlfriend to whom he was devoted. Her name was Ken-tee, which means 'Sunshine.' She told him where the mine was. Her own people killed her, horribly, for betraying the secret—or so the story goes. It doesn't explain why they didn't kill Walz, but they may have tried; he was a tough character, over six feet tall, built like a wrestler, and after his sweetheart's death he barricaded his house till it resembled a fort."

"Maybe they didn't feel he was as guilty as she," I suggested. "She had betrayed the tribe."

Jesse patted my hand. "It gets you, doesn't it? Wait till you hear the rest.

"In the years between 1879 and 1885 the Philadelphia Mint paid out over $245,000 to Walz for gold ore. Naturally people tried to follow him when he visited the mine, but no one succeeded. The terrain around the mountain is a wilderness of rocky canyons, bristling with cactus and dry as a bone. Walz was a crack shot, and if he caught anyone on his trail he didn't stop to ask why they were there. He died without passing the secret on, an embittered, lonely old man.

"That isn't the end of the story. Other people have found gold on Superstition Mountain. Some of them believed they had actually found Peralta's mine. Others believe it is still there. The search has never stopped."

"Wow." I sighed. "I love it. Want some help looking?"

"I'm not looking for the Dutchman mine," Jesse said coolly. "I just told you that story because it's the best-known treasure yarn of the Southwest. But there are dozens more. Arizona teems with such tales."

"That's not all it teems with," said a familiar voice. I turned. There he was, leaning against a sofa, his mustache quivering with contempt. "She's very gullible," he went on, addressing Jesse. "Shame on you for taking advantage of her."

"Ah, Tom," Jesse said. "You two have met?"

"He picked me up at the airport," I said. "But he doesn't know whether I am gullible or not. He has every reason to suppose I am not."

"You should have seen your face," De Karsky said. "Hypnotized. If I had handed you a fake Spanish map and a shovel, you'd have rushed out into the night and started digging."

"Is there something wrong with your spine?" I inquired. "I don't think I've ever seen you stand without support."

"I hope you are not under the delusion that I sought you out of my own free will," De Karsky said. "Hank told me to introduce you to some of the others. He was afraid Jesse might be monopolozing you."

"Hank's word is my command," I said wittily. "I've enjoyed this, Jesse."

"So have I. We'll talk another time."

He raised his glass in a graceful salute and sauntered off. I turned to De Karsky.

"I'm supposed to ask you if you want another drink," he said.

I looked at my glass in mild surprise. Sure enough, it was empty.

"Well. . . ."

"You'll need it if you're going to talk to the other nuts."

"Is that how you classify Jesse?" I asked.

"Yes."

"But that story was fact. Names, dates, places. . . ."

"Oh, the story is true—most of it. This is a melodramatic part of the world; no fictitious story is more unbelievable than some of the things that really happened out here. But Jesse's treasure-hunting theories are almost as impractical as Marcus's delusions of Atlantis. They'll never come to anything."

"There is a categorical difference and you know it," I said.

Tom handed my empty glass to the bartender and gave me a full one.

"Anyway," I said, "who are you to cast stones?"

"I'll throw stones at anyone I like. Save your sermons; you'll find them useful as we proceed."

So I was introduced to the lady in the turban, Madame Karenina, who told me about Hank's previous existence as a prince of lost Atlantis, and offered to find out who I had been; to Professor Ryan, who told me how America had been populated by the Lost Tribes of Israel; to Sam and Dee Ballou, who had spent three days with little green men from Arcturus in their flying saucer; and to a character named Horbiger who believed, if I understood him correctly, that the catastrophes of ancient times, such as the Flood and the plagues of Moses, were all caused by an old moon falling into the Pacific Ocean, or by a new moon rising up out of the Pacific Ocean. I know it doesn't make sense. Neither did Horbiger.

He was the only one of the group whom I could confidently classify as an out-and-out con man. He had tried to dress like a European professor, and he had a thick, affected accent, but the masquerade didn't quite come off. His gray eyes, magnified by thick glasses, were the coldest eyes I had ever seen.

I had my suspicions about the Ballous, too, at least about her. He was one of those blank-faced, smiling little

54

men who is not quite with it. If she had told him he had been kidnapped by Martians or hundred-legged worms, he'd have said, "Yes, dear." She was twice his size, a massive, faded blonde with arms the size of a strong man's thighs. It's not true that fat people are jolly. I remember seeing a picture of a nursemaid who had killed half a dozen children before they caught up with her. She looked a lot like Mrs. Ballou.

Ordinarily I do not drink much, but I needed something to dull the pain of talking to those people. I had finished my second drink and was halfway through my third when I started to feel funny. At first I thought it was mental nausea. Before long, however, the nausea became specific. I excused myself in the middle of a long spiel by "Professor" Ryan, describing the Semitic profiles of the ancient Mayans, and headed for the door.

Long before I got there I knew I wasn't going to make it up to my room. Instinct, and a draft of cool evening air, sent me blundering toward the French doors. There was a flagstoned terrace outside, fringed with shrubs. Like a sick animal I headed into the darkness, away from the lighted windows. When I tripped over an indistinguishable object I didn't bother rising; I stayed on my hands and knees and let it all come up.

It wasn't just my stomach. My eyes were fogged and my head was spinning like a flying saucer. I was so far gone I didn't realize I was no longer alone until an arm looped around me, supporting my heaving diaphragm, and a hand cupped my fevered brow. I knew who it was —I can't tell you how I knew, but I did—and I didn't care. Not at first, anyway.

"Is that it?" he asked, after the spasm had passed.

"For the moment," I mumbled.

I was as limp as a rag doll. My arms flopped helplessly as he tipped me back against his chest and held me with one arm while he wiped my face with his handkerchief. He was as efficient and impersonal as a doctor, but the warmth of his body felt wonderful; I was shaking with chill and the sweat on my face felt clammy in the night air.

As the shivering subsided and my insides settled back into place, I was able to savor the full humiliation of my position. If there is anything worse than throwing up all over a good-looking man whom you adore, it is throwing up all over a good-looking man whom you dislike. Let's be honest; the more a man despises us, the more we want to weaken his resistance. There is no finer revenge than to make him fall in love with you and then laugh at him. I hadn't admitted it to myself, but that was what I wanted to do to Tom De Karsky. I doubted that this incident had improved my chances. There is nothing less sexy than a woman who is vomiting.

"I was not drunk," I said.

"No," De Karsky said.

His voice sounded peculiar. I squirmed around till I could see his face. He wasn't looking at me. With his free hand he was groping for something that lay on the ground beside me. I couldn't see what it was in that dim light till he held it up.

"I can't take pills without water," I said querulously. "Besides, I don't want—"

"I should say you've had enough of them already," De Karsky said.

"What?"

"They fell out of your pocket, didn't they?" He picked up a few more of the pills.

"What?"

"Oh, for. . . ." He reached into my pocket. I was about to remonstrate when his groping fingers closed on something and brought it out. Another pill.

Capsule, I should say. It was one of those long thin plastic tubes filled with powder. I couldn't make out the color, but realization dawned with all the splendor of a stormy sunrise.

"Uppers?" I said weakly.

"That would be an appropriate term. I don't recognize the variety. That doesn't happen to be one of my specialties."

"Nor mine. I never—"

"Come off it. You must be thoroughly hooked if you can't even spend an evening without a pocketful of them. To take a risk like that. . . . You know this is the one thing Hank won't tolerate. He had an unfortunate experience with peyote some years ago, and since then he's been death on any variety of dope. If you want to get kicked out of here on your pretty behind, this is the way to do it."

I pulled myself away from him. I didn't look very dignified squatting on my haunches, with my hair straggling over my eyes and my recent performance fresh in both our minds, but I was so mad I didn't care.

"As it happens, I was unaware of Hank's feelings. It wouldn't have mattered. I don't take any kind of dope. I can't. Pot makes me break out and I'm allergic to amphetamines, I always have been."

De Karsky crossed his legs and stared at me.

"Is that true?"

"The evidence is before you," I said bitterly.

"Hmmm." He stroked his mustache meditatively. "That's undeniable. Then—"

"Somebody put these in my pocket and added another dose to my drink," I said. "It could have been almost anyone. I talked to lots of people, and part of the time my glass was standing on a table, unwatched—by me, at least."

"Almost you convince me, Abbott."

"It's an unconvincing story, I must admit. You can take those to Hank and tell him where you found them, if you really want to get rid of me."

"I do want to get rid of you. Even more, after this. . . . But I can't. Not that way."

"I don't follow you," I admitted.

He smiled. The smile curved the corners of his mouth but did not reach his eyes.

"If you're telling me the truth, you probably regard me as a hot suspect. I can't squeal to Hank without confirming your suspicions. Besides, it's your word against mine as to where I found the pills."

"That's right," I said, cheered.

"So. . . ." He got to his feet in one effortless movement and extended a hand to me. "I'll show you the back way to your room. You can say you suffer from morning sickness or something, and don't feel like eating—"

"Who says I don't feel like eating?" I stood up without his help. I felt wobbly, but not too bad. "Just lead me to a bathroom where I can wash up and comb my hair."

For the first time since I had met him I saw a human emotion cross De Karsky's face. The emotion was astonishment. His mouth actually hung open.

"You have nice teeth," I said. "You ought to show them more often."

Chapter Four

In one of her few relapses into sarcasm, my mother once said that if I was ever unable to eat she wouldn't call a doctor; she'd call an undertaker. By the time I returned to the living room, washed and brushed and outwardly composed, I had decided it was incumbent upon me to force down a little sustenance. Admittedly, greed was an element in this decision, but I had another motive. The dirty rat who had doped my drink might be disconcerted to see me going about my business unperturbed and unaffected. He might even be disconcerted enough to betray himself.

The others were beginning to drift into the dining room, and I blended with the crowd. Dinner was buffet style—the only way in which a staff of servants could deal with a transient group like that one. Besides, it suited Hank's casual life-style. There were little tables scattered around the room, overflowing onto a courtyard lit by wrought-iron lanterns, with a fountain tinkling in the middle.

When I saw the spread, my last pangs of queasiness vanished. I took a plate and waded in. Roast beef en croûte, ham with truffles, all kinds of Mexican food, like enchiladas and tamales. . . . I hesitated over a big pot of chili and then decided—what the hell—I might as well go out in style. After that my plate was full, so I looked for a table. As I headed toward the courtyard, I saw De Karsky watching me from across the room. His mouth was open again.

I found a nice table with a candle on it, and nodded affably at the houseman who came rushing up to fill my wineglass. It was champagne. Very good for the stomach, all those bubbles.

I was munching away when Hank came along. He was dressed in formal Western evening attire, in case I've neglected to mention that—jeans and a clean shirt and about twenty pounds of silver and turquoise. The silver plates of his concha belt were inlaid with turquoise and coral. Around his neck he wore a bola tie; the narrow braided leather strap supported a silver eagle-dancer figure whose outspread wings were masterpieces of inlay; the soft blue stones actually suggested the sweep of feathers. A lot of men in the Southwest wear jewelry like this; it might have looked strange at first, to eastern eyes, but it suited Hank perfectly. I twisted my pathetic little owl ring under so it wouldn't show.

"Got room for a couple more here?" he asked, looking approvingly at my heaped plate.

"Sure. Please join me."

"I've got to make sure all my guests are happy first. Just wanted you to meet these young folks. They're both dying to make your acquaintance."

If they were, they managed to conceal their rapture very well. There were two of them, male and female. The woman was about my age. She wore horn-rimmed glasses and a mean expression. Her hair was pulled back into a bun, her face was innocent of makeup, unless the freckles were painted on, and she was disgustingly thin. She wasn't bad looking, actually; her features were regular and she had pretty green eyes with long smudgy lashes, but she had evidently decided to make herself as homely as possible.

I didn't need Hank's introduction to know that the man was her brother. They were comically alike, even to the horn-rimmed glasses, except that he was a foot taller than she—well over six feet—and his expression was not quite as sour. Their names were Joe and Edna Stockwell and, Hank explained proudly, they were *anthropologists!*

"The anthropologists?" I said, before I could stop myself. Hank looked confused, and I went on, "Never mind me, I was thinking of something else. Glad to meet you. Call me D.J."

"You'll get along just fine," Hank assured us. He pulled out a chair for Edna, spread a warm smile over the three of us, and left.

61

Joe Stockwell looked at me over his glasses. "What does D.J. stand for?"

He really wanted to know. He had that kind of mind.

"That's a secret," I said. "And irrelevant, don't you think?"

"Perhaps. Yes. With whom have you been studying?"

I told him. He nodded gravely. Edna's face took on an expression of deeper scorn, if that was possible.

"My brother has his doctorate," she announced.

"Ah," I said. "And you?"

"I'll be getting mine next year. I'm doing my dissertation on Anasazi pottery."

"Ah," I said.

"Do you know anything about the Anasazi?"

"Very little," I said.

That finished me, so far as Edna was concerned. She nodded smugly and began to eat. Her plate was almost bare—nothing on it but salad.

Joe had been examining me with the critical attention of a paleontologist inspecting an old bone. Apparently he decided that the bone might have interesting features after all. He said,

"But Bancroft is a flint man. If you studied with him, you must have learned something about prehistoric Southwestern cultures."

I didn't bother explaining that Bancroft was only acting as my adviser this year, while Sakowitz, our "bone man," was on sabbatical.

"The Anasazi are too modern for him," I said. "He likes Folsom points."

"Yes, yes, of course." Joe took a bite of ham and chewed methodically. When he had finished his fifty chews (I caught myself counting them as, I am sure, he was himself), he spoke again. "Perhaps you'd like to join us for a few weeks. If you've had no field experience in the Southwest, I can teach you a good deal."

Edna looked up with such an agonized expression I thought she had found a worm in the lettuce. She had. I was the worm.

"But, Joe, she's had no experience—she'd just be in the way—"

"We can always use another pair of hands," Joe said, confirming my suspicion that his kindly offer had not been designed for my benefit. He wanted me for unpaid manual labor—washing potsherds and wielding a shovel.

"I certainly don't want to intrude," I said.

"No, no," Joe said, waving his sister to silence. "You—well, actually, you'd be doing me a favor too. We're on a limited budget, as you can imagine; thanks to Hank, we save on board and room by living here, but the university refused his offer of financial assistance—"

"I can imagine why," I said. Joe smiled at me. He looked nice when he smiled, but I was not deceived. He wanted my body. The parts of it necessary for digging, I mean.

"You know Hank," he said. "You're right; there were strings attached to the offer, and the university couldn't go along with his demands."

"He wanted us to look for dragon bones," Edna said in an outraged voice.

"Now, Edna, you exaggerate."

"I don't suppose she's exaggerating very much," I said, smiling sweetly at Edna. She didn't smile back. I gave up trying to be ingratiating and turned back to her brother. "Why dragon bones, for God's sake? I thought he was on a Martian kick."

"I don't try to keep up with Hank's ideas," Joe said, his

63

nose in the air. "Where Edna got the idea of dragons I cannot imagine; even Hank couldn't be that weird."

I started to contradict him—it seemed to me that nothing was too weird for Hank—but he waved me to silence with the same lofty gesture he had used on Edna. "That's beside the point," he continued. "We'd like to have you with us. The site is proving to be mildly interesting."

"Ah," I said. I had done all right with "ah" before; but this time Joe continued to look at me expectantly. "Honestly, Joe, I don't know," I went on. "I think Hank has something else in mind for me."

Edna pushed her plate away and gave me a gimlet-eyed stare.

"What is this mysterious discovery of his, anyway?"

"I was hoping you could tell me," I said.

"You mean you came here blind, without knowing what you're supposed to do?"

"I'm supposed to look at Hank's discovery and report on it," I said, annoyed by her hectoring tone. "If it's something big, you can't blame him for being secretive. Scholars are not above stealing other people's ideas."

"Hank's ideas aren't worth stealing," Edna said. "Merely being associated with him is a stain on a scholar's reputation."

"Then it's awfully brave of you to risk it, in return for this Spartan existence," I said gently.

Joe appeared not to notice the undertones of bitchiness in the exchange. He had his sister hypnotized or something; the minute he opened his mouth she shut up and fell into an attitude of respectful attention.

"It's not entirely impossible that Hank has found something," he said patronizingly. "Our own site is an example of what may exist in this area. Hank may have come across another village, or even a cemetery."

"I'm surprised he didn't ask you to have a look," I said.

"We haven't time for such nonsense," Edna snapped.

"Hank wouldn't consult me," Joe added. "He knows we aren't sympathetic to his ideas. But of course if you find anything deserving of my attention, I'd be happy to give you my opinion."

"Thanks," I said.

"There won't be anything," Edna said. She pushed her chair back. "Joe, wouldn't you like some coffee?"

"Yes, I believe I would."

"The waiter will bring it, I expect," I said.

"I prefer to get it myself."

She flounced off. I am not one to jump to conclusions, so I thought about her for another thirty seconds before I decided that I did not like her. I knew one of the reasons why she was mad at me. In spite of her sneers at Hank she was annoyed at his calling in an outside expert instead of consulting her and her sacred brother. I didn't blame Hank for not doing so. Joe was a pompous ass and his sister was worse. Both had probably patronized and insulted Hank while availing themselves of his hospitality. Hank was too much of a gentleman to kick them out, but it was no wonder he didn't care for them.

"I'm going back for seconds," I said to Joe, who was eating in placid silence. "See you later."

"We leave for the dig at five A.M."

If I had not yet made up my mind about joining them, that would have done the trick.

"I'll have to talk to Hank before I make any plans," I said. "I'll let you know."

I really didn't intend to eat anything else, I just wanted to leave Joe and his adorable sister. But when I went back to the buffet I saw a lovely assortment of desserts—apple pie, lemon chiffon pie, little cream puffs with whipped cream inside and chocolate sauce dribbled over them, fruit compote and chocolate cake and lemon Bavarian and. . . . I had some of the cream puffs. I would have had some apple pie, too, but I thought I'd better not tax my stomach too much, so I got a cup of coffee and wedged myself into a corner between the dessert table—in case I changed my mind about the pie—and the French doors. It was an excellent vantage point. I could see the whole room without being involved with the mob.

A few people were still eating, but most of them were on their feet. Hank's friends were a restless group. Marcus sat at a nearby table working on a slab of chocolate cake. I considered joining him; any man who could eat a piece of cake that size had to have some good qualities. But I decided I had heard enough about the Atlanteans for the moment.

Actually, I was looking for Jesse. I liked him better than anybody I had met so far, except maybe Hank. Eventually I saw him talking to Edna, of all people. I couldn't see her face, but he was obviously holding her spellbound; she stood gazing up at him as he talked, his smile brilliant, his head bent toward her.

So there was another reason why Edna might not care too much for little me. If she had something going with Jesse she certainly would have observed me, equally spellbound, at an earlier time. I was a little surprised at her interest, since she had given me the impression she wouldn't even spit on anyone with less than an M.A.; but love laughs at Ph.D.s, as the saying goes, and Jesse was indubitably gorgeous. Also, in spite of De Karsky's nasty cracks, Jesse was not a crackpot. His story had sounded very plausible to me.

The evening passed in what I was to find a quite characteristic fashion. There was no organized activity; people came and went, eating and drinking and talking. I wandered from room to room observing it all. There was a billiards room and a card room and a music room, with a grand piano the size of our kitchen back home, and various unidentified rooms in which other activities were going on. At one point the Italian coloratura gave an impromptu recital. I listened for a while and then drifted out and played pool with a young man in a white robe who was a Son of the Golden Temple or something like that. He was a rotten player. I won three games in a row, and then Golden Boy got mad and stalked out, his skirts swishing.

I went back to the dining room after my robed friend had deserted me, and I had a little piece of apple pie, and then I started out on another tour of exploration, in a different direction. Eventually I found myself in a long corridor lit by dim bulbs in antique sconces. The floor was of rough tile with the mellow brown glow of old brick. All along the whitewashed walls were objects that would have graced any museum of Southwestern art, but they were not organized, as in a museum gallery; Aztec masks of inlaid turquoise, modern paintings of Indian dancers and galloping horses, pottery of all periods were mixed together in a display that was obviously meant to be aesthetically pleasing rather than informative. At the end of the gallery stood a pair of double doors made of heavy dark wood studded with iron nailheads. They looked formidable, but they yielded to my tentative touch, swinging

67

back as lightly and noiselessly as if they had been formed of papier-mâché.

When the lights went on, I thought for a minute that some of the drug must have gotten to me after all. I was nose to nose with a three-foot-high character dressed in a loincloth and some beads and feathers. I speak figuratively; he didn't have a nose. He had a watermelon in place of a head.

The world is full of a number of things, as Stevenson once said, and I don't know very much about most of them. But I had done a little tourist-type reading to prepare for my trip, so I recognized this creation as a kachina doll, a particularly big and beautiful and elaborate specimen of the type. The dolls are not toys, though they were given to Hopi children; they represent the various nature spirits and demigods of that tribe. Masked dancers play the parts of the gods during the big religious festivals, so a well-educated Hopi child must know who and what the figures represent. I had seen some small, mass-produced versions of the dolls in the shop at the airport, but Hank's collection made those look like the cheap imitations they were. The shelves held row upon row of figures, varying in size, but all brilliantly painted and vibrant with life. The watermelon, I discovered from the label, was not a watermelon, but a gourd—one of the staple foods of the Hopi. Other dolls represented eagle and other bird gods, plants and animals.

The whole wing of the house was a little private museum. The room beyond the one with the kachina dolls had glass-fronted cases containing baskets and pottery, including some of the sensational black polished San Ildefonso ware. The next room had archaeological odds and ends—bones, scraps of fabric, arrowheads, and the like.

Everything was neatly labeled and displayed. There were no dubious artifacts and no references to Martians or Israelites or Atlanteans. In fact, it was a perfectly respectable, rather choice little museum, and the objects were considerably more impressive than the ones in most collections. It helps, of course, if you are a millionaire collector. It also helps to have a trained, hard-working assistant. I began to wonder if I had misjudged Tom De Karsky.

I was about to retrace my steps when I realized that the draperies at the far end of the room did not hide windows. Through a gap where they had not been completely closed, I caught a gleam of metal.

I didn't feel guilty about looking. The museum had been wide open, all the doors unlocked. The gleam *was* metal—a door like that of a bank vault, brightly polished steel.

I should have know this door would be locked. You don't build vaults unless you want to keep people out. But for some reason it irritated me to find that the handle wouldn't move. I kicked the door and swore.

Somebody laughed. It was a harmless-enough sound, but in that hushed, untenanted place, it startled me. I spun around. Tom stood there with his hands on his hips and his mustache twitching in his version of amusement. Not only did he look like an Indian, he moved like one— Cochise in person, not a twig snapping.

"You don't have to follow me," I said. "I wasn't going to steal anything."

"You couldn't, not from there. It would take a couple of pounds of explosives to blow that door. But go ahead and kick it again if it relieves any neuroses."

"What's in there?"

"Jewelry. Aha, that roused the old acquisitive instincts,

69

didn't it? Hank has one of the finest collections of turquoise and Indian jewelry in the world. Want to see it?"

"Yes," I said promptly.

He was an evil-minded man. He stood in such a way that his body hid the lock while he worked the combination. The door opened with a sinister-sounding whoosh of air. The lights must have been connected to the door, because they went on when it opened and I caught a mouth-watering glimpse of silver shimmering, of sky-blue stones. . . . But when Tom waved me in I hesitated.

"What happens if the door closes while we're in there?"

Tom's breath came out in an exasperated snort that made the hairs of his mustache wiggle.

"The door can't shut, you idiot. And if, by a million-to-one chance, it did, we push the button inside labeled 'alarm' and Hank comes and lets us out. Go on," he added, giving me a shove. "What do you think this is, the House of Usher?"

"I'm beginning to wonder," I muttered. But I went in.

I forgot my qualms in the first moment. The room was lined with display cases; more cases ran in a double row down the center, forming two aisles. The lights had been arranged to show off the exhibits to their best advantage.

Concha belts, squash-blossom necklaces, bracelets, rings, fetish necklaces and necklaces of strung turquoise nuggets, silver beads; deep rich red coral, and turquoise of every conceivable shade of blue, from pale azure Persian to deep aquamarine slashed by veins of dark matrix. There were figures of birds and animals and masked dancers formed of countless small stones cut precisely to shape and set each in its own specially designed compartment; pendants of needlepoint and petit-point technique, with dozens of tiny round and oval stones set in silver; heavy dark silver bracelets embellished with huge polished nuggets. . . .

Tom let me drool and slobber for a while, and then he started lecturing.

"The Indians have been working turquoise and shell for centuries, but they didn't use silver till after the white man came. The first jewelry was made of coins—Mexican pesos and American silver dollars—beaten flat and then hammered into shape. Now it's a complex modern art. The Navahos are the silversmiths par excellence. The Zunis specialize in inlaid work and in petit point."

I showed him my ring. He laughed.

"Indian jewelry has become popular lately, and a lot of junk is being turned out."

"I paid thirty dollars for it!"

"I'm sure you did, sucker." He indicated a fetish necklace, like many I had seen back home in department stores. You have seen them too, probably; tiny carved figures of birds and animals strung with small beads. This was a seven-stranded necklace, and the minuscule carvings were lovely blends of color—ivory bears, red coral birds, other animal shapes of turquoise and jet and a translucent amber shade. "That's worth about two thousand dollars a strand, at a conservative estimate," he went on. "It's by David Tsikewa, one of the modern masters. Hank has the best of the new and the best of the old. This"—he indicated a case where the objects were of heavier, darker silver, with fewer colored stones—"this is pawn jewelry—the genuine article, made by and for Indians. Men wore almost as much as women. Oftentimes they had to hock it when they needed food. That necklace at the end is one of the few pieces known to have been made by Beshthlagai Ithlini Athltososigi, who worked in the 1880's."

He rattled the name off with the ease of long practice, giving the strange syllables a melodious ring. The necklace was lovely. It had rows of the little flower forms called squash blossoms, and a heavy pendant like a crescent moon—the same basic elements you find in most squash-blossom necklaces, but there was a grace and elegance in the shapes that was quite distinctive.

"His name means 'Slender Maker of Silver,'" Tom added.

"Oh, that's beautiful," I exclaimed. I regretted this outburst of sentiment almost immediately, but to my surprise Tom didn't make a nasty crack.

"It's descriptive of the man and of his work," he said. "Those aren't squash blossoms, by the way, though everyone calls them that. They are probably derived from pomegranate flowers, by way of Mexico. You notice that they didn't use as much turquoise back then. It was always expensive, and today it's out of sight. A lot is imported from Persia, and the poorer qualities are treated to make them look like first-grade stone. If you want a really good piece, you'd have to go to a reputable dealer—and offer him your earnings for the next ten years."

"It's unlikely that I will ever be in a position to invest," I admitted. "But if I am, I'll consult you."

"I'm no expert. But like so many other subjects, the more you learn about it, the more interesting it is. The good turquoise is so rare and expensive these days that a casual shopper never sees it, so he fails to appreciate how beautiful the real article can be. Connoisseurs claim it has

72

a quality called 'zat'—a sort of soft, sensuous glow that is hard to define, but unmistakable when you see it. Look at that stone. It's Bisbee Blue—named for the mine where it was found. See how deep and glowing the color is? This variety, where the matrix takes the form of a webbed, over-all pattern, is called Old Burnham Spiderweb. The paler blue, with the iron pyrite matrix, is Blue Gem; this greener shade is Morenci."

"It's like diamonds," I said. "You can actually tell the mine where the stone comes from."

"Well, not always. But the finer types are easy to spot. For instance, this is fossilized turquoise from Lone Mountain—very rare."

Tom practically had to drag me out of that room. After he had closed the door and twirled the lock, I shook my head.

"That was frightening," I said.

"What? Being inside? Claustrophobia?"

"No. Greed. I never cared much about jewelry. But I wanted that. I wanted to touch it and wear it and feel it against my skin. How terrible!"

"If it's any consolation, Hank feels the same way. Though he's obsessively generous, he doesn't give away his turquoise. Fortunata has hinted often enough—"

"Fortunata?" I repeated incredulously.

"Haven't you met her? She's one of the more exotic birds of prey who fatten on Hank. Anyhow, Hank has a kind of . . . well, call it a mystique, about turquoise. It doesn't affect me that way, but I can understand it; I have similar feelings about other things."

"Such as what?"

"None of your business."

The tone, even more than the words themselves, was

like a slap in the face. He had been so nice up till then, relaxed and really friendly. Now I wanted to kick him.

II

Having had enough excitement for one evening, I went straight up to my room. One of the maids had been there. She had left a single lamp burning, just enough light to keep me from falling over my feet. The corners and the beamed ceiling were soft with gray shadows. On the bedside table was a brace of silver thermos jugs and a covered plate of miscellaneous tidbits. My bed had been turned down and my nightgown draped across the pillow. I use the singular advisedly; I only owned one nightgown. It was one of those virginal white eyelet things, with pale-blue ribbons dangling from various locations. Mother had given it to me for Christmas. Naturally I had never worn it, but I was glad she had forced it on me. The bed would have looked so naked without it.

Suddenly I was dead tired. I guess the quiet, restful look of the room was what hit me, but it had been a long day. I almost drowned in the bathtub, waking with a gurgle and a splash when I started to slide down into the scented water. I got into my virginal white nightie and started to crawl into bed.

Then I crawled out again. I went to the door and locked it. I took the top off one of the thermoses. There was coffee inside. I sniffed at it, and sampled a drop. It was a futile experiment, I couldn't tell anything from that and I was not about to risk getting sick again just to prove a point. The second thermos held soup of some kind, redolent of garlic and spices. I decided I didn't want that either.

I turned off the lights. Moonlight flooded the room. I

had planned to devote a few quiet moments to considering what had happened earlier, but it was a lost cause; I was asleep in two minutes. Just before I dropped off, a peculiar thought slid into my drowsy brain. Debbie's name. . . . What was it?

I was almost asleep before the answer came to me—not only the name, but my reason for wanting to remember it. Her Indian name was Ken-tee; the same name as that of the Dutchman's murdered Apache sweetheart.

Chapter Five

Sunlight woke me—dazzling, shifting light reflected from the whitewashed walls. There was no clock in the room, but I knew it must be early because when I went to the balcony to see what was happening outside, the air was bracingly cool.

The evening before I hadn't paid too much attention to the view except to notice that it was beautiful. The mountains had been swathed in shadows, their outlines indistinct. Now the sunlight fell full upon them, outlining barren crags with stark clarity, casting pastel shadows into the ragged canyons that had torn their sides. With each moment the light strengthened and the shadows changed color and outline, passing from lavender to rose to grayish pink. The lower slopes were dark with trees, tall green pines standing straight as soldiers.

Finally I tore myself away from the view and got dressed. I was about to leave the room when a thought occurred to me. I emptied the thermos of coffee down the drain and flushed away a handful of snacks. They were probably all right, but you can't be sure; you can get enough LSD on a postage stamp to send someone flying high. With people coming and going the way they did in that house, anyone could have entered my bedroom the night before.

There was no sensible reason why anyone should play such a trick on me. However, people are not sensible. Hank had a particularly ripe collection of loonies in residence, and any one of them might have decided they didn't want me around. Tom was a hot suspect too. I was not about to let his pretty face cloud my judgment. He had made no bones about his desire to get rid of me.

Breakfast was not being served in the dining room. I found a white-coated houseman, and he directed me to a courtyard enclosed by pillared loggias. Breakfast was laid out English style, with hot plates and silver chafing dishes.

On rereading these pages, I see that I have said quite a lot about food. So I will spare you a description of my breakfast. When I had finished I went looking for Hank. My miniature conscience was beginning to bother me. After all, I was being paid to work, not to loaf with the idle rich.

After I had wandered around for a while, finding new

wings and courtyards and rooms, and treasures innumerable, I realized I was fighting a losing battle, looking for one man in all that space. So I got smart. I cornered another servant and asked where I could find the boss. He said Hank was probably out in back, "with the animals."

I assumed the animals were horses. Wouldn't you? The place was a ranch, after all. I added a few dogs to my mental picture—Hank looked like the kind of man who would like dogs—and followed the directions I had been given.

Eventually I emerged from the house into a fenced enclosure with rich green grass and shade trees all around. I couldn't see any stables. However, there was a long, low white building on one side of the field. As I approached it I began to suspect what might be inside; the morning breeze carried sensory clues of various types, mostly smells. Even so, I was not prepared for the sight that met my eyes when I opened the door and looked in.

The floor was tiled. The bars of the cages that lined both walls gleamed like silver. They varied in size, from little cages big enough for a family of mice to huge enclosures suitable for. . . .

"My God," I said.

I looked again. It *was* a lion. Not the African type of lion, with a bushy mane; this was a puma or a mountain lion, or something of that sort. I love cats of all sizes, but I didn't like the look of this one and it obviously didn't like me; it glowered at me as I tiptoed gently past it.

The lion was the most exotic specimen in the little zoo. Most of the others were ordinary cats and dogs, but I saw a coyote and a couple of squirrels and some fuzzy fat little creatures that might have been prairie dogs or ground hogs. The cages were clean and well supplied with food and water; but almost all the animals had something wrong with them—bandages, or half-healed sores, or just a sick, mopey look. I was beginning to feel a little sick myself as I walked along the rows of cages toward a door at the far end. What was going on in this place? Did Hank's wild theories include experimentation on animals?

The door was open. I smelled antiseptic. As I approached, I could see what was in the room beyond the door, and what I saw strengthened my worst suspicions. It looked like a doctor's surgery—shelves of bandages and bottles of pills and such things. There was a table in the middle of the room. I could only see one end of it; the rest of the table, and whatever lay on it, were hidden by the bulky body of a man wearing a white coat. Hank stood at the other end of the table, so absorbed in what was going on that he didn't see or hear me till I stood in the doorway. Then he looked up.

"Good morning," he said, with a smile that now looked sinister, instead of good-humored. "Almost through here; just a minute. . . ."

"That's it," said the man in the white coat. He turned.

The light from the big lamp over the table struck full on his glasses; they shone like the eyes of a giant insect, or a monster from outer space. His hands were pink and pudgy and damp-looking.

On the table, tied down with cords, was the body of a rabbit. It was a big brown rabbit; its enormous ears lay limp and crumpled and pathetic on the table. Across one ear ran a row of neat black comma shapes.

"D.J., meet Doc Brandt," Hank said. "This is the young lady I was telling you about, Doc. The anthropologist."

Doc Brandt took a step forward so that the light no

longer reflected off his glasses. I could see his eyes now. They were soft brown eyes, like those of an amiable retriever. All at once the whole scene shifted focus, and I felt thoroughly ashamed of myself.

"You're a vet," I said brilliantly.

"Right. This is the first time I ever sewed an ear back on a jackrabbit, though. I hope it works. Those fellows need their ears to survive."

"I'll put him back in the cage," Hank said, untying the cords and lifting the rabbit in big, gentle hands.

The doctor turned to the sink and began to wash his hands.

"Are you the resident vet?" I asked, looking around the little operating room. It was small but very well equipped.

"Practically. I'm here every day. Hank keeps me pretty busy. Everybody for fifty miles around knows what a soft touch he is; they fetch hurt and abandoned animals here from all over the county."

Hank came back carrying a mangy-looking black cat. He held it as tenderly as if it had been a prize Persian. It put its ears back and hissed at me as he placed it on the table.

"She's had a bad time," Hank apologized. "It's no wonder she's a little suspicious of people. Have a look at her, will you, Doc? She came in yesterday. I think she's going to have kittens."

Brandt winked at me.

"You run along, Hank," he said, taking the cat. "I'm sure there are other things you ought to be doing."

"Are you trying to tell me I'm in the way?" Hank demanded.

"Yes. You're as bad as a nervous mother. You make me nervous too. Scram."

80

As we went back through the hospital, Hank pointed out the patients that particularly interested him. When we approached the lion's cage the big animal rose lithely to its feet and let out a noise midway between a growl and a snarl. I backed up a couple of feet.

"Nothing to worry about," Hank said. "He's just saying hello. Aren't you, old fellow?"

To my consternation, he put his hand between the bars and scratched the lion under the chin. It closed its eyes and tilted its head coquettishly. A grating sound like that of a rusty saw filled the room.

"It's purring," I gasped. "How do you do that?"

"Don't you try it," Hank warned. "Animals aren't naturally mean—most of them, anyhow—but when they don't feel good, they are apt to be quick-tempered. I don't know how I do it. I always have had a kind of rapport with animals. Some days I like 'em better than people, if you know what I mean."

"I know just what you mean."

"This old cuss was shot," Hank went on. For a moment his amiable face took on quite a different expression. "I don't hold with hunting for pleasure. Food's one thing; animals, including human animals, have to prey on each other, that's natural law. But man is the only animal that kills for fun. This place of mine is posted, no hunting allowed. If I catch anybody with a rifle. . . . Anyhow, the old fellow's getting along fine. In a week or so I'll take him back into the mountains and turn him loose. Come on out and see the healthy ones now. They cheer me up, after all this misery in here."

He had a fabulous setup—runs and kennels and luxurious quarters for a motley collection of pets, some mongrels, some show-quality animals. A few were caged—

"Not mean, just feeling strange and kind of soured by life, you might say. . . ." But most of the collection ran free, and they got along surprisingly well with each other.

I could have spent the day there, especially with the baby animals: kittens and puppies and deer, and a baby mountain lion that was absolutely adorable, though it left little holes in my hand when I played with it. I could see that Hank was reluctant to leave too, but eventually he said we had better go.

"It must be going on toward lunch time," he remarked.

"Already? I didn't mean to waste the whole morning. I came looking for you to ask when you want me to start work."

"Well, I certainly wasn't going to put you to work the very day after you got here," Hank said, looking hurt. "You just relax for a few days and take it easy. There's a pool, and horses, if you like to ride—but don't go out in the desert alone, it's not safe. And if you want to go to Flag, to shop or anything, take one of the cars, or—"

"But I didn't come for a vacation. I came to—"

"I'll tell you what, I'll just show you where things are, right now, and then you'll be able to amuse yourself. The pool's over this way."

It was Olympic size, of course, surrounded by flowering shrubs and by a low row of cabanas with red-tiled roofs and grilled windows. I said no, I didn't feel like a swim right now, so we went on to the stables. I was not surprised to see several sway-backed antiques among the thoroughbreds, tended with the same loving care. I had to admit I wasn't much of a rider. Hank's face fell and he said, well, how about the garage, maybe there was a car I would condescend to use. A Jaguar, maybe, or the Porsche? If I didn't want to go shopping, there was a pretty

82

good museum up in Flag, and also some Indian ruins that were kind of interesting. . . .

He acted like an anxious tour guide dealing with a bored, haughty patron who refused to be amused. As we walked he kept trying to think of other entertainments—the library, the sauna, the piano—and did I play the guitar, by any chance? He had a collection of antique stringed instruments. . . .

I wondered how I had fallen into this deal—and I wondered how this man had survived in the money jungle. All I knew about the world of high finance was by hearsay, but I had the impression you had to be mean as a mountain lion to get on. This man was a pussycat. It was a wonder someone hadn't eaten him.

I soon found out how he had survived.

We were some distance from the house, in what I would call the working part of the ranch. There were outbuildings galore, barns and tool sheds, and rows of little cottages where some of the help lived. It was getting on toward noon and the area was pretty quiet, so the sound, when it came, was quite audible, though it was not very loud—just a choked-off exclamation and a crash, as if some small breakable object like a vase had shattered.

Hank slid to a stop and swiveled around. There was nobody in sight, but the door of a nearby shed was half open; and as we stood, the crash was repeated, and was followed by another noise—a short, ugly-sounding expletive in a language I didn't know. The voice was a man's.

Hank reached the door in one long stride and kicked it open.

I've been using the word "shed" somewhat loosely. Like most of the other outbuildings, this one was of adobe and was neatly whitewashed. It had been fitted up as a laundry room, with rows of washers and dryers and iron-ing boards. Like all the work areas on the ranch, it had equipment for the comfort of the servants who would be using it—chairs and low tables, magazines, and a Coke machine. The crashes we had heard had been bottles. The remains of two of them lay on the tiled floor, glass shards glittering wickedly amid the pool of spreading brown liquid. Debbie had another bottle in her hand. She was backed up in a corner by the Coke machine. Her sleeve was torn and there were red marks on her arm. When she saw Hank, she lowered the bottle and relaxed, with a long sigh of pent breath.

The man had turned. His face was half covered by an unkempt dark beard, and more black hair showed through the gaps in his shirt, which had lost half its but-tons.

"Jake Smith," Hank said, in a purring voice like that of the big cat. "Something wrong with your memory, boy? I thought I told you to keep off my property."

The man licked his lips. He didn't speak. His eyes darted from one side to the other. But there was no way out. Hank blocked the door.

"Well, I take that back," Hank went on. "I'm not going to run you off this ranch. I'm going to run you clear out of the state. If I catch you again, I'll put you in the hospi-tal. This time I'm just going to cripple you up a little, so your memory will work better."

Hank started walking forward. He didn't speak to Deb-bie, he simply gestured, and she responded, moving to join me where I stood near the door.

"Hank, watch out," she said calmly. "He's got a—"

The knife arced glittering across the room as Hank

kicked it out of Jake's hand. His own hand went out, quick as a snake striking, gathered the folds of the wrinkled shirt, and lifted the man clear off the ground. Jake's face turned purple. He clutched at the arm that held him. Hank slapped him. The movement was so effortless it looked like the smallest of love taps, but it echoed like a pistol shot. Blood trickled from Jake's mouth into his dirty beard.

"Get out of here, girls," Hank said, without turning his head. "Close the door behind you."

I was too paralyzed to move on my own, but Debbie got me out of there and slammed the door. Then we ran, but not quite fast enough; I heard a couple of choked-off screams before we were out of earshot.

We went straight up to my room. We didn't discuss it, we just went. Debbie closed the door and leaned against it, panting.

"Sit down," I said, as soon as I got my breath back. "I'll get you a drink, or an aspirin, or—are you hurt? That looks like blood."

She glanced down at her bare shoulder and swore.

"It's just a scratch. That dirty pig never washes or cuts his nails."

"Lie down, sit down. . . . I'll get some iodine and—"

"Hey." She grinned at me, and I realized that she wasn't as upset as I was. She was only out of breath from running, and oddly excited; her eyes sparkled. "Keep cool, D.J., I'm fine. I'll put something on this—you could get tetanus just from touching that creep—but I don't need any nursing. You sit down, you look shaky."

I followed her into the bathroom and collapsed onto the edge of the tub while she dealt efficiently with her scratched arm.

85

"I'm shook," I admitted. "I just spent the morning watching Hank pat little bunny rabbits and pussycats. It's like seeing Jekyll turn into Hyde."

"There's no Hyde in Hank's personality," Debbie said. "He's incapable of viciousness. But don't cross him. Or anybody he is fond of."

"I wouldn't dream of it. I'd just as soon cross Marshal Matt Dillon."

Debbie laughed.

"The madder he gets, the more he sounds like John Wayne. It would be funny if it weren't so impressive."

"I suppose it's his true nature coming out."

"Well, not exactly," Debbie said drily. "His real name is O'Reilly, you know. His grandfather was an Irish contractor from Boston, and he's a graduate of Harvard Business School."

"You're kidding."

"It's not exactly a secret. Hank fell in love with the Wild West when he was a kid. He's spent most of his life, and a lot of money, building an image."

"That's the craziest—"

"Why?" She turned on me, fierce as a mother coyote protecting her pups. "Why does everything nice, and fun, and good have to be crazy? You wouldn't question his sanity if he sat in a fancy office on Wall Street and cheated his competitors and seduced his employees' wives and chiseled the government. He's created a beautiful image. Who cares if it's real? It is to him, and to the hundreds of people—and animals—he's helped."

"Right on," I said. "You're absolutely right. I couldn't agree more. Don't hit me."

She relaxed, smiling ruefully.

86

"We get defensive about him. He doesn't need defending, you know. God help the man or woman who does him dirt."

"Are you in love with him?" I asked.

Debbie flushed slightly, but she met my eyes without flinching. Her expression made me feel about ten years old.

"You're really sweet, you know that, D.J.? How did you grow up so innocent?"

"It's my parents," I said. "Mother reads Barbara Cartland and Dad thinks sex is a curious ancient Greek cultural trait. I've never been able to figure out how he engendered five kids. He was probably thinking of something else at the time."

I realized I had walked, uninvited, into a private part of her mind. I couldn't apologize, that would have made the intrusion more noticeable. All I could do was babble on, and ignore the error. But she was nice about it.

"Hank is twenty-five years older than I am," she said. "He thinks of me the same way he thinks about those animals out in back. Does that answer your question?"

"I'm sorry."

"That's okay." She smeared iodine on the scratches and grimaced as it bit in. "As for Jake, he used to work here, in the garage. He's a fair mechanic, but he is lazy and dishonest and he drinks too much. Hank hates firing people, that's why Jake lasted as long as he did; but he made a pass at me one day and Hank threw him out. He was drunk this morning, or he wouldn't have had the nerve to come back here."

"But aren't you afraid he'll come back again and—"

"He won't ever be back," Debbie said grimly. "I'd better change this blouse, and you had better go to lunch. By the way, don't speak about this to Hank. He doesn't like talking about such things."

"Are you kidding?" I said.

II

Lunch was a quiet affair. The public figures had gone, to do their public things, and the resident loonies were the only ones around. The first person to hail me as I sidled up to the buffet table was Joe.

"I thought you'd be out on the dig," I said.

"It's too hot to work in the middle of the day," he said, with that annoying air of patronage that permeated every word he said. "We've already put in six hours; I've got another six hours of recording, sorting, and general office work to do."

"No reason why you shouldn't do it here, in an air-conditioned room. And the swimming pool is at hand in case you need to refresh your weary brain with an occasional dip."

"Precisely. The written work is almost as important as the excavating. Too many archaeologists fail in this. The knowledge is of no use if it's hidden in scrawled notes that have never been published."

"Ah," I said. "I see what you mean."

"I thought you would. Do come and join Edna and me."

I looked around for an out, and saw Jesse coming in.

"I'd adore to, Joe, but I promised Jesse I'd talk with him about . . . about. . . . Maybe we can get together later."

I moved on down the buffet table, adding a dollop of potato salad and an avocado stuffed with crab to the other things on my plate, and thinking evil thoughts about Joe.

He was right, in a way. Excavation reports had to be published, so that other scholars could use the information. And yet, as everybody knows, publication has become an end in itself. "Publish or perish," as the saying goes. It doesn't seem to matter whether a scholar has anything to say, so long as he puts words together and gets them into print. But of course I wasn't being fair to poor boring Joe. His opinions repelled me because I didn't like him personally. I was ready to accept any far-out theory from handsome, charming Jesse. Oh, I know my weaknesses. Unfortunately, knowing about them doesn't cure them.

Jesse was putting salad on his plate when I accosted him.

"Can I sit with you? I do need rescuing this time."

"Rescuing from what?"

I gestured. Edna was moving toward us, pretending to select her lunch. Her plate held its usual assortment of rabbit food.

"You are going to need rescuing too," I said.

"Well. . . ."

"Don't be gallant. Of course, if you want to join Joe and Edna and hear all about their Ph.D.s and their crummy pots. . . ."

"Meow, meow," Jesse said with a grin.

"I'm not crazy about them," I admitted.

"I noticed that. Joe is a pain, I admit, but I feel a little sorry for Edna. She wouldn't be such a bad kid if she could squirm out from under her brother's thumb."

"Jesse, darling," I exclaimed. "You're so sweet."

Edna was close enough to overhear that. She turned scarlet, then turned and marched away. Jesse's brows drew together. Then he laughed and shook his head.

"You're something else. Let's find a table by ourselves. Does your disposition improve when you're fed?"

"Somewhat."

As we sat down, Tom came up. He gave Jesse a curt nod and turned to me.

"I've been looking for you all morning. I thought you came here to work."

"I spent the morning trying to get Hank to give me something to do," I said defensively. "He says I should rest for a few days."

"I have an appointment with him this afternoon—a formal appointment, in his office. If you would condescend to join the group, we might be able to get some information out of him."

"What time?"

"Four. After your siesta."

I would have told him what he could do with his siesta, but he left. Jesse patted my hand.

"Don't let him get to you. He majored in rudeness. If you aren't planning to take a nap, how about letting me show you some of my maps?" I gave him a speculative look, and he laughed. "I said maps, not etchings. Of course if you'd rather—"

"It's one way to get to a girl," I said. "Waving maps of gold mines under her nose."

I am bound to admit that initially my interest was not confined to Jesse's treasure-hunting theories. He *was* good-looking. But before long that deep, melodious voice of his had cast its spell again, and I was hanging on his every word.

During lunch he talked about the Seven Cities of Cibola, that glittering myth that had mesmerized the early Spanish conquerors. The seven golden cities, located

90

somewhere beyond the known world, were the stuff of legend, like El Dorado and the Garden of the Hesperides —a dream, a lure of treasure founded on nothing more solid than human greed and wishful thinking. But it had happened: not very often, just often enough to justify the dream. There was gold in the New World, the conquistadors knew that; many of them had shared in the rape of Mexico and the slaughter of Atahualpa, whose golden ransom had not saved him from Pizarro's treachery. Small wonder that they starved and died in the search for more loot. The San Saba mine, Dos Almagres. . . . The little Mexican girl herding her goats along the edge of the Arizona desert, caught in a sandstorm, finding heaps of gold nuggets—and unable to locate the spot again after struggling for her life back to civilization. Then there was the story of Yuma's mine, sixty miles northeast of Tucson, near the old Camp Grant—a story as wildly romantic as the Lost Dutchman tale with which Jesse had first touched my treasure-hunting instincts.

The man who had found the mine—or rather, talked Indian allies into showing him its location—was a cashiered army quartermaster who had married an Indian girl and become a member of the Yuma tribe. The allies of the Yuma, the Arivaipa Apaches, were the ones who knew the mine's location—a chimney of glowing rose quartz, so rich in gold that thirty pounds of ore yielded over twelve hundred dollars' worth of the precious stuff. If the rest of the ore was as rich as the sample, such a chimney might hold over a million dollars' worth of gold.

But the unlucky ex-army man and his bride were killed by Indians hostile to their tribe, and the only other white man who knew of the mine vanished, never to be seen again, on his second trip to the remote canyon where it was located. A few years later, in 1871, the Arivaipa Indians were massacred, man, woman and child.

"The Camp Grant Massacre raised a big stink in the national press," Jesse said. "Almost a hundred people were indicted for murder—Papago Indians, Mexicans, and whites. The jury turned them loose after less than half an hour's deliberation, but the President sent a special commission to investigate, and after that the Indians got fair treatment . . . for a while."

We were in his room by that time, and he had spread out some of his documents for me to look at while he talked. His room was down the hall from mine—a big, airy chamber fitted out as a combination bedroom and study. There were bookcases along two of the walls, and a long table was covered with books and papers. A small safe stood against one wall.

I am ashamed to admit that his philosophical comments on the evil nature of man fell on deaf ears as far as I was concerned.

"But you haven't told me what treasure you're looking for," I said. "Is it the Yuma mine?"

"If that's what I was after I wouldn't be here," Jesse said. "The general location of that mine is well known. It's about ten miles from the old fort, in the Yavapai hills. The only way anyone will ever find that treasure is by luck—or by tearing the mountains apart, rock by rock."

"I think I'd try," I muttered.

"You speak of that whereof you do not know. I'll take you out one day and show you the sort of terrain you'd be working in. You can't imagine until you've seen it how wild these mountains can be."

"Then what are you looking for?" Despite myself, my eyes strayed toward the safe.

"Yes, the documents are in there," Jesse said slowly. "D.J., I know I must sound paranoid, but—"

"No, that's all right. I understand. Even if you trusted me, I might let something slip."

"Nothing personal, you know. I just—"

Somebody banged on the door and opened it without waiting for an answer.

"I thought you might be here," Tom said. He stood with his feet apart and his hands on his hips and a look of cold disdain on his face. "Hank is waiting. Come on."

"It's not four o'clock yet," I protested.

"Is he paying for your time or not?"

"He is, but you aren't. I'll bet he didn't send you. Damn it, I am not going to be bossed around by—"

"Never mind, D.J.," Jesse interrupted. "You run along. We'll talk again another time. If you aren't busy with Hank later on, we might go for a ride into the desert."

"That would be lovely," I said, giving him a melting smile. *"Hasta la vista."*

"Hasta la vista," Tom repeated scornfully as he escorted me along the hall. "Where do you get that cheap Spanish stuff?"

"Why are you in such a bad mood?"

"You'll find out."

The conversation didn't seem to be getting anywhere, so I did not pursue it. Tom led me to a part of the house I had not seen before and opened a door.

The room was a library—not a rich man's formal apartment, with rows of matched leather bindings, but a working library. There were plenty of long tables and good lights, and groupings of leather chairs and low tables around the two fireplaces. The books were on two levels,

93

with twisted iron stairs leading up to a gallery above the main floor. The artwork in that room was fairly spectacular. I noticed a big wooden crucifix over one of the mantels; the figure was in a lighter wood that stood out starkly against the black of the cross. The carving was primitive, verging on crude, but the twisted limbs had a queer power. Flanking the crucifix was a pair of carved, painted masks like the ones the kachina dancers wore—not flat shells covering only the face, but more like rectangular boxes open at one end so that they rested on the wearer's shoulders and concealed the entire head. The colors were brilliant reds and greens and shiny blacks, and the mythological characters represented were a scary lot, with fangs and horns and feathers.

Hank was in his study adjoining the library. It was another marvelous room; supply your own adjectives. He was standing by the desk, fooling around with some of the papers on it. He looked up when we came in, and I saw with some relief that Dr. Jekyll was back; his brilliant blue eyes had the mild, apologetic expression they normally had, not the stony glitter that had hardened them when he dealt with Jake.

"She was with Jesse," Tom reported, thrusting me into a chair.

"Well, that's all right," Hank said. "I told you not to bother her, Tom. I'm not ready—"

"Then you'd better get ready. It's time this woman knew what is going on."

His tone was decidedly critical—strident, one might almost say. I wondered why Hank didn't pick him up by the shirt and hit him. Instead he sighed and looked at me apologetically.

"I guess you're right. I just didn't want to rush D.J.—"

94

"That's not the reason, and you know it," Tom interrupted.

"Then what is the reason, if you're so smart?" I demanded, turning in my chair so I could glare at Tom.

"If I knew, I'd say so. This whole procedure is very unlike Hank, and I want—"

"Who are you to make demands, anyway? It's Hank's business; if he doesn't want—"

"Children, children," Hank interrupted. "Don't fight."

The tolerant amusement in his voice reduced both of us to silence.

"Tom is right," Hank went on. "I have been unduly secretive. I have my reasons. D.J., in a few days I'll take you out and show you what I think is one of the greatest discoveries ever made in this country. I can't do it now because I'm waiting for certain equipment to arrive. I ordered it some time ago, but there was a manufacturing delay, and it's late in getting here. I'm expecting it any day, and when it comes, we'll use it."

"What equipment?" I asked.

Hank smiled at me.

"That would be telling." Then his eyes hardened, and I felt a distinct qualm, until I realized that his anger wasn't directed against me. "I've made a fool of myself before, jumping into things without investigating them first. I won't do it again."

"I warn you, Hank," Tom said. "If it's petrified dragons, or—"

"Who told you that?" Hank swung around to face him.

Tom stuck out his jaw and remained silent. I said, "Edna told me. At least she said something about dragons."

"Oh, Edna." Hank looked relieved. He even smiled

faintly. "Edna never gets anything straight, unless it has to do with her brother."

"Is that all you're going to tell us?" Tom demanded.

"It's only a few more days," Hank said mildly.

"A few days may be too late."

"Too late for what?" Hank's temper began to show signs of cracking around the edges. I really couldn't blame him.

"Why don't you tell this girl what has been going on around here?" Tom demanded. "You've got no right to get a stranger involved in your crazy activities without warning her—"

"Oh, good Lord, are you on that again?" Hank shook his head. "I told you that was an accident."

"Plural, accidents, not singular. You aren't that clumsy. Twice in one week—"

"What happened?" I asked.

"That damned mountain lion," Tom answered. "He got out. Hank says he may have forgotten to latch the cage properly. But something had roused the beast, he was in a nasty mood, and if Hank weren't a magician with animals. . . . The second time he fell on the stairs and knocked himself out cold. He heard noises in the night and went racing down to investigate, instead of calling the security people, like any sane man—"

"It sounded like somebody crying," Hank said, blushing. "A baby, or a small animal. . . ."

"But there was nothing there," Tom said. "If you can't admit someone set that up—"

"Why the hell should they? Even if I believed that someone wanted to damage me, that's a damned-fool way to go about it. I admit I'm not as young as I used to be, but people don't usually break their necks falling down a flight of stairs."

"They could easily break a leg, though," I said. "Or some other vulnerable part. . . . What about the mountain lion?"

"Look here, you two, if I wanted to kill somebody I'd get a rifle and shoot them," Hank said in exasperation. "I wouldn't count on a poor dumb animal doing the job for me."

A queer little shiver ran through me. It was that word "shoot." I had forgotten about the gun Tom had picked up in Phoenix—if it was a gun, and not my overactive imagination.

If Tom was genuinely concerned about a threat to Hank, he might have procured a weapon in order to protect his exasperatingly unsuspicious employer. Certainly that is what he would say if I accused him—if it was really a gun I had seen. He must know I had not gotten a good look at it. All he had to do was deny the accusation. . . .

The ifs and ands and buts were getting too complicated for my simple mind. One other point occurred to me, though. The pills in my pocket and in my drink—could they be considered another "accident"? Apparently Tom hadn't said anything about that to Hank. I saw no reason to add to the confusion.

All this passed through my mind quicker than it takes me to write it down, but I am not the world's fastest thinker; the two men had gone on arguing while I brooded, and I started paying attention again when Tom said,

"I don't see why you need your damned mystery tool.

Why can't we go out tomorrow and have a look at the place?"

"Because it's a hell of a long, hot trip out there for nothing. D.J. needs time to get acclimated before I take her on an expedition like that."

"Is Tom going along?" I asked sweetly.

"He can come if he wants to," Hank muttered.

"Just one more question," I said. "Not that I'm not enjoying all this, but I can't help wondering why you needed me. Why couldn't Tom check your find?"

"Tom?" Hank looked at me in innocent surprise. "He wouldn't be any use to me; it's not his field."

"I thought he was an archaeologist."

"He is. But he's the wrong kind of archaeologist. I'm not sure precisely what is out there, D.J., but one thing I know: it isn't a Roman temple."

My brilliant brain began to click slowly into gear. Wheels and cogs ground around and around and a-round. . . .

"I should have known," I said hollowly. "He's a classical archaeologist. That's it, isn't it? Romans and Greeks and. . . . I bet he speaks Greek like a native. I'll bet he. . . . Why didn't you tell me?"

I bounced up out of my chair and pointed an accusing finger at Tom. He was, characteristically, leaning against the desk. His eyeballs converged as he looked at my finger, which was touching the tip of his nose.

"What difference does it make?" he asked.

I was about to tell him when Hank said firmly, "Now you two run along. . . ." I think he was about to add, "and play," but he thought better of it. "You can amuse yourself for a few days, can't you, D.J.? If there is anything you want—"

"I have everything I could possibly want," I said. "It's okay if I use the library, isn't it?"

"Sure, anytime. But don't tire your eyes reading; have fun. I'll let you know the minute my—er—equipment arrives."

He was not the sort of man you argue with. I might have tried, if I hadn't been so depressed. As I walked toward the door, my shoulders must have had a discouraged sort of slump, because Hank said suddenly, "D.J."

"What?" I turned.

"I'll give you a hint." His eyes twinkled. "Edna wasn't as far off as you might think."

He went out the door at the other end of the study before I could reply.

I kept underestimating him, which was not too bright of me; he wasn't a stupid man. As soon as I mentioned the library, he knew what I wanted to look up. His reaction to Tom's crack about dragon bones had been a dead giveaway. The final comment hadn't told me anything I didn't already know; it was a good-natured dare.

I turned to Tom, who was still supporting his feeble frame against the desk. I meant to say something caustic about classical scholars. Unfortunately the connection between my brain and my mouth comes unhitched from time to time.

"What did you do with that gun?" I demanded.

Tom's eyes widened innocently.

"What gun?"

"I suppose you know my father," I said.

"I fail to follow your train of thought," Tom said. "Why should the mention of a fictitious gun lead inevitably to your father? I know of him, of course; he's one of

99

the hoary old monuments of my field, not the type to fool around with guns, surely?"

"I should have known," I muttered. "There's something about classical archaeology. . . . Does the discipline turn people into monsters, or are monsters attracted to it?"

"That's not a very nice way to talk about your father."

"I'm very fond of him, but there's no denying that he is a monster. Any man who would name his daughter—"

I stopped just in time. Tom's head had lifted alertly and he was hanging on my words.

"I wondered about the initials," he said interestedly. "Do go on."

"Like hell," I said, and turned toward the door.

"Where are you going?"

"To the library. To look up dragons."

Chapter Six

You would not believe how many grown-up, supposedly sensible people have written books about dragons. I should have anticipated this, because I had recently discovered that a lot of grown-up, supposedly sensible people had written about flying saucers and Atlantis and things like that. But I had hoped I could zip through the basic references in an hour or two and maybe get in a swim before dinner.

Wrong. When Jesse came looking for me, to tell me it was almost cocktail time, I was still listing bibliography.

I had read Willy Ley's chapters on the Dragon of the Ishtar Gate and on Javanese tree lizards, which may have inspired the dragons of European legend; I had checked on Saint George and the other famous dragon slayers; I had skimmed through a little book of Chinese fairy tales, in which benevolent dragons figured prominently; and—I blush to admit—I had gotten sidetracked onto sea serpents, which are related to dragons in that both are reptiles. At least they would be reptiles, if either one of them really existed.

Fortunately the book was open to the picture of the *Daedalus* sea serpent when Jesse's beautiful face peered over my shoulder. There was no reason why I couldn't have told him about the dragons, but I was oddly reluctant to do so. Hank hadn't sworn me to secrecy. Yet, like Debbie, I was getting protective about him. I could criticize him, but I didn't like to hear other people jeer.

I jumped nervously when Jesse's lips brushed my ear. The friendly gesture might have been an accident, but it wasn't; when I turned my face toward him his mouth skimmed neatly down, avoiding my nose, and fastened on my mouth. It was a long kiss and I reacted more enthusiastically than I had planned to.

"Well, now," he said, putting his arm around my shoulders and getting a better grip, "let's just try that again from this angle. . . ."

"Not now," I said, pushing him away. Tom had already walked in on us once that afternoon. I wouldn't have put it past him to be peeking through the keyhole. There is something very undignified about being caught making out in a library.

Jesse went up another couple of steps in my regard when he accepted my rejection without argument or sulking. He perched himself on the edge of the table and reached for the book.

"Sea serpents?" he asked, raising one eyebrow. "Lunacy seems to be contagious. If you stay here long enough, you'll acquire a crazy theory too. Sea serpents are even worse than buried treasure."

"I don't know about that. Lieutenant Drummond, Mr. Barrett, Midshipman Sartoris, and Captain M'Quhae of the *Daedalus* saw one sixty feet long on August fourth, 1848, at longitude nine degrees twenty-two inches east—"

Jesse burst out laughing.

"Not to mention," I went on, "the serpent seen in 1906 by two Fellows of the Zoological Society, and the monster that was run down by the S.S. *Santa Clara* in 1947, in broad daylight, and was seen by all three of the mates. I mean, fellows of learned societies may not be reliable witnesses, but officers of Her Majesty's navy. . . . I wonder if Hank would like to finance an expedition."

"Even Hank wouldn't go for that one. Where would you start looking? The Atlantic is a big ocean, and the Pacific is even bigger."

"True. Maybe I'll go in for something more practical."

"We might start by searching for a good martini," Jesse suggested.

So we had the martini, and another of those fattening dinners. Jesse and I were among the early birds, and as I watched the others file in and select their food, I was struck by the fact that they all ate like starving people. Maybe they felt they had better stoke up while they had the chance. It seemed to me, too, that the attitude toward me had hardened; I felt a chill antagonism that made me wonder if I was getting to be as paranoid as they were.

Nobody spoke to me until I had almost finished eating. Then I heard a muffled exclamation from Jesse, and looked up to see a woman bearing down on us.

She had not been present the previous evening. I would have noticed her if she had been. She was practically a caricature of a lady professor, a type that exists almost entirely in fiction. She was short and massive; not fat, but heavily built, with an enormous thrusting bosom and solid legs. Her feet, in thick, laced oxfords, hit the floor in a series of reverberant thuds. Her thick gray hair was pulled back in a bun. Her suit was gray, too, mannishly cut, with a white blouse and a man's tie. Her gray coloring, her tree-trunk legs, and her long drooping nose were elephantine; but most elephants have pleasanter expressions.

Thump, thump, thump; she marched up to us, put her hand possessively on the back of my chair and barked, "Frau Professor Doktor Doktor von Stumm."

The repetition of "doctor" was not due to nervousness on her part, no such thing. In Germany a woman bears her husband's scholarly titles, and if she has a Ph.D. herself, that title is added to the others. It's one case, rare in this man's world, when a woman gets more than she is entitled to, instead of less.

I was tempted to reply in kind. I can invent titles too. I decided to try a little reverse snobbism instead.

"Call me D.J.," I said.

She smiled. She shouldn't have done it. Her teeth were too big for her mouth, large and inhumanly even and brilliant white. They gave the impression that an inexperienced museum worker had put her together wrong, adding an outsized jaw to a small brain pan.

"Good. We are colleagues. You may call me Frieda."

I couldn't imagine doing it. At least she hadn't offered to shake hands. Hers were bigger than Jesse's, and looked capable of tearing telephone books in half. She sat down. The chair buckled, but held.

"I was indisposed last night," she explained. "I did not meet you. So I came at once, as soon as I was able, to offer my services."

I was almost afraid to ask what she had in mind.

"Services," I repeated blankly. Jesse's face had gone blank too. He leaned back in his chair and stared at the ceiling. I couldn't decide whether he was trying to control laughter or outrage.

"You will be going with Hunnicutt, to investigate his prehistoric site," Frieda said. "I too will come. I will assist."

"Is that what it is—a prehistoric site?"

She leaned forward, thrusting out her jaw. Close up, her face was even more terrifying.

"He keeps his secret," she said, with a rumble of gargantuan laughter. "But I suspect. I know what is to be found. You have of course read my book?"

I glanced at Jesse. He was no help at all. The corners of his mouth were twitching, but he kept his eyes on the ceiling. My own eyes roamed desperately, and caught another glance. From a table not far away Tom was watching. He rose immediately and came toward us.

"Hello, Frieda," he said. "Tummy ache all better?"

She turned to him. A look of pure animal greed came into her eyes. I might have had my doubts about her sexual habits before that; we do tend to stereotype people by outward appearance. But when I saw the way she looked at Tom I felt sure she was heterosexual, at least part of the time. I found the idea repulsive. Not because she was ugly and fat and twenty years older than Tom. . . . At least I don't think that's why.

He didn't seem to be disconcerted by her leer. He pulled out a chair.

"I thought I had better referee," he said. "Have at it, girls, whenever you're ready."

"Referee?" Frieda tilted her head and tried to look kittenish. I tried not to gag. "But why should we quarrel, you foolish boy? This child would not be here if she did not have a scholar's mind. She will find my arguments irresistible. She has, I am sure, read my book."

By God, I had read it. I don't know why her name took so long to register, or why it chose that moment to drop into the slot; but I remembered. She had written one of those enormously popular pseudoscientific books about ancient mysteries and spaceships and such. There had even been a TV special based on it. I had hated that book —probably because it was so successful. I wondered why Frieda was sponging on Hank. She couldn't need the money, she must have made a bundle. But I guess nobody ever has enough money.

"I read it," I said.

"Good. Then when you with Hunnicutt go, I will accompany."

I should have said something tactful, like, "That's up to Hank." But Tom was watching me, a gleam of white teeth showing under his mustache. If I backed down now, after all the harsh words I had hurled at him, I would look silly. Besides, the woman annoyed me.

"No, you won't," I said pleasantly.

"Ah." She had been expecting that reaction; her false friendliness was a ploy. She leaned back, drawing a deep

breath. The shelf of her bosom swelled to alarming pro-
portions. "Why do you reject my help?"

"Because I think you and your theories are a crock of—"

Jesse let out a whoop of unrestrained laughter, and Tom
said reprovingly, "Watch your language. Frieda doesn't
approve of vulgarity."

"No, no, let her speak." Frieda waved a hamlike fist. By
pure accident, no doubt, it passed within an inch of my
nose. "I am accustomed to the skepticism of scholars. I
had hoped. . . . But I am prepared for disappointment. You
may deny and doubt, young woman, but I tell you that
Hunnicutt has found confirmation of my theories in the
great desert. As if further confirmation were needed! The
evidence is overwhelming, the visits of those ancient
space travelers to the awestruck aborigines of this
planet—"

"Pure fiction," I said. "Not even entertaining fiction.
Heinlein and Ray Bradbury do it much better."

Frieda banged on the table. Every dish on it jumped and
rattled.

"The legends of fiery chariots, carrying godlike
beings—"

"Meteors, volcanic eruptions, thunder and lightning," I said. "Plus the creative imagination of human
beings aching for reassurance about death. If you can
imagine spaceships, why couldn't they imagine fiery
chariots?"

"The ancient paintings and rock drawings showing men
wearing space helmets—"

"Masks. Hank has a couple of them in the library right
now. We've found the masks. Why haven't any of your
space helmets survived?"

We had attracted a crowd. I had kept my voice down

107

—well, fairly much down—but Frieda boomed like a bittern, and I suppose it was obvious that we were arguing. I wondered if she and the other nuts had held a meeting and elected her their spokesman. They were all standing around, listening avidly. Jesse had given up his pretense of detachment and was following the conversation, his head swinging back and forth like that of a tennis fan watching a hot match. Tom was clearly enjoying himself.

"Thirty love," he chanted. "You can't win, Abbott, but go on talking; it's good exercise for the vocal cords."

Then I lost the last vestige of my cool.

"Your theories are so stupid, only a moron could fall for them," I said. "You set up straw men so you can knock them down. I read your book. You claim Egyptian and Sumerian civilizations sprang up out of nothing, full blown. That's a lie. There's solid evidence of centuries of prehistoric development, consistent and documented. You claim we can't duplicate ancient buildings or technical processes. Lies again. Any jackass can build a pyramid, the same way the Egyptians did, if he can afford to hire the laborers. There are no lost sciences."

I had to stop for breath at that point. Frieda's face had turned an alarming puce. Now she said softly,

"And the scientific achievements of the ancients? The fact that the height of the Great Pyramid, multiplied by a thousand million, corresponds to the distance between the sun and the earth—"

"Why pick a thousand million? Multiplied by a hundred it corresponds to the distance between Schenectady and Boston. That's a mystically significant figure, because I was born in Schenectady and—"

"It is, of course, good scholarly technique to sneer,"

Frieda said, with a pretty good sneer of her own. "None of you can explain what moved the ancients to erect great buildings that had no useful function—"

"Like cathedrals and fancy tombs," I interrupted. "Or do you claim that the towers of Chartres are also beacons for space travelers?"

Frieda's lips drew back. (My, what big teeth you have, Grandma!) I braced myself for a bellow of rage. Instead, after a momentary, almost unnoticeable sideways glance, she bowed her head and said gently,

"You cannot admit the truth. The young are the true reactionaries. I pity you."

Forewarned by that quick flicker of her eyes, I rolled my own eyes to the side. Sure enough, there he was—Gary Cooper trying to calm the mob, Hank Hunnicutt afraid his friends were going to be rude to one another. Frieda was no dummy, she knew he wouldn't like it if she roared at me. I decided to try some rhetoric myself.

"Why do you deny man?" I cried in my most ringing soprano.

Tom did a beautiful doubletake and Jesse's eyes opened wide. Pleased at this reaction, I went on, "Why are you afraid to admit he is a genius as well as a murderer? A species which produced *Hamlet* and the *Choral Symphony*, the Theory of Relativity and the electron microscope couldn't invent a pyramid? Why do you have to denigrate humanity by inventing gods and superior beings? Could it be because you are afraid—afraid of death and dissolution, unable to accept the inevitable end?" My voice dropped to a thrilling whisper. I put on a compassionate smile and held out my hands, like Anita Bryant talking about Jesus loving everybody. The gesture finished Tom, who had caught on to what I was doing. He hid his face in his hands, but he couldn't keep his shoulders from shaking.

"Don't be afraid," I said. "We are all alone, from birth unto death. That is the lot of man, his tragedy and his triumph. Let me show you the true wonder of life, more marvelous by far than your petty godlings and antique spacemen—the wonder of man's frail body and towering spirit!"

In the hush that followed I swooned limply back in my chair and covered my eyes with my hand. It was a good gesture. I'd learned that from Anita too. From under the shelter of my fingers I saw Hank retreat, as noiselessly as he had come. That struck me as a good omen. He hadn't even waited to hear Frieda's rebuttal. Though if I do say it myself, mine was a hard act to follow.

She didn't try. She, too, had seen Hank leave, and she let her mask drop.

"That was low," she snapped. "Okay. You want war, that's what you'll get."

Her German accent had disappeared. I didn't suppose her name was von Stumm, or that she was a professor's wife, or that she was European. Everyone in the place was a fake. Nobody used his right name. Not even me!

"It would be tilting with windmills," I said loftily. "Excuse me. I need more dessert."

Jesse followed me to the buffet. "Maybe you shouldn't have done that," he said.

"You didn't try to stop me."

"Two reasons. First, I wouldn't insult your integrity in that way. Second, I couldn't have stopped you if I had wanted to."

"Correct. I'm sorry I got mad. Idiocy always annoys me.

110

But I'm not sorry I argued with her. I feel much better after getting that off my chest."

"She's not a nice woman," Jesse said.

"How very inadequate!"

"I mean it."

"What can she do? Ambush me in a dark corner?" Jesse's face remained grave, and I stopped laughing. "Oh, come on," I said. "Don't be silly."

"She's quite serious about her beliefs, you know. Paranoid schizophrenics are capable of violence for rather flimsy reasons."

"If you're trying to scare me, you are succeeding," I said hollowly.

"Just stick with me." He put his arm around my shoulders and gave them a quick, comforting squeeze. "I'll protect you from the wicked lady."

"Thanks." I added a few more cream puffs to my plate. Food is so reassuring.

We took another table, as far from the first one as we could get. Frieda was still talking to Tom. The others had dispersed. Naturally, I assumed they were on Frieda's side, so I was naively surprised when, a few minutes later, Madame came billowing toward me and gave me a big smile.

"That was well done," she said, with a genteel nod in Frieda's direction. "She is overbearing, that one; it is time she was put in her place."

I should have realized that the crackpots were as hostile toward one another as they were toward genuine scholars. Hank's crackpots had good cause to hate one another; they were competing for his attention, and for the crisp green stuff he could dole out.

"She is a materialist," Madame went on contemptu-

111

ously. "You were right to point out that she denies the great capacity of the human spirit and the human mind."

"That's your bag, isn't it?" I asked. "The human spirit."

Madame refused to take offense. I found myself responding to her overtures. Compared to Frieda she was a model of courtesy and good sense. After we had chatted awhile, she offered to do a life reading for me.

"What's that?" I asked, scraping up the last puddle of chocolate sauce.

Madame started to answer, waving her plump hands, but Jesse cut her short.

"She'll tell you who you were in your last ten lives," he said. "Just give her a clue. Would you prefer a Spanish princess of the Middle Ages, or maybe Cleopatra?"

Madame's eyes flashed. "You joke," she said. "You mock at mysteries you do not understand."

"Are you a theosophist?" I asked.

"No, no, that is old-fashioned. I have gone beyond that. This is science that I do; the science of the mind, the unexplored frontier."

"What would I have to do? I won't be hypnotized."

"Anyone can be hypnotized," said Madame scornfully.

"I didn't say couldn't. I said won't."

"Bravo," said a voice. It was Tom again, sneaking around like Natty Bumpo. "The girl has some rudiments of intelligence after all."

"It is not intelligence to refuse knowledge," Madame said.

"She's got you there," I said, continuing to scrape my plate.

Tom's hand came over my shoulder and grabbed the plate away.

"Why don't you just lick it?" he inquired rudely.

112

"There's plenty more where that came from, if you think your figure can stand it."

I had not intended to eat any more, but after that I had no choice. I came back from the buffet table with another plate of cream puffs and chocolate sauce to find a full-blown battle raging. Edna and her brother had joined the group, and Edna had agreed to have her life history read.

"It can't do any harm," she insisted.

"You're crazy," Tom said. "Joe, can't you—"

"My dear fellow!" Joe lifted his sandy eyebrows. "She's a free agent. It's her decision."

"Are you sure, Edna?" Jesse asked anxiously.

"Yes, I'm sure."

"You are a true scientist," Madame murmured. "You have the open mind, the willingness to learn."

So that was how she had gotten to Edna. No doubt my closed mind and my refusal to learn had been discussed while I was gone. Edna gave me a look so naively triumphant that I felt a little sorry for her.

"Hypnotism is dangerous unless it's done by a professional," I said.

"You say I am not a professional?" Madame snapped. "I, who have sent thousands back into time?"

"Shut up," Tom said to me, as I continued to expostulate. "Can't you see you're only making it worse?"

Whatever else she was—and I can think of several names for it—Madame was a showman. Excuse me, a showperson. By the time we reached the small parlor where the experiment was to take place, she had collected a good-sized audience, including Hank. He looked at me in mild surprise when I took him aside and voiced my doubts.

"Why, honey, it's perfectly safe. She's sent me back a

number of times, and I've watched her do the same for others. I know you're a skeptic, but try to—"

"Keep an open mind? You know, Hank, if you leave your mind too wide open, all sorts of nasty things can crawl in."

He laughed and patted me on the head and went off to talk to Madame. I turned to find Jesse behind me. He was looking grave.

"I'm not so sure this is a good idea," he said.

"I think it's a rotten idea. But what can we do?"

Jesse shrugged. "Sit down and watch, I guess."

A fire flickered on the low hearth. The nights got surprisingly cool in that high altitude, but this fire was for emotional comfort rather than physical, and it gave a homey touch to the bizarre proceedings. Madame had placed Edna in a comfortable chair. She fussed over the girl, arranging a lamp so that the rays left her face and her hands softly illumined, without glaring. Edna was enjoying herself, though she tried to appear cool. I suppose she wasn't often the center of attention. But I noticed that her hands were clenched into tight fists. She was scared as well as excited.

Tom joined us on the couch. He was annoyed and was making no attempt to hide his feelings.

"What a damned-fool stunt," he said, without lowering his voice. "Tampering with a neurotic personality like hers—"

"Sssh." I jabbed him with my elbow.

"She is neurotic. I tell you—"

"You don't have to tell me. I agree. But we're probably worrying needlessly. People do this all the time."

"They also drive cars all the time. What were the highway fatalities last year?"

Having arranged Edna to her satisfaction, Madame straightened up.

"I must ask for silence," she said. "Is that understood? Do not speak until I give you leave. It is difficult, what we do here—difficult for me and for the subject. Interference can cause great harm."

"Clever," Tom muttered. "If Edna flips her lid, Madame can blame it on us."

"Oh, she isn't stupid," Jesse said morosely.

I hate to admit this. I would rather admit to first-degree murder, or beating my husband. But against all my common sense, I was secretly fascinated by what was going on. Madame put on a good show. The lights were dimmed, the silence grew till it filled the room like a fog. Her technique was the same one all hypnotists use, the low, soothing voice, the concentration—in this case on a bright silver locket—but it was practiced, and very effective. Watching her, I could understand why Mesmer had such a hard time convincing his contemporaries that his technique was scientific, and why people still think of hypnotism as related to magic.

It didn't take long to put Edna under. Her clenched hands relaxed. Her eyes remained open, but they took on a blank stare. Finally Madame asked softly, "Do you hear me, Edna?" The girl said tonelessly, "Yes, I hear you," and I felt cold, in spite of the fire.

You've probably read about how this sort of thing is done. It has been the subject of several popular books. Madame took Edna back in time, with statements like "You are now six years old. It's your birthday, Edna. Do you have a birthday cake?" I had heard about this method, which is a perfectly acceptable psychiatric technique, nothing weird about it; but when Edna's high,

115

child's voice described the flowers on her cake, my spine crawled.

Back and farther back, till Edna was babbling, barely able to articulate words like "mama" and "da-da." Madame had no need to caution us to remain silent; even those who had seen the performance before were awed. Then she said softly, "Rest awhile; sleep till I waken you." Edna's eyes closed. Madame turned.

"Now," she whispered. "Now is the great leap, the step into mystery. Whatever she says, do not cry out, do not interrupt. I tell you again; it can be disaster."

She was impressive. Her face shone greasily in the lamplight. I had heard of actors who could cry when they wanted to, but I had never met anyone who could sweat on cue.

Then Madame turned back to her—I almost said "victim."

"Now," she intoned. "Now, Edna, we go back, farther back. Back before the time you have told us of. Back, far, far back. . . . What do you see?"

There was a long pause. Edna's eyes were still closed.

"Dark," she said finally. "Dark. Water. Nothing."

"She is still in the womb," Madame explained, *sotto voce.* I had a sudden crazy desire to laugh.

"Farther back," she said. "Back, back in time. . . . Are you going back, Edna? Do you hear me?"

"Yes," Edna murmured. "Back. . . . Ah!"

It was a gasp, so sharp and unexpected after her earlier hollow whisper that most of us jumped. Not Joe. His face still wore a supercilious smile.

"Tell us," Madame said. "What do you see now?"

Then I did feel crawly. Edna's face changed, not slowly but all at once, in a split second. It was the face of a

116

different woman—older, broader, flatter . . . I can't possibly describe it. From her parted lips came a harsh babble of sound, completely unintelligible to me, resembling no language I had ever heard, but rising and falling in the unmistakable inflections of intelligent speech.

Joe leaped to his feet as if he had been jabbed hard from behind.

"Holy—"

"Quiet!" Madame hissed like a snake; even her movement was reptilian, as she swung around to face him. "Not a sound. Wait."

"But she's speaking. . . ."

His voice died away. Edna was still talking. When she stopped, Madame said softly, "What language is it? Be calm, speak quietly."

"Yuman," Joe muttered. "Some form of it. I don't know all the words."

"Ah." It was a hiss of satisfaction this time. "Can you translate, Doctor?"

"What?" Joe passed a hand over his forehead. He looked dazed. "Something about the fire. The fire wouldn't burn because the wood was wet. I didn't follow the rest."

"Then we will go on. Edna."

There was no reply. Edna sat slouched in the chair, her face flat and unresponsive.

"You who will be, in a later life, Edna Stockwell," Madame crooned. "Speak to us now in English and tell us your name."

The muscles in Edna's thin neck jerked, as if she struggled against an invisible obstacle to speech. When the words finally came out, they were strained and distorted.

"My name . . . Running Deer."

117

"How old are you, Running Deer?"

"I . . . do not know. Many summers. Many winters."

"Do you have a child?"

A flash of emotion crossed the stolid face.

"Strong sons. Daughters, too. . . . I have given strong sons to the tribe of my people."

I felt Tom stirring beside me. I reached out and grabbed at him.

"Shut up," I muttered. "Wait."

The obscene dialogue went on.

"Where do you live, Running Deer? Describe your house."

"It is a cave." The words came more fluently now, but they had a thick, guttural undertone totally unlike Edna's normal voice. "There are many holes in the rock, many homes. We climb on ladders. The stream is below; it is hard, hard to carry the water jars so high."

"Walnut Canyon?" Joe's voice was shrill. "Ask her if it's Walnut Canyon."

"Idiot," Tom muttered.

"Be still," Madame said sharply. "Where is the rock where you live, Running Deer? Is it a high place or a deep place?"

"Deep, very deep," was the prompt reply—and I began to think that "prompt" was the right word. "The path goes up and up for many steps, a long walk. The homes of the people are below, on either side."

"Ask her about the cooking pots she—" Joe began. Hank shut him up this time, leaning forward to put a hard hand on his shoulder.

"No, let him ask," Madame said. "This is what we need to know. This we can check."

118

When the question was asked, Edna went on to describe her kitchenware quite fluently.

It was at this point, when even Joe was panting with excitement, that the performance lost its charm for me. When you realized what was happening, the whole thing became embarrassing and pathetic. The chatter about strong sons and fair daughters was bad enough, but when Edna began to murmur about the embraces of her warrior, her chief, who had given her those strong sons and so on, I started to squirm.

"Wake her up," I said. "This has gone far enough. It's disgusting."

"You must overcome your Judaeo-Christian sexual hang-ups," Joe said. "The people of her tribe did not—"

I surprised the group, including myself, with a well-chosen Anglo-Saxon expletive.

"She's right," Tom said. "Hank, will you please—"

Edna was still muttering to herself. Her face wore a fat, greedy smile. Hank looked at her uneasily.

"Yes, well. . . . Madame?"

"Very well. It is tiring, to dwell long in the past. I will bring her back."

The journey was condensed this time. First Madame took Edna back into the womb, then step by step up to the present. She ended with, "Now I am going to count to three, slowly, and when I finish counting you will awake to the present. You will not remember what you have said. You will be happy, peaceful, filled with the light."

Edna's face was her own again. Her eyes were closed, her mouth drooped open. She looked feeble-minded, and she was snoring. But when Madame finished the count

119

she awoke; and if she wasn't filled with the light—whatever that might mean—she looked peaceful enough. I didn't realize how worried I had been until she spoke, and then I went limp with relief.

"What happened?" she asked sleepily. "I thought you were going to hypnotize me."

"She did." Joe jumped up, unable to contain himself any longer. "Edna, it was absolutely amazing. You spoke Sinaguan!"

"How do you know?" Tom demanded. "The Sinaguan language hasn't been spoken for over five hundred years. We can't even be sure they were a Yuman-speaking tribe."

"Well, it was Yuman—an archaic form. The Patayan cultures *probably* spoke a Yuman language, and the Sinagua were *probably* related to the Patayan. . . ."

"And I'm probably a damned fool," Tom murmured. "Oh, hell, why bother?"

I knew why. A smothering, heavy feeling came over me. I felt just the way I did when I realized it would have to be me who told my little brother about the birds and the bees, because nobody else was going to do it. Believe me, I have few sexual hang-ups, Judaeo-Christian or otherwise. I balked at telling Don the facts of life because, first, I knew he would be embarrassed, second, I knew he would be bored, and third, I knew he wasn't going to believe anything I told him. I did it, though. People have to be *told.* Whether they accept the truth or not is their problem.

I rose slowly to my full height—five feet and a couple of inches. I cleared my throat. I stood there till everybody stopped talking.

"In case any of you fail to understand the mechanism

involved in this procedure, I will explain it to you," I said. "Edna was not reliving a previous life. She was producing information out of her subconscious about a period she had studied intensively. The specific facts she gave us are well known to all archaeologists. The other facts were so vague as to be meaningless, or not susceptible to proof. The Sinaguans didn't keep records of births and deaths and marriages."

The audience's reaction was just about what I expected. Bored, embarrassed, and unconvinced. There was a murmur of "hear, hear," from Jesse, and a growl from Tom; and a patronizing smile from good old Joe.

"D.J., I admire your skeptical approach. But I assure you, Edna does not know the language. She doesn't know any Yuman dialects."

"Do you?"

"Yes, of course. Not as well as I'd like, but. . . . She did not study it. She might know half a dozen words, no more."

"But the books were available to her. She was with you when you were studying. The subconscious absorbs everything, Joe, you know that. Don't you remember the case of the servant girl in Europe, during the nineteenth century, who spoke fluent German and French while under hypnosis? It was proved that she worked for a professor who was a linguist. Her conscious mind couldn't recall any of the material she had seen and heard while working around the house, but when she was under hypnosis—"

"You're jealous," Edna said, spitting out the words. "You can't admit that anybody knows anything except you."

For a minute I had thought I was making an impression

on Joe. Any echo of Freud impresses the young and callow; when I mentioned the good old subconscious mind he looked a little shaken. But the illiterate European maidservant didn't impress him. Obviously he had never heard of the case. It was only known to psychologists and occultists, the latter of whom still consider it one of the proven cases of reincarnation.

"Naturally I will take your hypothesis into consideration," Joe said stiffly. "But it is unscholarly to dismiss a theory simply because it contradicts all the known facts."

"Is it really?" I snapped. "I would have thought that was a damned good reason."

Joe was one of those maddening people who refuse to lose their temper. He smiled patronizingly.

"I'm afraid I can't be quite so dogmatic," he said. "But I think we had better end the discussion for tonight. Edna looks a little tired. Go to bed, Edna."

No wonder it was easy to hypnotize that girl. Her brother did it all the time. She stood, swaying a little, and my damned conscience rose up again.

"Somebody should go with her," I said. "Edna, would you like me—"

Edna just looked at me. Madame took her arm.

"I will care for her," she said. "Have no fear, she is full of—"

Tom's lips shaped a word, and again I fought back an uncouth desire to laugh. The group broke up. Madame led a drooping Edna away. Hank followed them, looking worried. Joe sauntered toward me.

"Would you care to join us tomorrow?" he asked, taking a pipe and tobacco pouch from his pocket.

"You would smoke a pipe," I said.

"I beg your pardon?"

"Never mind. I don't think I will come, Joe."

"Another day, perhaps."

He walked away, radiating complacency.

"I need a drink," Tom said. "Do you want anything, D.J.?"

"No, thanks. I think I'll go find the Professor and argue about ancient Lemuria. 'Now, now, sinking, black ink over nose. . . .' "

Tom gave me a startled look and burst out laughing. It was the first time I had seen him overcome by genuine, robust amusement. His mustache quivered and his eyes sparkled and he looked divine.

"Very apropos," he said, between chuckles. "Where on earth did you find a copy of Le Plongeon?"

"I do my homework," I said gloomily.

I don't know whether Jesse recognized the reference. He was sunk in a brown study. I wondered if he had noticed, as I had, that Edna's description of the great chief, the virile warrior, the father of her strong sons, had borne a striking resemblance to Jesse himself.

Chapter Seven

After the smashing production starring Edna and Madame, Jesse suggested we go for a little stroll around the grounds. If he had anything else in mind beyond a stroll —and I most certainly did—we never got to it, because Tom insisted on accompanying us. I gave up finally and said I was going to bed. Jesse asked me if I'd like to do some exploring next day.

"Great," Tom said enthusiastically. "I'll join you."

"We have to leave early," Jesse said. "About seven."

"I always rise at dawn," Tom said, beaming at us like a young mustachioed Vincent Price.

Actually it was after seven thirty before we left. I had come down to breakfast in shorts and a halter; the two men let out a united cry of protest and sent me back to collect a hat and sunglasses and more covering.

We hadn't been on our way for long when I realized why they had objected to my attire. The sun beat down through the rarefied air like an ultraviolet lamp. If I hadn't had something over my shoulders I would have been burned to a crisp.

Jesse was driving a vehicle of the jeep type, with four-wheel drive and a jaunty little canopy to ward off some of the sun. Five minutes after we left the grounds there was no sign of a road; we bounced merrily along a track that was distinguishable from the surrounding desert only by its relative freedom from large cacti.

The ranch and the underground springs that made its existence possible were located in a basin. We had not gone far before the mountains began to close in around us. Strictly speaking, the highest peaks were not an isolated mountain range but part of a plateau that stretches across northern Arizona and New Mexico. The Grand Canyon is the largest and most spectacular of the myriad rocky trenches that split this tableland. It is a tumbled mass of rock, hardened into strange formations. The lower slopes are clothed in the living green of towering evergreens, with willow and oak and other deciduous trees in fertile valleys; but when you get away from water the slopes are almost bare of vegetation. I began to understand why the fabled lost mines of the Southwest were still lost.

"The old maps mention landmarks," Jesse said. He

pointed. "See that rock? It looks like a sombrero, doesn't it?"

"A camel," I said.

"Yes, well, that shows you what I mean. Any outcropping of that approximate shape looks like a camel, or a sombrero, or any other image that happens to strike you. Even if you could locate the specific landmark some old prospector had in mind, it would take forever to search the surrounding terrain."

We stopped for lunch in the shade of a bizarre pinnacle of red rock that Jesse called the Devil's Thumb. I was about to sit down when Tom grabbed my arm.

"Wait a minute." He took a stick and poked it into some of the holes that riddled the rock.

"I guess it's okay," he said finally.

"What were you looking for?" I asked.

"Snakes."

"Snakes!" I jumped back and looked wildly around. The dusty ground shimmered in the heat.

"It's all right." Jesse lowered himself to the top of a convenient rock and began unpacking the picnic basket.

"I told you you should have worn boots," Tom added, stretching out his long legs. Like Jesse, he was wearing knee-high boots and heavy jeans.

"I didn't bring boots," I said sullenly. "Where I come from, we only wear them when it snows. What kind of snakes live in these parts?"

"Rattlers, mostly," Tom said. "Big ones. This particular variety doesn't always rattle before it strikes."

"Stop teasing her," Jesse said. "Sit down, D.J., there's nothing to worry about."

I squatted and accepted a ham sandwich.

"It's not worth it," I said.

126

"What?" Jesse asked.

"Hunting for treasure."

"There are risks," Jesse admitted. "The snakes are the least of them; they don't bother you unless you bother them. The greatest danger is getting lost. It doesn't take the body long to become dehydrated. But," he added cheerfully, "at least these days you probably wouldn't get shot in the back by bushwhackers."

"Do you just ride around like this all day, or do you have a specific goal in mind?" I inquired, reaching for the water bottle. Talking about dehydration made me thirsty.

"Oh, I have a goal." Jesse glanced at Tom, who had leaned his head against the rock and was apparently preparing to take a nap.

"Your secret is safe with me," Tom mumbled. His eyes were slitted and sleepy-looking, but I caught a very alert gleam from under his drooping lids.

"Remember that peak I showed you, the one that's shaped like a sombrero?" Jesse asked. "That's my starting point. Have a look at this."

I leaned forward eagerly, forgetting snakes, as he reached in his pocket. The object he produced was disappointing. I had expected a piece of human skin or a battered parchment, with maybe some rusty, faded bloodstains on it. What I got was a folded sheet of paper—a Xeroxed copy.

"The original is in my safe," Jesse explained, with another wary look at Tom. "This copy gives the essentials, though. If you can make any more of it than I can, you're welcome to half the treasure."

At first all I could see were vague lines, twisting like—well, like snakes. Then I made out printed words.

"Dry . . . what's this? Oh, I see. Dry riverbed. Twenty miles north. . . ."

Jesse's hand flattened the map against my knee.

"Here's the peak shaped like a sombrero," he said, pointing. "We're about twenty miles north of it now."

"But that's an awfully vague direction."

"Very true. See this line? It's a dry riverbed. That's what I'm looking for. If it was dry back in 1887, when this map was made, it may have vanished altogether now. But if I can find that, I'll have a fix."

Tom opened one eye. "How do you find a ninety-year-old riverbed?"

"Ah, well, there are ways," Jesse said.

"Are you a geologist or something?" I asked.

" 'Something' is more like it. I never got my degree."

"Who cares about degrees," I mumbled. I was beginning to get drowsy too.

"Take a nap," Jesse said, getting to his feet. "I'm going to have a look along this arroyo. I'll be back before you start to sizzle."

I had every intention of going with him, but when I tried to get up, my legs wouldn't obey.

"Have fun," I said, yawning.

I woke up when Jesse shook me.

"Any luck?" I asked, rubbing my eyes.

Jesse shook his head. He looked remarkably cheerful.

"I didn't expect to find anything. This was just one of the possibilities I mean to check out, but there are others. Are you ready to head back?"

"I want a swim," I said. "And a gallon of iced tea, and a bath and a couple of bottles of lotion. . . ."

The experience brought home to me, as no warning could do, the dangers that lurked in the austere, beautiful

128

landscape. We had been amply supplied with liquid, yet after a few hours in the heat my body craved water, inside and out. The hot, dry air was strangely exhilarating, and the barren terrain had the exotic beauty of an extraterrestrial landscape. I told Jesse I had enjoyed it, and he looked pleased. He glanced over his shoulder at Tom, who was snoring in the back seat.

"I'll take you out again whenever you like," he said. "But you'd better get yourself some boots. Not only because of snakes; if you want to go with me you'll have to hike, maybe do a little rock climbing. Can't do that in sneakers."

I had already reached the same conclusion. It was dumb of me not to have thought of boots, but we don't have many rattlesnakes around Cleveland.

Jesse offered to drive me to Flagstaff next morning, and I accepted. I wanted to spend some time at the museum. I had a letter of introduction from Bancroft to one of the curators there. But when we arrived at the house, Hank had a surprise for me. His mysterious piece of equipment had arrived. He was just about to leave for Flagstaff to pick it up.

II

Hank could have sent one of the servants to pick up his machinery, but that wasn't his style. Tom offered to drive —with, I thought, a touch of desperation in his voice and manner—but Hank refused in no uncertain terms. When I mentioned boots, he slapped his forehead.

"I should have thought of that. You certainly will need them where we're going. Better come with me, you can buy your boots while I tend to my errand."

I took a quick shower and changed into something a

little more appropriate for city shopping. I did it faster than any man could reasonably have expected, but when I came down Hank was pacing the hall.

The car out front was a grubby little blue Volkswagen.

"Not the Rolls?" I said.

"If you want—"

"No, no, of course not. But I do love all those buttons."

The car was air-conditioned, but that was the only amenity it boasted. It was very short on springs. After we had gone a short distance, I understood why. I also understood why Tom had offered himself as chauffeur.

It wasn't that Hank was a bad driver. The problem was two-fold. One, he went too fast. Two, he never watched the road. He was one of those people who has to look at the people he's talking to, and he never stopped talking, except when I was talking, and then he felt courtesy demanded he keep his eyes on my face.

When we were on the local road it didn't much matter. You couldn't tell the road from the desert anyhow, and when we ran off onto what might laughingly be called a shoulder, it was only a little bumpier than the surface of the road. But when we reached the main highway I started to die. The road climbed, in a series of swooping loops that crisscrossed the cliff side. The low stone parapet was the only thing between me and a hundred-foot drop. It did not inspire any confidence.

After a harrowing half hour, marked by the blaring horns of the other cars we met, as Hank appeared to drive straight at them down the middle of the road, we finally reached the top of the plateau and roared along a wide highway between forested fields. At least it was flat. Once I saw a deer. It was running like mad, away from the road. The warning probably went out among the wildlife as soon as Hank took to the highway: "Cheese it, fellows, here comes that man Hunnicutt."

Hank dropped me in the center of town, promising to pick me up in half an hour. It took me that long to find my boots. I had been given specific instructions as to what kind to buy, and I had to try two stores before I found some that fit. They were not stylish. They laced up the front, and had big thick soles and flat heels. I couldn't bend my ankles. On the advice of the clerk I wore them, hoping to break them in somewhat, and as I stalked straight-legged up and down the streets of Flagstaff, I felt like Frankenstein's female monster.

When Hank picked me up, I looked in the back of the car. There was nothing there, so I assumed he had his prize in the trunk. It couldn't be too massive, then; the front compartment of a Volkswagen isn't very big.

I tried to interrogate him, but got nowhere. He had picked up "the thing," yes; it looked all right, yes. That was all he would say. I could see that he could hardly wait to get home. He was as tickled as a little kid with a new toy; he didn't want any of the other kids to play with it till he'd had his turn. He drove even faster on the way back, and when we went down the mountainside I just gave up and closed my eyes.

Hank dropped me at the front door of the house and drove on around to the back. It did not improve my temper any to find Tom waiting, full of questions. I had to admit I still had no clue as to the nature of the mystery device, and Tom's contempt was unconcealed. I went up to my room and sulked and read some more about dragons.

Tom wasn't the only one who was curious about Hank's new toy. That evening, when I told Jesse I wouldn't be available next day, he asked about it, and Joe, who had overheard our conversation, also expressed mild interest. (He never expressed keen interest in anything except his own fascinating self.) We started speculating on what the item could be.

"He's probably ordered a miniature carbon-14 dating lab," Jesse said with a grin.

Edna had been sitting with her back ostentatiously turned to me, working on a revolting piece of embroidery.

"But Jesse, you couldn't miniaturize that equipment; you'd need a whole lab; and besides—"

"I know, dear, I know," Jesse said. "I was joking."

"Oh," Edna said. She held up her embroidery and looked at it. The design wasn't bad; it was a geometric pattern, probably derived from Indian weaving; but the colors she had chosen were garish reds and purples.

"I like that pattern," I said, trying to be nice.

"It's going to be a pillow," Edna said. Her tone was a trifle less unfriendly than the one she usually employed when she was talking to me, and I was about to go on being ingratiating when Joe spoke. She swiveled toward him like a sunflower facing the sun.

"I'll bet it's some new variety of dowsing rod," he said, glancing at me as if to say, "See, I can make jokes too."

"No, he was into dowsing last year," Jesse said seriously. "The dowsing rod worked just fine when it was over known sources of water, but when they took it out in the desert, it died."

"Maybe because there wasn't any water," I said.

We were sitting around the living room waiting for dinner, and some of the other guests had drifted in while we talked. One of them was unfamiliar to me—a young-ish female with a flaming mop of red hair done Afro style, wearing skintight slacks and top and lots of feathers. I had to admit her figure justified the slacks, but the bunch of peacock feathers sticking up out of her hair made her look like one of those exotic African baboons.

"Don't tell me you are open-minded about dowsing, Ms. Abbott," she said in a shrewish voice. "I'd have thought you would dismiss it as just another superstition."

"I don't believe we've met," I said.

"This is Fortunata," Jesse said. "She's been away."

"Fortunata what?" I inquired.

The woman made an impatient gesture with her long fake-jade cigarette holder.

"I need no other name. There is only one Fortunata."

"I can well believe it," I said politely. "What's your gimmick, Fortunata? Reincarnation? No, Madame has that cornered. Spiritualism, astral projection—"

Fortunata's eyes were so buried in mascara and eyeliner it was hard to see them, but the part I could see was very hostile.

"You would call it a gimmick, no doubt. I am trained in historical biology. I seek out the new men who are arising from the dying Fifth Race."

"Aha," I said, pleased. "You're a Lemurian."

Fortunata's drowned pupils flashed.

"The Lemurians of the Third Root Race were gross, shambling apemen, Ms. Abbott. You intend to be insulting, of course."

"They were also hermaphrodites, who reproduced by fission," said Tom, who had made his usual unobtrusive entrance and was now leaning on the back of my chair. "Take another look at the—er—lady, D.J."

"I didn't mean to be insulting," I said. "I meant that you

133

must be a follower of the Lemurian idi—— I mean, theory. Aren't there Seven Root Races?"

"Five have passed, the Sixth is now in the process of arising," Fortunata said. "The Fifth Root Race was the Aryan; out of its sixth subrace the new men will come."

"How nice," I said.

"Hank is one of them," Tom said. "I'm not."

"I don't suppose I am either," I said.

"Some degenerate examples of the older subraces still exist," Fortunata said. "It is they who lead the world to destruction from which only the new men can save it."

"It's a fun parlor game," Tom said. "On dull evenings we sit around and try to figure out what subrace we and our friends belong to. The Rhoahals were the first subrace of Atlantis—twelve feet high and coal black. Then there were the Semites—bright kids, but very sneaky. The Toltecs drank blood—"

"The skeptics may joke. They are the first who will die," Fortunata said. The threat was directed at me. I protested.

"I wasn't making fun of you, Fortunata. Tom was the one—"

"Always he jokes," Fortunata murmured throatily, batting her sticky eyelashes at Tom.

Dinner was announced then, so the group broke up, leaving me to reflect sadly on the injustice of it all. There I was, trying to be nice and noncommital, and she didn't like me a bit. Apparently she had heard about me from the other crackpots and had decided that offense was the best defense. But beautiful Tom could sneer all he wanted, and she smiled at him.

Hank did not appear at dinner. I figured he must be in his room playing with his toy. He had said we would get

134

an early start, so I excused myself after dinner and went to my room. I took with me an armload of books from the library. I don't know why I was so intent on getting a clue to Hank's discovery; in another twenty-four hours I would know what it was. I suppose I felt he had challenged me. It would be one up for me if I could find out what the enigmatic dragon clue meant before I learned the truth. It was like a game.

But it wasn't a game, and I was soon to find that out.

My reading got me absolutely nowhere. Clues weren't lacking; in fact, to an imaginative mind there were all too many clues.

Fossil bones of dinosaurs and other large prehistoric animals were believed to be the remains of dragons, back in the unenlightened Middle Ages. Paleontologists used to search Chinese pharmacies for such bones, since they were considered cures for every known ailment. Dragons appear in the mythologies of many countries, including England; remember Uther Pendragon and the red dragon of Wales? Not to mention Siegfried fighting a dragon and acquiring immunity from wounds by bathing in its blood. Traditionally, dragons are the guardians of treasure, and except in Chinese mythology, they are malevolent. Well, they are reptiles, after all, and we know that snakes are evil—sometimes Evil with a capital letter, as in the Garden of Eden. That line got me off onto Serpent Cults and Snake Gods, an enormous subject in itself. Not all snake gods were bad news. Snakes were sacred to Athena, the goddess of wisdom. Some North American Indians worshiped rattlesnakes. Then there was the biggest of all snakes, whose name I can't remember at the moment— the one Thor wrestled in Scandinavian mythology, which symbolized the earth itself.

135

Considering the way Hank's mind seemed to work, any or all of these dragon-snake references might contain the key to what he thought he had found. He might have been looking for dinosaurs, or proof that the western United States was colonized by the Chinese, or even for the tomb of Saint George. The fact that none of these interesting items could possibly exist in the Arizona desert would not deter him from looking, or even concluding that he had found one or all of them. He might be on his flying-saucer kick; old myths describing flying creatures spouting fire could refer to spaceships, couldn't they?

No, they couldn't. But Hank and Frau Doctor von Stumm didn't believe that.

Finally I tossed the reference volumes aside in disgust and turned for refreshment to another book, which I had borrowed from Hank's excellent collection of fantasy and science fiction. (I was not surprised to find that he had a taste for that genre.) There is a very fine dragon in *The Hobbit,* and I figured that Smaug was as likely a candidate as any for Hank's elusive dragon.

Chapter Eight

Dragons pursued me all night. I woke up when one of them—a medium-sized green dragon with bright-red eyes—started pounding on my door.

It was still dark in my room, but the windows to the east were gray, heralding the approach of dawn. I rubbed my eyes and tried to wake up. I could still hear the dragon beating on the door.

"D.J.—Abbott! Open this door, damn it. Are you all right? Answer me, or I'll kick it down."

The dragon shriveled up and vanished with a pop like

137

a breaking balloon. The voice was Tom's, so I deduced, cleverly, that it was he who was pounding on the door.

I had not neglected to lock my door the night before. I have a well-developed sense of self-preservation, verging on cowardice, and somebody had already tried once to drug me. I doubted that I had endeared myself to the lunatic fringe since that time. If they had not liked me to begin with, they had good reason to loathe me now.

I yelled, "I'm coming, stop that," but he didn't hear me; the door was actually shaking under the thunder of his assault. It sounded as if he were throwing himself against it—a stupid move if there ever was one.

So I got up and unlocked the door, and opened it, and caught Tom as he flung himself against what was now thin air. I don't know why I didn't let him fall flat on his face. It was pure reflex. We both went staggering back and collapsed onto the bed. For a minute or two things were very chaotic. He kept yelling, "Are you all right?" and clutching me, and I kept trying to roll out from under him, because his elbows were in my diaphragm. Besides, I wasn't wearing much, and most of what I was wearing was wound around my waist. Finally I got my own elbow into his Adam's apple and shoved. Blessed, blessed peace ensued. I pulled my nightie down over my knees.

"You are all right," he said, after an interval.

"Healthy as a horse," I agreed.

"Then what took you so long to answer the door?"

"I was asleep. Selfish of me, I know, at this hour, but—"

"Don't be sarcastic. I can't stand it this early in the morning."

He was lying on his back. I sat up cross-legged and finished arranging my garment. Then I studied Tom, who

138

was clutching his throat and making pained noises. He was wearing even less than I was, above the waist, at least, and in the light from the open door I saw his brown chest heave up and down like that of a man who has been running.

"What happened?" I asked.

He rolled his eyes toward me but didn't answer. I knew he could talk, so I figured he was just acting martyred. I hadn't hit him that hard.

"I assume something must have happened," I persisted. "If you had come for what my mother would call purposes of lust, you wouldn't have announced yourself by trying to kick the door down. I know my beauty drives men to madness, but you don't strike me as. . . . Hey! Is somebody hurt or something?"

Tom stopped rubbing his throat.

"I can't figure out whether you are naturally stupid or just so loquacious you can't stop talking long enough to think. Obviously something is wrong or I wouldn't be here at this hour. Your frivolous comments would be disgusting if someone *had* been injured."

"Not if I didn't know about it," I said; but I felt a little subdued, all the same. "What made you think something had happened to me?"

"Something did happen to you a few days ago. You were the first person I thought of when Hank rousted me out a few minutes ago. He was so mad he was barely coherent."

"He's not hurt?"

"Nice of you to ask. No, he's all right. But his precious machine has disappeared."

"What?"

"You heard me. It's gone. He had it in his room last

night; I gather he was playing with it till after midnight. It was there when he went to bed. When he woke up it was gone."

I slid off the bed and reached for my jeans. Tom watched interestedly as I slipped them on, under my nightgown, so I went behind the bed before I put on my shirt. Jeans and shirt were both tighter than they had been when I arrived at the ranch. In fact, my shoes were the only item of clothing that still fit right.

"Let's go," I said.

"Where?"

"What do you mean, where? To help Hank look, of course. You were bursting with energy a few minutes ago."

"I used it all up." Tom rose with a sigh. "Oh, all right. I suppose we'll have to look for the damned thing."

He led the way to Hank's room, which was on the floor below, in another wing. The door was wide open and the lights were blazing, but the room was empty—empty of people, I mean. It was full of other things—the usual bedroom furniture plus bookcases and tables and cabinets and chests and a couple of display cases. The walls were hung with Navaho rugs and with masks like the ones Hank had in his library. Apparently he was fond of the grisly things. *Chacun à son goût.*

"He's not here," Tom said blankly.

"Obviously. Where was the damned thing? Now that I think of it—*what* was the damned thing?"

"I never stopped to ask," Tom said with chagrin. "He was yelling and cussing so much. . . . It was over here, on the chest by the window. So he said. I wonder how the thief got in. Hank's a light sleeper. I'm surprised he didn't wake up."

"What about the window?"

"You do reason occasionally, don't you? He probably did come in the window. There's a balcony."

The windows were French doors, actually. They were wide open. The morning breeze made the draperies sway. Tom pushed them back and I followed him out onto the balcony. It was light enough now to make out the dim outlines of objects below, and I realized that Hank's balcony was not self-supporting, but rested on the roof of one of the columned loggias that surrounded most of the courtyards.

"Simple," Tom said, peering over. "Any agile person could shinny up one of the posts and climb onto the balcony. The chest is practically within arm's reach of the French doors."

"The thief was lucky, then," I said. "Or else. . . ."

"Or else he was out here watching while Hank was operating the gadget," Tom agreed. His voice was grim. "Maybe Hank was the lucky one."

We were speaking softly, but in the hush of early morning our voices carried. There was a sound down below, and a flicker of something pale, moving.

"Who's there?" Tom called.

"It's me." The voice was Hank's. It was very calm, but it held a note that would have made me quake if I had done anything to irritate him. "I've found it, Tom."

"Where was it?"

"Right here in the courtyard. It's smashed to smithereens."

"We'll come down," Tom said.

"Who's with you?"

"It's me—D.J."

"D.J.? Oh. Er—wait a minute. Don't come down yet."

"Why not?" Tom leaned forward, trying to see him. "Where are you, Hank?"

"Over here." The voice came from the right side of the loggia, but I couldn't see a human form. "Uh—Tom. . . ."

"What the hell is the matter with you?"

"Nothing, nothing. Before you come down. . . ." The voice dropped to an agonized whisper. "Tom, could you just toss me my pants?"

II

I didn't laugh till we were out in the hall, with Hank's closed door and a considerable distance between us and his embarrassment.

"Did he really go rushing out of the house naked?" I asked, chortling.

"I keep telling him he's taking chances sleeping in the buff," Tom answered, with equal amusement. "It wouldn't matter if he weren't so modest. He got caught once before, when we had a thief in the house. The poor thief got so frantic with Hank chasing him, he tripped and rolled down the stairs and woke half the house. We had a distinguished congresswoman staying that night, and when she rushed out to see what was happening, Hank ducked into the music room and hid behind the piano. We tore the place apart looking for him, thinking he'd been hurt."

"What happened to the thief?" I asked, fascinated.

"Oh, he got away in the confusion. Hank swore after that that he'd wear pajamas, but I guess he's relapsed into his old habits."

My sense of humor deserted me when we got downstairs and found Hank crouching over the battered heap of scrap that had been his precious piece of equipment. I poked experimentally at a jangle of wire.

"What was it?"

Hank winced at the past tense. He didn't say anything. It was Tom who finally announced accusingly, "It looks like a magnetometer. What the hell were you planning to do with that?"

"This is a new type," Hank mumbled. "Even more compact, even more sensitive. It's supposed to be good in any terrain."

I had heard about these devices, though I had never seen one used. I don't understand electricity—or machines of any kind. All I know is which button to push. But as I understand it, this gadget measures the conductivity of the soil. When you move it along over the surface of the ground, a needle jiggles up and down and makes a line along a piece of graph paper. If you know how to read the graph, you can tell where the underlying soil has been disturbed. It is something like a lie detector, I guess, and it is useful in excavation because any change in the quality of the soil will show up—foundations of buildings, for example, and filled-in post holes, even when the posts themselves have rotted into dust.

"Is it a village site?" I asked curiously. "Is that what you found, Hank?"

The sun was well up now, and the light was clear. I could see the graying stubble on Hank's leathery cheeks, and the lines around his eyes. I felt sorry for him till I observed the way his mouth was set.

"I guess you'll have to wait a little longer, D.J.," he said.

"Now look here, Hank," Tom began. Hank waved him to silence.

143

"That's enough, Tom. You're a good man and a good secretary, and I trust you, but I've said all I'm going to say for now. You kids go back to bed. I won't need you today, D.J., but don't make any plans for tomorrow."

His voice had lost its studied Western drawl. It was quick and incisive, with an underlying note of command that shut me up as effectively as a shout. It didn't shut Tom up.

"Tomorrow?" he repeated. "But how—"

"I said go back to bed. And don't worry. The old man has got a trick or two up his sleeve yet."

He scooped up the wreckage of the machine and strode away. Tom and I stood staring after him.

"He can't possibly repair that thing, can he?" I asked.

"Nobody could repair it. I wish I knew what the old devil has in mind."

"Why is he being so mysterious?"

"I can understand that," Tom said slowly. "He's like a kid in some ways; he likes his little mysteries. Also, he's been ridiculed unmercifully by the academic types. He's good-natured about it, but he's a lot more sensitive than he lets on. No, his secrecy is understandable, if you understand Hank. The mystery is not why he's acting as he is, but why someone is determined to keep you from seeing what he has found."

"Maybe he's found something really important this time," I said. We started toward the house.

"What's that important? A pile of rotted adobe bricks, or a cave full of bat manure and Folsom points? There are unknown sites out there in the mountains waiting to be discovered—villages, cemeteries, maybe even the remains of Paleolithic man. Something of that nature would certainly cause a scientific sensation; they have never found

144

human bones to go with the earliest flint tools. But even granting he's found anything unusual, why would someone want to suppress it?"

"I don't know," I said.

"Of course you don't."

"We may be on the wrong tack altogether," I said. "Suppose these incidents have nothing to do with Hank's find? He must have enemies. Maybe a business rival is trying to get revenge on him for cornering the stock market."

"Oh, go back to bed," Tom said disagreeably. "You're no help. I don't know why I bothered waking you up."

He went through the door and let it shut in my face.

I was wide awake, so I figured there was no point in going back to sleep. Need I mention what I wanted? No, I am sure I do not. Early as it was, the breakfast buffet was spread out on the tables in the courtyard. I wasn't the first customer. Edna was brooding over a cup of black coffee while Joe loaded his plate with eggs and bacon and ham.

He greeted me with flattering enthusiasm.

"I thought you and Hank were off on the great hunt today."

"It's been postponed," I said.

"Oh, really? What about joining us, then? We're a little late this morning, but we're leaving as soon as I finish breakfast."

"I won't have finished breakfast for a long, long time," I said, helping myself to eggs Benedict and orange juice.

"Take your time," Joe said amiably. "I can afford to lose a few more minutes if we have another pair of hands at work."

His unusual affability roused my suspicions, which were already inflamed; but except for that he looked normal enough. Even Edna looked normal—hostile, I mean. She obviously didn't want me, and that enabled me to make up my mind.

"Okay, I will," I said.

Joe finished his breakfast while I was still eating. He went off on some errand or other, leaving me and Edna tête-à-tête. She had taken out her horrible embroidery and was stabbing awkwardly at it with a needle. I suspected she was pretending it was me she was stabbing.

"Why don't you like me?" I asked pathetically. "I haven't done anything to you."

In her surprise she stuck herself with the needle and let out quite a human-sounding yelp. She put her thumb in her mouth and sucked it.

"What makes you think I don't like you?" she mumbled.

"The way you act. Honestly, I haven't any designs on your work, or your brother—he's a nice man, I'm sure, but he's not my type. So why don't you relax and enjoy me? I'm rather nice myself."

A reluctant smile curved her mouth. "Are you always so—so—"

"Tactless?" I suggested. "Candid? Blunt? Adorable?"

"Well . . . candid."

"No. I lie whenever I feel the need. But I don't see any point in hating people unnecessarily. It's tiring."

"That makes sense, I guess."

"I've only had a survey course in Southwestern archaeology," I said. "I'm very ignorant and humble and anxious to learn. So let's be pals, okay?"

"Okay."

"Great. I will go and assume my professional costume."

When I came clumping downstairs in my big new boots

and a broad-brimmed straw hat, the Stockwells were ready to go. We piled into the jeep. I was happy to observe that the back seat held a very large picnic basket and half a dozen thermos jugs.

Joe drove with a panache I would not have expected from him, fast enough to make coherent speech impossible over that bumpy terrain. I concentrated on holding on to myself and my hat. The drive took about half an hour. At the rate we had been traveling I calculated that the dig must be fifteen or twenty miles northwest of the house.

It was located in a narrow canyon. When Joe stopped the car I looked around. I couldn't see anything except rocks.

"Where is everybody?" I asked.

"I told you, I don't have the money to hire help," Joe said somewhat self-consciously. "During the weekends some of the students from Flagstaff come down to lend a hand, but the rest of the time. . . ."

"I see." Literally, that was inaccurate. I understood the situation, but I couldn't see a thing. Nothing that looked like an archaeological dig, anyway.

"This way." Joe got out of the jeep and started walking. I followed, leaving Edna to deal with the gear. If Joe didn't see fit to lend his sister a hand, why should I?

I had a good idea of the situation. Presumably Joe and Edna had wangled a grant of some sort, but it had not been ample enough to allow them to hire help. Most graduate students were dependent on aid or on their own earnings; few of them could afford to give up a summer to dig for free. Joe's dig must be very small potatoes. If it had amounted to anything, the university would have found the funds to work it.

In spite of my modest comments, I did know a little

something about Southwestern archaeology. I knew, for example, that the Arizona–New Mexico area had been occupied by three major cultural groups. The Mogollon of the eastern region, the Anasazi of the northeastern highlands, and the Hohokam of southern Arizona, who had been able to raise crops in a barren desert because of the irrigation ditches they had scraped out with stones and shells. The most impressive culture of the three was the Anasazi. They were the people who had built the pueblos, those amazing apartment-type cliff dwellings.

Among my vast storehouse of knowledge was the awareness that this particular part of Arizona was a sort of crossroads between the main cultural types. And I do mean crossroads; prehistoric people didn't squat around the pueblos staring at the ground; they traded and traveled and visited. There were cultural influences from both Anasazi and Mogollon in this part of the state, but the people who had lived here about a thousand A.D., give or take a century or two, were the Sinaguans Joe had mentioned the night Edna put on her show. Compared to the Anasazi, they were a rather dull lot, but they had built pueblos, like the one at Montezuma's Castle, and they had had the courtesy to bury their dead instead of burning them and scattering the ashes. (Cremation burials are very annoying to archaeologists.)

As I clumped along, stiff-legged, following Joe down the rocky floor of the arroyo, I wondered if he had dragged me out into this dusty hell to look at bones. That was my specialty, after all, if I had one. But man did not enter the Americas until long after his bony shape had settled into the form we call Homo sapiens—erroneously, perhaps; who says we are so wise? There are no Neanderthals or Olduvai-type hominids in North America. If Joe had found bones, all I could do with them was determine the sex and age and like that; and I could do it much better in a museum than out among the rocks.

I flattered myself. The job Joe wanted me for could have been done by a subnormal Neanderthal.

What he had found was a tiny pueblo consisting of three rooms built into a declivity on the canyon face, and a cemetery. Compared to the multistoried fantasies of Mesa Verde and Montezuma's Castle, this place was a disaster—an ancient slum, shoddily built and crumbled almost to unrecognizable heaps of dust. What's more, it had been abandoned by the inhabitants, who had presumably moved to a nicer neighborhood and taken all their belongings with them. Joe's total loot consisted of a pile of brown potsherds.

The concavity in the rock, with its crumbled walls, was twenty feet over my head. I viewed it without enthusiasm. The rock appeared to be sandstone, which is not exactly the most solid type of stone to climb on. As I stood staring up, some little bits of the cliff dropped off and dribbled down on me, narrowly missing my hat. I decided that if Joe suggested I climb up there, I would politely decline.

However, he and Edna had already exhausted the possibilities of the house remains. The cemetery was his current project. He had found two graves, on a ledge below the pueblo. The old Indians liked to keep their dead relatives close by—or else they were too lazy to carry the bodies any distance.

I felt a faint stir of interest when Joe mentioned graves. No, I'm not a ghoul at heart; bones are just cast-offs, like old clothes, only more sanitary. And people often buried the choice treasures of the dead with them; you can find

149

jewelry, pottery, tools, even cloth in that dry climate. But when Joe stooped over and showed me the first grave, my excitement died. There was nothing in the hole except a broken pot and a couple of greenish thighbones.

"Ick," I said.

Edna had caught up with us. She looked like a Near Eastern peasant woman, loaded down with baggage; now she dumped it in a heap and gave me a contemptuous look. Our pact of friendship hadn't lasted long.

"You were expecting a gold-inlaid mummy?" she inquired.

"I thought this climate preserved objects better than that," I said, waving a disparaging hand at the remnants of the Sinaguan. "Running Deer, I presume?"

Edna glowered at me. Joe was, as usual, oblivious of other people's feelings.

"There was water here at one time," he explained. "Seepage has destroyed the matting in which the body was wrapped. I found traces, but couldn't preserve any of it. As for the bones. . . ."

"Ick," I repeated. "You don't expect me. . . . There's not enough left of Running Deer to bother with, Joe."

Frankly, I didn't believe his wild story about water. The rock walls were chalky dry, the floor of the arroyo was all brown dirt and barren rock, except for some scrubby plants that looked like vegetable skeletons. Then I remembered what I had read about flash floods and the brief, incredible blossoming of the desert after the spring rains; and I looked up again, and sure enough, there were water marks on the canyon walls above my head. God knows how old they were; but the canyon itself had been water-carved at some immemorially ancient period.

"We'll search along the slope for more graves," Joe

150

le's got himself a new magnetometer—or
nfernal device is called."

here? How?"

e yet," Tom said. "But it should arrive at
le called New York this morning and or-
own out by special jet. It was due to arrive
ew hours ago."

him so long to get the first one!"

ew, that's why. He got the first one off the
A couple of universities also ordered them,
s arrived in the U.S. at about the same time
ught one from Columbia."

e offered them three times what they paid

d interested me enough to stop my forward
orarily, but we were close to the dining
:ing odors were tickling my nose.

1 me more while I eat," I said, proceeding

on to repeat what he said in reply. It was
ld not really true.

le where I could sit by myself. Before long,
ame came up and asked if she could join
other crackpots was with her—the fat man
hecked suit.

d unenthusiastically. "What is this, a dele-

ked at me pityingly. "You hurt me deeply,
 can you speak of such—"

" the fat man said. "You're wasting your
e with this kid. I don't think we ever got

went on. "Hopefully they will be beyond the seepage area. I'll just lay out a section for you, D.J. Er . . . you do know the basic principles of excavation, I assume?"

"Certainly," I said haughtily.

Well, I did know. The basic principle is that you dig.

Joe trotted around pushing in little pegs and stringing rope around them, bounding an enclosure about eight feet square. He took out a notebook and scribbled in it.

"This will be section A-four," he muttered. "Section B-four is to your left as you face the cliff. . . . Let's see. We'll form our dump there."

The spot he indicated was twenty yards away from section A-four. I started to protest, visualizing a busy morning running back and forth with baskets of dirt. I had done enough gardening with Mother to know how heavy dirt can be. But I saw Edna watching me with malicious enjoyment, so I closed my mouth.

There was nothing in square A-four except dirt. It took me most of the day to find that out. Joe insisted I dig down farther than I had intended to dig, in case some energetic ancient gravedigger had buried Grandpa good and deep. The only thing that consoled me was that he and Edna didn't find anything in sections B-four and A-five either. I suppose it was just as well I didn't come across anything important. I do not, in fact, know much about excavating, except for a few vague principles I'd read in a book. I watched Edna out of the corner of my eye and imitated her. There's nothing to it, but it is slow work. You can't take a shovel and go at the job, because you might hit something crumbly and break it, so most of the actual digging is done with a trowel and/or bare hands. Did you ever try to dig out a hole eight by eight by six feet deep with a trowel? I do not recommend it.

I should have realized, when I saw the picnic basket, that Joe was up to no good. It wasn't until midmorning that I remembered he and Edna usually came back to the house for lunch. But he was not the lad to fail to take full advantage of his extra pair of hands; it was late afternoon before we quit, with only an hour's break in the hottest part of the day. By that time I was a moving statue of dust and sweat and stiff muscles. And I was sunburned. All the way back, I kept consoling myself by considering the educational value of the day's work. I had learned something important: I did not want to major in Southwestern archaeology. In fact, I was beginning to think very kindly about the Eskimos.

I wallowed in my sunken tub for almost an hour. Then I fell on the bed and zonked out.

It was twilight when I awoke, stiff as a board and still thirsty. When I speak of twilight, I speak loosely; there really was no such time of day. The light lingered clear and bright until the sun dropped behind the mountains, and then it was night. I put a robe on myself, and a lot of ice cubes as well as other things in a glass, and wandered out onto the balcony.

The mountains were rough amethysts, against a sky like a giant stage backdrop—layers of gauzy scarlet and gold and amber, lit from behind by mammoth spotlights. I sat there drinking and relaxing, enjoying the play of cool evening air on my face, and I knew I was caught. Heat and dust and sunburn be damned, I loved the place. I wouldn't want to give up the lush green spring of Ohio, or even the blustery winters, when snow frosted every surface; but the desert was part of me too. I would have to come back to it, not just once but again and again.

It would be nice, of course, if I could come back to a

place like thi
swimming po
me.

The food in
invisible pixie
cheese and th
started thinkir

Fortunata a
around the liv
her flaming b
made of the s
to-here dress.
the front of th
was hanging a
draped over he
age. When he
called to me. I
saw no reason

He caught up
"Wait a minu
you hear me cal
"Yes, I heard y
seemed to be en
"I hear you sp
"It was very ii
"I'll bet. Your
that? Stand still.
"Talk while I
"You're always
ous about what H
it."
"I'd believe any
Is the expedition

"It sure is.
whatever the
"He has? V
"It's not he
any moment.
dered it to be
in Phoenix a
"But it too
"It's brand
assembly line
so several oth
his did. He b
"I suppose
for it."
"Probably
The news
progress ten
room and er
"You can
on my way.
I see no r
rude, crude,
I found a
however, M
me. One of
in the flash
"Sure," I
gation?"
Madame
my child. I
"Can it,
time being

introduced, Miss Abbott. My name is LeFarge—Sid Le-Farge."

"It would be," I said. "Never mind. What's your racket, Sid? You can call me D.J."

"Right." He smiled at me. I suppose the expression was meant to be pleasant, but it wasn't; he had a fat, round, red face, which might have been good-humored if his eyes had not resembled small unpolished pebbles. When he smiled, the fat on his cheeks swallowed up his eyes and reduced them to dull slits.

"I figure we might as well put our cards on the table," he went on. "You've got a pretty big mouth yourself—"

I laughed.

"I didn't mean it exactly like that," Sid said.

"That's all right. I do have a big mouth. Yours is not precisely tiny. Go on."

Sid glanced at Madame.

"I told you, Liz, the way to talk to this chick is straight from the shoulder."

"Right on," I said. I was fascinated. I had not heard such a collection of antique slang since I saw a Jimmy Cagney revival at the Bijou.

"Okay, then." Sid put his elbows on the table—preparatory, I presumed, to putting his cards on the same surface. "We've got a pretty nice deal going here, kiddo. We want to know if you're planning to queer our pitch. Wait. . . ." He raised a fat, admonitory finger. "I'm not finished. We aren't gonna take any interference sitting down, you know. There's maybe a dozen of us, and only one of you. Not that we always see eye to eye, but we can get together in case of trouble. Oh, I admit it. You could be trouble, all right. You're Hank's new pet, and if you're

155

like the rest of these university types, you could be pretty nasty to us. But I figure, what the hell, you're young enough to know what side your bread is buttered on, and maybe smart enough to realize you aren't all that different from us."

"How do you mean?" I asked, as he paused for breath.

"You're living off of him too," Sid said simply. "And it's a good life, kiddo. Now, isn't it?"

"It sure is," I said, fondly contemplating my empty plate, which had once held filet mignon sitting on chunks of pâté and little toast slices. "And I see your point, Sid. But there's one big difference between me and the rest of you. You're professional crooks, and I'm just a beginner."

He was not at all offended. His fat cheeks pouched up till his eyes disappeared. A wheezy, heaving sound that might have been laughter puffed from his mouth. It took him some time to get over his fit of boyish mirth. He mopped his face with his napkin before he went on.

"You're right about that, kiddo. But basically we aren't so different. Whatever idea it is you're pushing, it's just an idea. You can look down your nose at us all you want, but how can you be so sure we're all wrong and you're right? You think you know everything, maybe?"

"Not quite everything," I said modestly. "But—"

"That's what gets me so mad," Sid said, warming to his theme, with righteous indignation in every line of his face. "All you damned professors and Ph.D.s sit around sneering at us like you were God Almighty. You've made plenty of mistakes yourself. Look at Galileo and Lister and people like that."

"Oh, everybody drags in poor old Galileo," I said in disgust. "There was only one of him for a thousand characters like Donnelly and Velikovsky and Edgar Cayce. I'm no crusader. And Hank is no innocent, to be guided by a person like me. If he wants to go on supporting you leeches, that's his business. But I am damned if I am going to become one of the gang. Go on your merry way and leave me alone."

"We leave you alone, you leave us alone," Sid said.

"No deal. You people aren't merely wrong, you lack the feeblest remnants of reason. I'll tell Hank precisely that if he asks my opinion."

"But—" Sid began.

"Shut up," Madame said. "I told you it was no good, Sid. You think you're so fascinating all you have to do is grin at some girl and she'll fall for you."

"That certainly was an error on your part, Sid," I said.

"Okay." Sid pushed himself back from the table and stood up. His piggy little eyes had gone dull again. "We tried to play fair with you, kid. If you won't play, that's your tough luck. Don't blame me for what happens."

And off they went. They should have looked comical —the squat little woman in her worn theatrical draperies and the fat little man in his horrible suit. But they didn't. There had been real menace in Sid's voice.

I decided I would have some dessert, to raise my spirits. When I stood up, I found myself face to face with Tom. His mustache was quivering the way it did when he was amused or moved in some other way. It was some other way this time.

"Big mouth is not the phrase," he said. "Did you have to threaten that hoodlum?"

"I didn't threaten him, he threatened me."

"Oh, you noticed that, did you? Have you got rocks in your head? First the von Stumm, then Sid—"

"I'm not afraid of those creeps," I said, wishing it were

true. "But it was nice of you to rush over to protect me."

"Dream on. I was looking for you to tell you Hank wants to see you when you've finished dinner. If ever."

There were none of the little cream puffs with chocolate sauce, but there was a cake like a trifle, soaked with brandy and covered with whipped cream, with fruit and nuts sticking out of it. I ate slowly and with relish, savoring every bite, while Tom watched, tapping his fingers impatiently on the table. He didn't say anything till I went back for a second helping. I won't tell you what he said then. When I'm not with Mother my vocabulary is not the most refined in the world, but I have a phobia about typing words like that. It's Mother's fault, of course.

"Naughty, naughty," I said. "Why don't you relax? Hank wouldn't want me to rush. He likes me. You know, I think I'm getting to him. Last night, when I put on my performance with Frieda, he was really impressed. I didn't see his face when he left, but—"

"I did," Tom said. "He was laughing."

"He was?"

"Not aloud, he wouldn't be so rude. He bolted because he was about to burst holding it in. Don't underestimate him. He's a much more complex person than you realize."

Feeling properly squelched and rather thoughtful, I got myself a cup of coffee. Tom followed me and snatched the cup out of my hand.

"That's enough," he snarled. "Get moving."

"Sid has better manners than you do," I said.

Hank was in his study. He said he hoped I hadn't rushed through dinner and I said no, I hadn't. Tom had carried my coffee into the study, probably because he was so mad he had forgotten to put it down. He set the cup on a table with exaggerated care, and pulled up a chair for me. Hank smiled approvingly at this demonstration of gallantry.

"I was going to offer you coffee," he said. "Wouldn't you prefer espresso to that?"

"This is fine," I said.

"I'll just have a cup myself, then," Hank said. "Tom?"

"Why not?" Tom said disagreeably.

I expected Hank to ring or yell for service. Instead he threw open the doors of a handsome carved cupboard, and what to my wondering eyes should appear but a huge metallic contrivance bristling with knobs and faucets and dials. I thought at first it was his magnetometer. Then he started pulling levers and pushing buttons. The machine gurgled; and I recognized it for what it was—an espresso machine, one of the big commercial models. I suppose the servants kept it loaded up with coffee and water and whatever ingredients such monsters require (as I keep reiterating, I do not understand machines, or like them). Hank obviously loved them. His face glowed as he manipulated the device. Eventually it produced coffee, together with a rather vulgar series of sounds, and Hank filled two cups.

He sat down behind his desk with his coffee, after offering a cup to Tom. The lamplight fell full on the turquoise in the massive bracelet he wore on his left wrist, and I said involuntarily, "That looks like Morenci."

"Very good," Hank said in surprise. "I didn't know you were an expert on turquoise."

"I'm not. Tom showed me your collection the other night, that's absolutely all I know about it. But I recognized the color. It's beautiful."

The stone was a polished cabochon fully four inches

159

long. I touched it with a reverent finger. The surface was warm, not cold like most stones; it almost felt alive.

Hank slipped the bracelet off his wrist. The stone was set in a simple silver mounting. A single silver leaf shape, with roughly stamped veining, curved around one side of it. The band was bent to fit the curve of the wrist, and was open at the end. Hank squeezed the ends in, decreasing the diameter; the soft, virtually pure silver bent easily. Then he held it out to me.

I put it on. For a few minutes I just sat and purred, moving my arm around so that the light brought out the velvety blue of the stone—the mysterious "zat" of the turquoise. Then I started to take it off.

"Keep it," Hank said, watching me. "It's yours."

I heard a soft, quickly suppressed sound from Tom, who was sitting beside me.

"Oh, no," I gasped. "I couldn't."

"Never accept expensive gifts from strange gentlemen, dearie," said Tom, in a peculiar voice.

"Don't be disgusting," I said angrily. I couldn't help it if the dialogue sounded like an excerpt from a Victorian novel; people do talk in clichés when they are moved. "That's not it," I went on awkwardly. "I. . . . It's too valuable, Hank. I'd be afraid to wear it."

I thrust it at him. He had to take it.

"I'll put it in the safe while you're here," he said, in the voice that brooked no argument. "I can see why you might not want to leave it lying around. But it's yours. Now, let's not discuss it. We have more important things to talk about."

I was afraid to look at Tom. I decided I would deal with the problem if it came up again; maybe Hank would forget about the offer by the time I was ready to leave.

160

"I hear you have another magnetometer," I said.

"Right. And this one is going to spend the night with me, in my room, same as the first one."

Tom was slouched deep in his chair, in his usual spineless fashion. "What's wrong with the safe in here?" he demanded, sitting upright.

"Nothing, but—"

"You're hoping someone will try to swipe it," Tom said in an outraged voice. "I suppose you told everybody in the house that it had arrived, and where it was going to be?"

"I don't know what's come over you, Tom," Hank said. "I swear you're inventing plots. I can't figure out why someone took the first one, but I'm assuming it was only a malicious gesture. Nobody would try the same stunt twice. But if they do, I'll be ready for them."

Tom was ready to go on arguing, but Hank raised his voice and drowned out his protests.

"No more foolish talk, Tom. If you want to come along tomorrow, you're welcome. I just wanted to tell D.J. I plan to leave early, before it's light. Is that all right with you, D.J.?"

"Whatever you say. But I agree with Tom that—"

"Tom's an old lady," Hank said, grinning at his secretary. Tom slid down in his chair and looked very unladylike. "I'll have somebody wake you in plenty of time, D.J. You'd better get to bed now. It will be a long day. Don't forget to wear your boots."

I have never been in the presence of royalty, but I imagine they use the same tone of voice when they dismiss people from their presence. I stood not upon the order of my going, but went.

The dismissal included Tom too. He closed the door of

161

the study after him and stood there frowning, his hands in his pockets.

"What are you—" I began.

"Sssh." He grabbed my arm, and we walked down to the other end of the library. A fire was burning on the hearth. Tom gestured toward a chair and took one himself. They were big, high-backed leather chairs placed close to one another, and I felt like a character from an old-fashioned English mystery story as we sat there cheek by jowl, conversing in low voices.

At first I was afraid Tom was going to bug me about the bracelet. If he had told me the truth, the gift had meaning that far transcended the value of the jewel, which was of course considerable—though insignificant to Hank. However, he had other things on his mind.

"Did you tell anyone about the new whatever-it-is?"

"No," I said. "I did mention to Joe and Edna that the trip had been postponed. I don't think I told them that tomorrow was the day, but. . . ."

"It doesn't matter. If I know Hank, he's broadcast the news all over the ranch. He doesn't really believe my warnings, but he wouldn't mind a chance to slug somebody."

"He had a fight the other day with a man who was hassling Debbie," I said.

"Jake Smith?"

"I think so. Debbie said he used to work here, in the garage."

"That was Jake. I thought he'd left the area." Tom looked thoughtful. "I wonder if Hank could be right. Jake is the type to smash things for the fun of it. He wouldn't dare tackle Hank personally, but if he saw him fondling his new plaything, he might have wits enough to know it would hurt Hank to lose it."

"He pulled a knife on Hank," I said.

"Any rat will bite when it's cornered. But he's no killer, our gentle Jake. He's a coward and a bully."

"Could he have been responsible for the other accidents? Hank said he had warned him off the property once before."

"It's possible. Getting at the lion's cage would be no problem, and everybody knows Hank spends most mornings out there with the animals. The stairs would be trickier. I think someone stretched a cord across them. After Hank fell it wouldn't take long to remove the evidence. Yes, Jake might have done it—but it doesn't seem his style, somehow. Anyhow, he couldn't have put the pills in your drink."

"Need we assume that was part of the same plot?" I asked. "Hank's pet loonies seem to see me as a threat. Maybe doping me was a separate piece of spite."

"Oh, hell, I don't know." Tom groaned. "It's all too amorphous. But I'll tell you one thing: I am going to spend the night outside Hank's door."

"Noble man," I said admiringly. "Enjoy yourself. I am going beddy-bye."

I was almost at the door before he spoke again.

"Abbott."

"Yes?"

"Lock your door. And the balcony doors."

Chapter Nine

Having nothing of any magnitude on my conscience,
I sleep very soundly. Normally I don't wake up till somebody kicks me out of bed. I know now what it was that
woke me at the crack of dawn next morning; but at the
time I was amazed at myself. My first emotion, as I lay
blinking at the bright morning light, was fear that I might
be turning into one of those horrible people who bound
cheerily up at 6 A.M. every morning.

Something was bothering me. You know how it is,
when you wake up and think, What was I worrying about

last night? After a few hazy minutes I realized what it was. Hank had said he wanted to leave early, and he had promised to have me awakened. Early in this house meant *early*—before dawn. But sunrise was bright in the sky, and nobody had pounded on my door. I had locked it—I didn't need Tom's reminder to do that—but I would have heard someone knock. The room was utterly silent except for the whir of the air conditioning and the chatter of birdsong, muted by the closed windows.

Believe it or not, I was halfway down the hall before I knew why I was running. I don't really believe in ESP; but I am willing to concede the possibility that, in moments of extreme stress, minds that are in rapport can occasionally communicate. However, that wasn't what drove me at top speed toward Hank's room. I had good, sensible, rational reasons to expect the worst.

It wasn't the worst, but it was bad enough. Tom was lying on the floor outside Hank's door, face down; his arms and legs were bent at such uncomfortable angles that it was obvious he wasn't snatching a nap. I had turned him over and was slapping his face, not too gently, before I realized that something wet and sticky was soaking through my thin nightgown onto my lap, where his head rested.

I knew what it was, but I put my hand under his head. When I removed it, my fingers were red.

I took a deep breath and remained calm. His color was good and he seemed to be breathing normally. All the same, it was mildly alarming that my rough handling hadn't produced the faintest trace of returning consciousness. There was a sizable lump, as well as a cut, on his head, but his skull seemed to be in one piece. That was one thing I knew about—skulls.

I slapped him again and got no response, so I lowered his head to the floor and stood up. The servants didn't come upstairs until later in the morning, but the kitchen staff was on duty early. The kitchen was the most logical place to go for help. There wasn't a doctor in the house, not a real one. Besides, the villain who had slugged Tom might be one of the guests.

I ran down to the dining room. The smell of frying bacon led me to the kitchen. It was the first time in my life that the smell of food made me feel sick.

The room was full of people. I had believed myself to be quite calm up to that point, but all at once the faces seemed to blur into a haze of staring eyes and open mouths. I suppose I was a sight to startle any assemblage, white as my bloodstained nightgown, waving my arms and keening like a banshee. That's Debbie's description. Hers was the first face that took on recognizable outlines from amid the general haze.

"What's wrong?" she demanded. "Has something happened to Hank?"

I stared stupidly at her. "Hank," I said. "Oh, my God. I never even looked."

I turned and ran out again.

Most of them followed me, in an insane parade; Debbie was right on my heels most of the way, but I was running so fast it took the vanguard some time to catch up. Tom was still lying where I had left him. I bounded lithesomely over his prostrate form and flung myself at the door.

It wasn't locked. The draperies at the window waved in the breeze.

The room was empty, but it took me some time to convince myself of that obvious fact. I looked under the bed and in the closet, I peered into the bathroom. Debbie stopped me when I heaved up the top of an old Spanish chest and began tossing out blankets.

"He's not here," she said. "Where is he?"

"I don't know." I took a deep breath, focused my eyes on the bridge of my nose, and started muttering—well, never mind the word, it's my secret mantra, and you aren't supposed to tell anybody what it is.

"Stop that!" Debbie grabbed me by the arms and tried to shake me. "Are you going to have a fit or something? D.J., this is no time for—"

I uncrossed my eyes.

"I'm all right. What we need now is a doctor."

The servants were standing in a whispering group. One of them was kneeling by Tom.

"My brother, Juan," Debbie said. "He's a premed student."

"What's wrong with Tom?" I asked.

Juan looked up. "He got a knock on the head; that's obvious. It isn't too bad, but there's something else— some kind of drug. Debbie, you had better call Doc Parsons."

"You had better call the police, too," I said.

"Assault and battery," Juan said cheerfully.

"Not just assault." Debbie, already at the telephone, turned to look at me. I went on, "The rest of you spread out and start looking for Mr. Hunnicutt. But I'm afraid . . . I'm afraid we've got something worse than assault on our hands."

II

"Kidnapping?"

"Kidnapping," I said.

The sheriff eyed me skeptically. He was a real, honest-to-goodness sheriff, and under other circumstances I would have been thrilled to make his acquaintance. He even looked like a sheriff, all lean and bronzed and leathery, with silvery-white hair and a big star on his leather vest. His name was Walsh, and he was beautiful, but he was dumb.

"Now, see here, Miss—"

"Abbott," I said. "Ms. Abbott."

His eyes narrowed, and I could see him sorting through his mental labels: "Feminist . . . liberated . . . damn pushy woman. . . ."

He was polite, though.

"Okay—Ms. Abbott. What makes you think Hank has been kidnapped? He goes off like this all the time."

"Does he always hit his secretary on the head before he takes off on his little jaunts?"

The sheriff sighed. "You heard what Doc Parsons said, young lady. Your friend took some kind of sleeping medicine. He probably fell and hit his head. As for Hank, he's a bit—er—"

"Eccentric," I said. "Millionaires are eccentric; poor people are crazy."

"Crazy, eccentric, I don't care what you call it. The point is, he's done this kind of thing before. Why, you just got through telling me he had some nutty idea about a big discovery out there in the desert. He's always wandering around discovering things. Sounds to me as if you got him all riled up, with your worries and your fussing at him, and he just decided to take off on his own. He'll be back, waving some fool bone or chunk of rock, telling you it's a piece of a Martian spaceship."

He beamed paternally at me. I did not beam back.

"That is not how it was," I said.

"Well, that's how it strikes me."

The sheriff and I were in the library. The servants were still looking for Hank, although a search of the immediate area had produced no trace of him. That relieved some of my worries, and substantiated my belief that kidnapping, not murder, was the issue. As for Tom, the doctor had confirmed Juan's tentative diagnosis. The bump on his head was not too bad, but he was doped to the eyeballs with sedatives. He had not had anything like a lethal dose, and there was nothing to do but let him sleep it off. The idea that he had hit his head falling was Sheriff Walsh's contribution. I knew, and the sheriff knew, that nothing near the scene of the accident could have caused such a wound.

Walsh had his own theory, and I was pretty sure what it was. Hank was a power, not only around here but internationally; I could imagine that he could be very unpleasant if someone got in his way. Walsh didn't want to annoy Hank. He believed that Tom had tried to keep Hank from leaving, and that Hank had slugged him. That's what a reputation for eccentricity, and several million dollars, can do for a person. He can get away with everything short of dismemberment, and other people will just shrug tolerantly.

In a way I didn't blame Walsh. The series of incidents that had culminated in Hank's disappearance sounded trivial when you considered them one by one. Yet I was convinced they made a pattern. I was also convinced that whatever the provocation, Hank wouldn't have attacked Tom.

Walsh and I were sitting there staring at each other in mutual distrust and dislike when one of the sheriff's men came in carrying a piece of paper.

"Here you go, Chuck. This should settle it."

I made a grab for the paper, but the deputy eluded me and handed it to his boss.

Walsh was a slow reader. I think he deliberately prolonged the process in order to frustrate me. I kept jumping up and down saying things like, "What is it? What does it say? Let me see." Nothing aggravates a man so much. It finally got to Walsh. Scowling, he handed me the paper.

The message had been typed. It read: "I've gone to have another look at the place. I may be gone a few days. Sit tight and don't make a fuss."

It was not signed.

"I told you so," Walsh remarked.

"That is a really mean, catty remark," I said. "If I had said that to you, you would have classified it as a typical female crack."

"I guess I would," Walsh muttered. "Okay, young lady, I apologize. You owe me an apology too. Was I right or not?"

"No, you were wrong, wrong, WRONG, and this doesn't make you right. It isn't even signed. The kidnapper typed it on Hank's typewriter—"

"Kidnap notes say things like 'Bring ten thousand dollars to the arroyo at midnight,' " Walsh protested. "They don't say—"

"They say that if the kidnapper wants ten thousand dollars. This kidnapper doesn't. He wants to keep Hank out of circulation for a few days so he can. . . ."

Walsh waited while I fumbled for a fitting end to the sentence. I couldn't find one. I didn't know the reason.

"Well?" he said, after a while.

"I don't know why he wants Hank out of the way. But it has something to do with his discovery—"

Walsh's temper finally cracked. He let out a roar that made me jump.

"What am I doing, arguing with you? Arguing with a woman is the damnedest-fool activity a man can engage in, and you are the worst. . . . Who's the sheriff around here, anyway?"

"You are," I admitted. "But—"

"No more 'buts.' You want to do something useful, get on up there and tend to your boyfriend. That's what a woman is supposed to do, tend the sick and things like that."

Boyfriend, indeed. I had never met such a man for clichés. Walsh had it all figured out. Tom was one of the rotten younger generation, doping himself with pills; Hank was an eccentric millionaire who did peculiar, unaccountable things; I was just another dumb female, flying into a panic when she saw a little blood, inventing soap-opera drama to account for her "boyfriend's" condition. . . .

"You are a stupid male chauvinist," I said; but I didn't say it till after the door had closed on Walsh. In the old Westerns John Wayne and Gregory Peck sometimes spanked the heroine when she got uppity. I wouldn't have put it past Walsh to do the same.

I decided I might as well go up and have a look at Tom. Not that he needed any TLC from me; if he came to and found me swabbing his wounded brow, he'd probably pass out again from sheer surprise. But he might have some idea as to what had happened to Hank.

Doc Parsons, who was still in attendance, wasn't quite as irritating as Walsh. He admitted he couldn't account for the lump on Tom's head; he even admitted, when pressed by me, that it might have been caused by the

171

conventional blunt instrument. (Not all that blunt; there had been a sharp edge on the instrument.) But, like Walsh, the doctor refused to believe that Hank was in any danger. He brought out one telling point to support his idea.

"I glanced into Hank's room," he said. "No sign of a struggle, was there? No chairs overturned, nothing like that. Well, young woman, you wouldn't get Hank Hunnicutt out of there against his will without a fight."

I threw up my hands, literally and figuratively.

"How long is Tom going to be unconscious?" I asked.

"Depends on how much he took and how much he's accustomed to taking," was the cautious reply. "I'd guess he's got a good twelve hours yet to go."

"Oh, damn," I muttered. "Isn't there anything we can do to wake him up?"

"There is plenty I could do, but I'm not going to do it. He's in no danger. Just let him—"

"Sleep it off," I said. "Good-bye, Doc.

After he had gone I stood by the bed and looked at Tom. He looked so comfortable I had to restrain a strong impulse to hit him again. His lips were curved sweetly, as if he were having a beautiful dream.

The door opened and Debbie peeked in.

"I thought maybe someone should stay with him," she said. "Doc Parsons said it wasn't necessary, but—"

"I had similar ideas," I admitted.

"We'll take turns. You haven't had breakfast, have you?"

"You may not believe this, but there are occasions in my life when I think of something else besides food."

"You aren't even dressed."

"True." I glanced in mild surprise at my dishabille. "I

172

wondered why the sheriff kept looking over my left shoulder and blushing. I'll get dressed and eat something. I also want to have a look at Hank's room."

"The police looked already."

"They weren't looking for the same things I am looking for. Debbie, you know Hank better than I do; would he act like this?"

"He's gone off alone before, plenty of times. But he'd never hit Tom. Not from behind, anyway."

"Keep an eye on Sleeping Beauty, then. I'll be back soon."

I was about to go upstairs to my room, to assume more fitting attire, when it occurred to me that the maids might be about to tidy up Hank's room. I wanted to see it before they did so. I had been in no condition to notice details when I was there before.

Tom's room was in the same wing, but on another corridor, around the corner from Hank's. When I turned the corner, still fetchingly attired in my bloodstained nightgown, I saw Jesse coming toward me.

"My God, D.J.," he said. "You look like something out of a monster movie."

"Thanks," I said.

"You know what I mean—the heroine after the Horrible Shrinking Man has tried to carry her off. Not that I'm complaining, but shouldn't you get some clothes on?"

"I will. I wanted to search Hank's room first, before the maids got to it."

"I had the same idea."

"Where have you been?"

"With the search party, of course."

"No sign of Hank?"

"Not a trace. One of the jeeps is missing, though."

"Naturally. They would need some means of transportation."

"They? D.J., don't you think it's barely possible that Hank has gone off on his own?"

"Just barely," I said. The door of Hank's room was closed—by the police, I guess. I opened it.

The maids had not been there yet. I saw a pile of blankets on the floor, and started to exclaim; then I remembered that I had thrown them there myself. Except for the disarray caused by my wild search, there was no sign of a disturbance. The bed had been slept in; the sheet was thrown back as if the sleeper had awakened and gotten out of bed in the normal way.

"What are you looking for?" Jesse asked.

"Clothes. What would he wear?"

Jesse frowned.

"I think he usually puts his clothes out on a chair or something before he goes to bed. I don't see anything lying around, do you? That suggests he dressed himself."

"Nonsense. If you can steal a man, you can steal his clothes too."

We prowled the room, looking aimlessly around.

"I don't see anything unusual," Jesse said.

"I also don't see his new magnetometer."

"His new what?"

"Something like that. I don't know what its official name is."

"Oh, yes. Someone told me he had a new one. How big is it? Where would he have put it?"

I started pulling out drawers. There were a lot of them. Dresser, chest of drawers, a couple of filing cabinets . . . Nothing. I opened the Spanish chest and tossed out the rest of the blankets. Still nothing.

"I'm pretty sure it would have been in this room," I said, opening the closet door. "Tom suggested he should put it in the safe and he said no, he wanted it with him."

"It doesn't seem to be here," Jesse said.

"They took it, too."

Jesse folded his arms and cocked his head. His eyes were twinkling with what I could only regard as inappropriate amusement.

"D.J., don't you think you're getting a little paranoid about your mysterious 'they'?"

"No." I kicked a pair of shoes back into the closet and closed the door. "The fact that the magnetometer is missing doesn't affect my case one way or the other. Hank certainly would have taken it with him if he wanted to look at his discovery again. But, damn it all, one magnetometer already got smashed. That does bear out my theory. Somebody will stop at nothing to keep us from seeing his find. Jesse, we have to go on looking for Hank! He could be hurt, drugged. . . ."

My voice cracked, and Jesse's smile vanished.

"You're absolutely right. I won't say I subscribe to all your theories, but we certainly shouldn't leave any stone unturned. I'll take a jeep and go out myself, right away. I know this country as well as any of the men. Only promise me you won't try to search on your own. We don't want to lose you too."

"I won't. But if I knew you were looking, I could rest easier."

"Then rest. I'll find him, I promise, if. . . . I'll find him. You relax."

I couldn't relax. Every passing moment made me more and more uneasy; it was as if some part of my mind knew something awful was about to happen, something I couldn't prevent. I got dressed in a hurry and went down to breakfast. The body needs nourishment.

Despite everything that had happened, it was only midmorning—too early for most of Hank's pampered guests to have left the sack. Madame was one of the early birds. She found me eating breakfast and took a chair—uninvited, I hardly need add.

"What is this I hear, that Hank has run away without you?"

"He's gone, anyway," I said.

"And Tom. They say he and Hank had a terrible fight and that he has a fractured skull, broken bones—"

"Is that what they're saying? It's a lie. Tom hit his head, but he's not seriously injured. You know Hank wouldn't hurt him."

"I do not know what our esteemed patron would do," Madame said smoothly. "He is a most unpredictable man, and the potentiality for violence is there."

I couldn't deny that. I had seen him with Jake. But I didn't like the implication that Hank had flipped his lid and run amok. A very nasty suspicion slid into my mind. I wondered if Hank had left his fortune to his various crazy causes.

The idea upset me so much I left half a western omelet and four sausages on my plate. A few days ago, I would have sworn that the gentle, philanthropic man had no enemies, except perhaps abstract business rivals; and in spite of all the sensational movie plots I had seen, I doubted that the presidents of General Motors and Shell Oil had taken to assassinating their business adversaries. But now motives were swarming up out of the dirt like maggots.

When I got back to Tom's room, Debbie was sitting by

the window, her hands folded in her lap. Her Indian heritage was suddenly very apparent; but I knew that the passivity of her face concealed torrential emotions. She looked up when I came in, and nodded approval.

"You look a hundred percent better."

"I feel a hundred percent worse. Any change?"

"No." Debbie looked at Tom with something like hatred. I knew how she felt. A possible clue to Hank's whereabouts might be lurking behind that peaceful face.

"Why don't you get something to eat?" I suggested.

"I've eaten. But if you'll stay here, I'd like to go out."

"Where?"

"To look for Hank."

"Debbie, you can't do that. The others are looking—"

"No, they aren't." Her reserve broke down. Her face twisted like that of a little girl trying not to cry. "The sheriff called off the search."

"Damn him! I'll go and tell them—"

"You can't. Nobody has the authority to order them to do anything—except maybe Tom." She added, glaring at the bed, "I'd like to grab him and shake him. . . ."

"Now, now," I said. "Maybe we're getting all worked up about nothing. Surely nothing could happen. . . ."

But my voice trailed off weakly. I couldn't convince her when I didn't believe it myself.

"Let's make a deal, D.J.," she said quietly. "Let's not kid each other. We're the only ones who are really worried. Talk—and let me talk. It's easier to face things head on, and try to figure out what we can do about them."

I let out a sigh and dropped into a chair facing hers.

"My view exactly. All right, then. I don't think Hank is dead. I also don't think he left under his own steam."

"Agreed so far. Go on."

"Tom was drugged," I said. "Hank was too. He must have been. They couldn't have gotten him out of the house otherwise. Something in the espresso? Tom drank less than Hank, so they had to knock him out in order to reach Hank. Tom planned to stay on guard last night."

Debbie nodded. She was taking it well. She said, "One of the jeeps is gone."

"Jesse told me."

"You know what that means."

"That the kidnappers are not outsiders, or they would have brought their own means of transportation? I think they are members of the household, but the conclusion doesn't necessarily follow. They would have to steal a jeep if they wanted us to believe Hank left of his own accord."

With one detached part of my mind I marveled at the way we were talking—quickly, quietly, like dispassionate observers. Only Debbie's eyes betrayed her feelings.

"Look," I said awkwardly. "I honestly don't think Hank is in danger. If I'm right about the motive for this, some unknown party is trying to prevent us from visiting Hank's mystery site. There have been a number of incidents designed to accomplish the same thing, but no violence, Debbie; nothing really lethal. They wouldn't dare kill Hank. The murder of a man of his prominence would bring police swarming all over this place. That's the last thing our friend seems to want—publicity. He's gone to a lot of trouble to keep a low profile."

Debbie shook her head.

"You're a stranger here," she said flatly. "You don't understand this country. It's easy to commit murder here. Two days out in that sun, and you'd have a dead body, with not a mark on it to show anything but accidental death."

The same thought had crossed my mind, but it was so horrible I didn't want to admit it even to myself.

"Hank is desert trained," I argued. "Nobody would believe he—"

"It could be arranged," Debbie said, in the same dull voice. "I've been thinking how. They wouldn't want to tie him up. Ropes leave marks. If he were drugged and unconscious, they could just dump him in some isolated spot. The drug would be absorbed long before he was found."

"But if the drug wore off too soon, he could—"

"He couldn't walk, or even crawl, very far with a broken leg or two."

I stared at her, speechless with horror, and she added, "It happens, even to the old hands. Rock crumbles, there are avalanches. . . ."

I stood up. My legs felt wobbly, as if I were coming down with flu.

"Get your brother up here," I said, and turned purposefully toward the bed.

III

Even with Juan helping, it took us hours, and a gallon of black coffee, to awaken Tom. We walked him up and down that room till I thought my arms and legs would drop off. Debbie moved with the steely efficiency of a robot. She was smaller than I was, but she never faltered.

Juan wasn't enthusiastic about what we were doing. He kept muttering about Hippocratic oaths and other extraneous matters. Brother and sister said very little, but I could see they understood one another, and Debbie's distress was probably the only thing that could have moved Juan to act against Dr. Parsons' orders.

It was midafternoon when he finally dropped into a chair, panting. He had been doing most of the work for the past hour, and although Tom was a lot steadier on his feet by then than when we had started, he was a heavy load.

"He should be coming around soon," Juan said heavily. "I hope to God Parsons never finds out about this. It's hard enough to get into med school these days."

"He'll never learn the truth from me," I said. I bent over the bed. Tom lay sprawled where Juan had dropped him, his arms extended like the wings of a dead bird, his legs dangling off the bed. His eyes were still closed, and his mustache drooped damply. We had poured a lot of water on him.

"Wake up," I said, and slapped him.

"Ouch," he said distinctly.

Debbie grabbed his shoulder and shook him. Tom opened one eye.

"Debbie?" The eye rolled in my direction and then closed. "You," he muttered. "Go away."

A few more minutes of mingled threats and cajolery and he got with it. His eyes flew open.

"Hank," he said.

"He's gone. Kidnapped." I sat down on the edge of the bed. "You were drugged. It's been hours, and Hank is still missing. What happened last night?"

"I don't remember."

"Temporary amnesia," Juan said. He added, with the gloomy satisfaction some doctors display when they are stating an unpalatable fact, "He may never remember. It's a common symptom—"

"Shut up," Debbie said.

"Dragons," Tom muttered.

"He's still groggy," Debbie said, and reached out to give him another shake.

"Maybe not," I said slowly. "What are you talking about, Tom?"

"It's gone," Tom mumbled. "Damn, my brain's all full of cobwebs and dust. . . . Get out of the way, D.J. Got to get up. Walk. No, don't help me. . . ."

I had not crossed Tom off the list of suspects just because he had been drugged and slugged. But as I watched him reel up and down the room, grabbing at the furniture to keep from falling, my suspicions withered and blew away, along with several other preconceptions. I don't think it was because he looked so heroic and romantic—all that beautiful bare brown muscle showing, and bandages on his head, and his face pale and set like Errol Flynn facing the Inquisition. . . . I simply decided that nobody would go to that much trouble to give himself an alibi.

"Want some coffee?" I asked, as he passed me on his second tour of the room.

"God, no." He stopped, holding on to the bedpost, and looked blearily at me. "My face hurts," he said accusingly.

"I slapped you some," I admitted.

"You're a monster."

"Tom, this is serious. Honest, I wouldn't have hit you—"

"I know." He dropped onto the bed and put his head in his hands. "I'm trying to remember. Was there something in the coffee?"

"Probably."

"It tasted funny. I only had one cup. . . . Hank always drinks three or four cups after dinner."

181

"You were hit on the head too," Debbie said. "Did you see who did it?"

"Is that what this is?" Tom felt the bandage and winced. "Wait a minute, it's coming back. I heard something inside the room. I was so damned sleepy. I was walking up and down to keep awake. . . . I opened the door and looked in. . . . Yes, by God, there was something there, bending over the bed. All in black. It had a face like. . . ."

"Not a dragon," I protested. "Don't tell me—"

"Something monstrous," Tom muttered. "Striped black and red, with fangs. . . ."

"You're hallucinating," I said.

"It might have been a mask," Debbie said.

"Yeah." Tom looked at her as if she had said something brilliant. "I guess it might have been. It was startling, though; caught me off guard for a second. . . . I can't remember any more."

"There were two people, then," I said. "I didn't think one man could handle Hank, conscious or unconscious. The second man was behind the door. He hit you. So you don't have any idea who they were?"

"Not the foggiest." Tom started to shake his head, and then thought better of it. "When did all this happen? What time is it?"

"Late afternoon. I found you outside Hank's door at about five thirty or six o'clock. He said he'd have someone wake me, but nobody did. I guess my own subconscious alerted me."

"He meant to wake you himself," Tom muttered, cradling his head tenderly in his hands. "He's always considerate of the servants. . . . Holy God, you mean he's been

182

missing all this time and you're sitting around here? Let's get—"

He started to stand up. I caught his arm.

"You're in no condition to go anywhere. You'd better lie down. We were hoping you had seen something that could give us a clue, that's why we worked you over; but you haven't been much help. Relax, will you? Everything possible is being done."

It was a lie, but there was no sense in telling him the truth. He fell back against the pillow and closed his eyes. There were purple marks, like bruises, under the sunken sockets. I didn't feel too pleased with myself.

"Okay, you female leeches," Juan said. "That's enough. Leave the guy alone."

"We had to do it," I said, trying to convince myself as much as Juan.

"I guess so. But you're not going to get anything more out of him tonight. He'll be okay in the morning. We can't do much till then anyway; it's getting late."

Debbie dropped into a chair and stared at her feet. Juan said awkwardly,

"I'll go out and look some more first thing tomorrow morning, Deb, I promise. If Hank has been kidnapped— which I don't for a moment admit—we'll be hearing from the kidnappers. If we find a ransom note, we call his lawyers; it's that simple."

"But Tom said—" I began.

"Tom was barely coherent, lady. As a witness he isn't worth a plugged nickel. A blow on the head can produce all kinds of weird symptoms. He needs rest."

Debbie didn't say anything. After a minute Juan shrugged and went out. His skepticism showed me what

183

we were up against. Nobody took our fears seriously, not even Debbie's brother.

"I hate to admit it," I said, "but I'm about to drop."

"Take a nap, why don't you? Juan was right; it's too late to do anything today."

"I'll rest if you will. You worked the hardest."

"I'll stay with him," Debbie said. Tom was asleep again, breathing heavily.

"He's told us everything he knows," I said, smothering a yawn. "He's in no danger now."

"The person who slugged him may not know that," Debbie said.

Chapter Ten

I slept for several hours. The light was fading when I woke up; by the time I had showered and dressed it was dark, except for a few bars of luminiscent crimson streaking the west, like neon signs pointing the way to heaven.

I looked into Tom's room on the way downstairs. They were both asleep, Debbie curled up on the big bed next to Tom.

It was like another world down on the first floor. The usual evening activities proceeded merrily, as if everything were normal.

Fortunata was the first of the crackpots to greet me. I couldn't help noticing her clothes. They got more outrageous every time I saw her. Tonight it was a black sequined jumpsuit that looked as if it had been painted and glued on. The black feathers topping the coppery aureole of her hair were the same ones that had adorned the silver-lamé turban—an economical little touch I found sourly amusing.

"The messenger has come," she cried, lifting her glass in a mocking salute. "Now we will hear the truth. Rumors have been circulating all day. What has happened?"

"Nothing that concerns you," I said.

She caught me by the wrist. I wasn't going anywhere, so I stood there and let her dig her nails into me.

"Concern us? Our friend, our patron is in danger, and you say it does not concern us? We wish to help."

I let my eyes wander insolently over the assembled group, lounging at ease in their comfortable chairs, holding their glasses of expensive booze.

"I noticed how upset you all were," I said. "Hank will be very touched when he learns how much you've helped."

"How can we be useful when we do not know the facts?" Madame demanded.

"The facts are simple," I said. "Hank is missing. We'd like to know where he is."

"We could maybe form a search party," Sid suggested unenthusiastically.

"Search party?" I slapped Fortunata smartly on the bicep, loosening her grip, and threw out my arms in what was meant to be a mystic gesture. "How can you suggest anything so mundane? Here you all are, with your private pipelines to the Infinite World Consciousness; why don't you ring up one of your contacts and ask where Hank is?"

No one spoke. "Oh, come on," I said. "Don't be modest. Here's your chance to prove your claims. How about a little séance?"

"Yeah, Fortunata," Sid said. "How about it? That used to be a sideline of yours, before you got scientific. Maybe that Indian spirit of yours can locate Hank."

Fortunata gave him a withering look.

"What about you, Sid? You claim you can locate gold with your dowsing rod; why not a missing man?"

"Oh, is that your racket, Sid?" I asked. "You walk around with a little pointed stick, and dig when it wiggles? How much gold have you got stashed away?"

"Sneer all you want," Sid muttered. "Radiesthesia is a science. It locates the magnetic currents—"

"Giving it a fancy name doesn't make it a science," I said. "But I've got to admit I don't see how you can locate Hank with a dowsing rod."

"It is possible, however," Madame said smoothly. "The divining rod has been used to locate missing persons. In France, in 1947, Gramenia was awarded fifty thousand francs for locating the body of a young man who had fallen in the Alps. He used a pendulum, and a map of the area."

Sid gave her a look that should have made her blush. The grand alliance of nuts was breaking down; they might stick together against a common enemy, but if they saw a chance to put a buddy on the spot, they wouldn't hesitate. Madame was in the clear; she couldn't be expected to locate Hank by means of her peculiar hobby, so she had no qualms about embarrassing her colleagues.

Sid didn't say anything at first. He had the blank, trained face of a professional poker player, but I didn't need ESP to know what he was thinking. It wouldn't do him any harm to try. If by chance he did find Hank, or even came close, his stock would go up about a thousand percent. If he failed—well, he was probably very good at inventing excuses. All mystics are.

"I will do my best," he said portentously. "But the conditions are not good—"

"Why aren't they?" I asked.

"Negative thoughts interfere with my performance," Sid said, staring at me.

"Mine are very negative," I admitted.

"See?" Sid spread his hands and looked appealingly at the others. "With such skepticism it is hard to work. But I'll take a crack at it. I'll need a large-scale map. . . ."

"Maybe the Martians have seen Hank," Mr. Ballou said suddenly. His wife stepped heavily on his foot. He yelped.

"I'll get you a map," I said.

"After dinner," Sid said.

"I thought you weren't supposed to eat before a performance," I said.

"That doesn't affect the divining rod," Sid answered. "If Fortunata is going to have a séance, though, she isn't supposed to load up her stomach."

He and Fortunata glowered at one another.

"I will try, of course," she said, between her teeth.

"How about you, Frieda?" I asked, turning toward that person, who was standing with her arms folded viewing us all with impartial contempt. "Don't you want to dissociate yourself from all these goings-on? I mean, a serious historian like yourself surely doesn't approve of séances and radiography, or whatever it is."

Sid started to correct me. I brushed his protests aside with a lordly air.

"I don't care what you call it," I said. "It's all balderdash. Right, Frieda?"

As I intended, the question put her on the spot. All the crazy theories overlap; a mind weak enough to invent hypotheses like the ones she endorsed was open to any feebleminded idea. Besides, she was curious. She wanted to be present at the performance, in case anything interesting happened. Add to all that her dislike of me, and her automatic rejection of anything I said, and it's no wonder the woman was at a loss for words. She contented herself with a mutter and a scowl. I shrugged.

"I'll see you all later, then."

They could hardly wait for me to leave. As soon as I closed the door, the voices began. It sounded like a dogfight in there.

I found Jesse in the dining room, hunched over a plate of untouched food. He didn't look up till I touched him on the shoulder.

I didn't need to ask what he had been doing, or what the results had been. I had estimated his age at somewhere in the late twenties. Tonight he looked ten years older.

"No luck?" I asked. I knew the answer, but I had to ask.

"No. Any news from this quarter?"

"Fortunata is going to hold a séance," I said, trying for a touch of comic relief. "And Sid is about to try some map dowsing."

"Good God."

"I suppose it can't do any harm. Sid needs a map. I thought you might have one."

"Sure. I'll get it for you in a moment."

189

"Eat something," I said, as he poked distastefully at his food.

"I'm too tired," Jesse said. "You aren't eating either. You look a little weary yourself."

"Not as weary as you do—I hope. I haven't done much, except drag Tom around his room a couple of million times."

Jesse's eyebrows shot up.

"Isn't that a rather brutal thing to do to a man with concussion?"

"He doesn't have a concussion. Well, not much of one. He does have very thick hair, luckily for him."

"All the same, D.J.—"

"Oh, stop it," I said irritably. "You men all act as if I were Lucrezia Borgia. It had to be done. If he had seen something or recognized a face—"

"I take it he didn't."

"How did you know?"

"You'd have blurted it out right away." He smiled at me. "You're not exactly phlegmatic."

"True. Well, you're right, he was no use at all. All he saw was a weird figure with the head of a dragon."

"What?"

"Debbie thinks the kidnapper was wearing a mask," I explained. "Juan thinks Tom was hallucinating. He's got dragons on the brain, just as I do."

"Why dragons?" Jesse asked warily.

"Oh, I forgot you hadn't heard about that."

I told him about Hank's hints. There was no point in being coy about them now. He started eating mechanically; at least the story was taking his mind off his immediate worries. But when I had finished he shook his head with a smile.

190

"Hard to know with Hank. He's crazy enough to believe any of the theories you have proposed. He is also capable of trying to throw you off the track. Are you just going to sit here and watch me, or are you going to eat?"

"I guess I had better force myself," I said.

I got a plate and started along the buffet table, but the food didn't look as good as it usually did. I was helping myself to roast beef when the Stockwells made their appearance.

"We've just heard the news," Joe said. "What's been going on around here?"

"You must have left before the fun began," I said. "I don't know what you heard, or who told you, but the truth is, Hank is gone and Tom has a lump on his head —and a stomach full of sleeping pills."

I told them the rest of the story, as succinctly as possible. Joe's reaction aggravated me. Oh, he said all the right things, expressed shock and surprise. . . . But I could sense the avid curiosity under his facade of concern.

He and Edna followed me back to my table. During the thirty seconds or so that this took, Joe thought the situation over and formulated a theory which he proceeded to expound.

"I'm inclined to agree with the sheriff. Hank is a very unpredictable person. If he doesn't communicate with us in the next day or two—"

"He could be dead by that time," I said.

Edna had not spoken. She just sat there looking paler and blanker than usual. Now she suddenly exclaimed, "Oh, no. No one would hurt Hank. Don't you think you're getting rather melodramatic?"

She was talking to me, but I noticed she didn't use my name. People don't when they dislike you.

191

"If you had seen Tom, you wouldn't think I was over-dramatizing," I said angrily. "You don't seriously believe, any of you, that Hank would hit him over the head—from behind?"

"No, no," Joe said soothingly. He gave Jesse one of those "you know women" looks. "But it could have been an accident, D.J. If they had struggled—nothing serious, just a friendly tussle—and Tom fell . . . he'd hate to admit Hank got the better of him."

"So he made up a story about midnight intruders and dragon faces," I said. "Maybe you're right, Joe. Maybe a man would be dumb enough to do something like that."

"You're impossible," Edna exclaimed. She pushed her plate away and stood up. "Ever since you came here, there's been nothing but trouble. We were getting along fine till you arrived. Why don't you get out?"

I was too dumbfounded by this outburst to respond immediately. Before I could think what to say, Edna turned and ran out.

"You've upset her," Joe said accusingly.

"I certainly have," I said. "I wonder why."

The lunatic fringe had been drifting into the room while we talked. They ostentatiously avoided us, and I concluded that another temporary alliance had been formed.

I said as much to Jesse, adding, "Are you going to attend the performance?"

"Oh, I suppose so. I'll just run up to my room and get that map."

"What performance?" Joe demanded.

So I told him. Again he said the right things, expressing the proper academic contempt and amusement. The university had programmed him well; if you punched the right keys, you got the right answers. But his eyes were bright with an emotion other than laughter. Under his coating of skepticism the man was a potential sucker. I had suspected as much when I watched him react to Edna's performance as Running Deer. I wasn't surprised. Many brilliant scholars have fallen for spiritualism, and every nutty new theory about wandering comets and little green men from Venus acquires one or two "scientists" who defend it.

After a while I stopped listening to Joe, because he was very boring. Finally Jesse came back with the map, and Joe said,

"I'll go find Edna. She may be interested in this display. It should be quite amusing, don't you think?"

"Oh, yes," I said sourly.

II

I gave Sid the map and received a formal invitation to join the party.

"I thought you didn't want any skeptics jamming the air waves," I said.

Madame answered.

"We will need your testimony if the experiment succeeds, to convince other doubters. Even you cannot deny what you yourself have heard."

"Maybe not, but I'll do my best," I said pleasantly.

Von Stumm, glowering in the background like a solid gray thundercloud, remarked softly, "And there you speak the truth. You do not want to believe, or to think."

"Whose side are you on?" I asked. "I thought you claimed. . . . Oh, hell, why do I bother?"

The nuts started to leave, so I went back to my table and

had a cup of coffee with Jesse, to give them time to arrange the scene. While we were sitting there, Joe came back dragging his sister. Edna's mouth was set in an ugly pout, which didn't surprise me; what did surprise me was the unmistakable evidence that she had been crying. Since she scorned makeup, she had made no attempt to conceal the redness of her eyes and nose.

I could have been catty. I could have asked a lot of embarrassing questions about why she was so upset about a crazy millionaire for whom she felt nothing but contempt. I didn't ask any questions, and I think I deserve some credit for kindness. I certainly didn't get any thanks from Edna, then or later. The fact is, my compassion was stupid. I didn't know how stupid until it was almost too late.

Anyhow, I ignored Edna's swollen eyes, knowing that neither of those oblivious men would notice. We headed for the parlor.

The screwballs were out in full force. They were a colorful crowd, I must admit. The parlor resembled the exotic bird cage at the zoo.

Fortunata was like a *Mad* magazine caricature, an insane blend of the Dragon Lady and Little Orphan Annie, with her skintight black outfit and her flaming red hair. Sid was wearing a jacket of red-and-green plaid—the tartan of some fictitious Scottish clan, perhaps. A "diamond" the size of a lima bean glittered greasily on his fat hand. Madame looked like a burlesque queen in her gauzy draperies of mauve and purple; von Stumm like a character out of an old World War II spy drama— "Speak, you English pig, or Doctor von Stumm will apply the electrodes!" The Ballous, in their cheap mail-order clothes, were just as unreal as the others. Mrs. Ballou was trying for the simple-country-folks image, but her calico print dress didn't suit her hard face.

They were all clustered around a big mahogany table where Jesse's map was spread out, its corners held down by various pieces of bric-a-brac.

"Here we are," I said briskly. "Let the play begin."

Sid had sense enough not to make a big production out of it. He claimed to be a scientist, not a mystic.

"Sit down," he said curtly. "All of you sit down and keep your mouths shut. This isn't easy. I need to concentrate."

It was a large table. There was room for all of us around it, though we had to bring chairs from various parts of the room. Sid remained standing, his hands on the table, his head bent over the map.

When the rustle and buzz of conversation had died, he glanced up.

"Okay, here we go," he said. "Remember—no talking."

In his right hand he held a strange object. It looked like a small metal ball attached to a cord about eighteen inches long. Slowly, almost hieratically, he raised his hand. The metal glittered in the lamplight. So did the cord; it must have had metal strands woven into it. The ball was not a perfect sphere. It came to a point at the bottom.

I don't know about other people, but I find that keeping quiet is a strain on my nerves. My ears start to ring after a while, and I get dizzy. Sid leaned forward slightly, his left hand on the table; his right, holding the pendulum, was rock-steady. No one spoke, but there were sounds; small surreptitious noises like rats in the skirting: the rustle of cloth, as someone shifted position; the varied harmonies of breath; the far-off mutter of voices as the servants cleared the tables in the dining room.

195

I didn't understand how Sid could keep his hand so still. The cord hung rigid as a steel rod. Finally it began to move. The movement was tiny, almost unnoticeable, but it broke the concentration that had held me; I let my breath out and looked at Sid's face. His upper lip was beaded with sweat and his thick lips were moving.

The pendulum began to swing in small circles. I didn't feel that Sid was making it move. In fact, he looked as if he were trying as hard as possible to hold it still. The drops of moisture on his face coalesced and began to trickle down his chin.

I forced my eyes away from Sid's face and looked at the map. I was sitting sideways to it; I couldn't make out the lettering. Suddenly Sid's arm jerked, not much; but the movement was so abrupt, compared to what had preceded it, that it gave the impression someone had caught his arm. The circular motion of the pendulum continued, but now it was narrowing. The metal ball swung in ever-diminishing circles, till finally it hung as motionless as it had originally.

"There." The fat man's voice was barely recognizable. "Get it, quick . . . someone. . . ."

A hand shot out—a long, thin, prehensile hand with sharp crimson nails.

"Here?" Fortunata asked. Her index finger stabbed a spot on the map.

Sid nodded. His expression was that of a man at the limit of his strength. He dropped into the chair behind him and drooped forward, his head bowed.

"Here," Joe said shrilly. "Here, I've got a pencil—watch out, I'll get it—"

There was a sort of scuffle in the middle of the table, a jumble of fingers and pencils.

196

"You pushed me," Fortunata exclaimed. "I have lost the place."

"No, I've got it," Joe insisted. "Here. This was the spot right here, wasn't it?"

Fortunata shrugged and examined her nail.

"I cannot be sure. You jostled me. I think you have bent my nail."

Joe had put a neat penciled cross along a jagged contour line. I'm not good at contour lines. I looked for some print. The nearest name read "Dead Man's Gulch." The general direction was northwest of the ranch.

"Nicely done, don't you think?" Jesse said softly.

"What? Oh. Oh, yes; I see what you mean."

I looked at Fortunata, who was still pretending to examine her fingernail. She had provided Sid with his excuse, if he needed one—and he almost certainly would. I wondered if they were all in league together, or if it was only Fortunata and Sid who had agreed to help one another out.

"How about you, Fortunata?" I said. "Are you going to have a crack at it, too?"

"But it seems that Sid has found the place," Fortunata said.

"Far be it from me to cast the cold water of skepticism on the fire of inspiration," I began. "But—"

"That's okay," Sid mumbled. "I don't know. . . . For a minute there I had the power, but. . . ."

Joe was poring over the map.

"I know this area," he said excitedly. "It's not far from our excavation site. We could have a look tomorrow."

"We certainly could," I said. "But it won't do any harm to let Fortunata try, will it? There's a lot of empty landscape out there by Dead Man's Gulch, partner."

Sid reached for a handkerchief and mopped his face.

"You go ahead, Fortunata. The girl is right; I can't pinpoint the spot exactly."

Fortunata shrugged. The light ran up and down her sequins like greedy hands.

"I will try, then. Madame, the lights, if you please."

I don't know much about séances. I guess there is an established routine. All I can say is that they moved like seasoned actors performing a well-rehearsed scene. Madame turned out all the lights except one lamp in a far corner. The others moved their chairs closer to the table and clasped hands to form a circle. Jesse and I and the Stockwells formed a small pocket of doubt at the lower end of the table. I was between Joe and Jesse, with Edna on Jesse's other side.

As the silence deepened, I wondered why all the spiritual forces demanded that everybody keep quiet. If they could work at all, why couldn't they work through a light, genteel murmur of conversation? I didn't ask, because I knew what the answer would be. Concentration. We all had to pour our mental powers into a common pool, seeking, searching. . . . Hell, I thought disgustedly; I could do this sort of thing. All it takes is a little study of the jargon, a little common, garden-variety psychology—and a few nitwits like Joe to work on. He was so excited his palm was sweating.

Darkness increased the semihypnotic effect. I started multiplying mentally, to keep my mind occupied. Jesse's hand was warm and dry; his fingers closed firmly over mine.

I won't bore you with the routine. Fortunata started panting and puffing, and finally went into a trance. So that there would be no doubt about this, Madame exclaimed, "Hush! She is in a trance!"

Fortunata's puffing and panting went on for quite a while. Suddenly a voice said, "Good evening, all. How are you?"

Prosaic words—but the voice was that of a stranger, deeper than a woman's voice, not as deep as most men's, with an indefinable but pronounced accent.

"It is her control," Madame whispered. "Black Eagle." Then she said aloud, "Good evening, Black Eagle. We are all well. How are you?"

"Well," Black Eagle said. "It is well with me, and with my brothers and sisters in the land of—"

"My foot is going to sleep," I said. "Tell Black Eagle to skip the small talk."

A murmur of annoyance ran around the circle. Fortunata groaned theatrically.

"You will break the trance," Madame hissed. "Be still."

Fortunata heaved and moaned and twisted around for a few minutes. Then we got Black Eagle back again.

"You are troubled, my friends," he intoned. "I am here to bring you peace."

"We don't want peace, we want information," I said.

"You seek one who is lost," Black Eagle said.

"Good boy," I encouraged.

"None are truly lost," the peculiar, androgynous voice went on, with a hint of reproach. "The one you seek is not with us. Nor is he wholly in your world. His spirit wanders. . . . He seeks the light. . . ."

The comments were just about what I had expected— vague and cryptic, like the pronouncements of the Oracle of Delphi.

"Give us a clue," I said humbly. "Where does the lost spirit wander, O great chief?"

A flood of light burst upon us, so bright after the dimness of the room that we were all momentarily blinded. A voice thundered out, "Hell and damnation!"

The accidental appropriateness of the comment made me want to laugh. I knew the light came from the open door, and I recognized Tom's voice. But poor Joe almost fainted. His wet hand went limp and cold, like a dead fish. I released it and wiped my own hand on my thigh. Tom flicked on the overhead lights.

"What are you doing out of bed?" I demanded.

He had put on a shirt, but he had not buttoned it or tucked it in; it flapped sloppily around his hips. His ruffled hair was inky black against the white bandage, his eyes were wild, and his face was red. He was mad at everybody, so naturally his rage focused on me.

"What kind of a ghoulish performance is this?" he yelled. "Who the hell do you think you are, Abbott?"

"It wasn't my idea," I protested. "At least. . . . Well, I guess it was at that. I don't think you should be—"

Now that my eyes had adjusted to the light, I could see Debbie behind him. She put her hand on his arm; he shook it off. The movement made him wobble visibly.

"I'm sorry, D.J.," Debbie said. "I tried to restrain him, but he's awfully stubborn."

"Put him in a chair, then," I said disgustedly.

Tom's angry color had faded into a shade as pale as a heavily suntanned man can show. He didn't object as Debbie guided him to a chair; he seemed to be concentrating on some absorbing and difficult problem, like how to walk.

The others were staring, including Fortunata. She was wide awake and perfectly calm; I noted that she had neglected to go through the "coming out of the trance" routine.

200

Madame, whom I had long since recognized as the sharpest of the group, was the first to spot this tactical error. She bent solicitously over Fortunata.

"My dear, are you all right? You could have been seriously injured. I do hope—"

"I feel weak," Fortunata said.

"You don't feel up to trying again, I guess," Sid said.

"It is impossible. The rapport has been broken—shattered."

"Next time you talk to Black Eagle, tell him we apologize for not saying good-bye," I said.

The party broke up. With more tact than I would have given them credit for, the crackpots departed, leaving the five of us hovering over Tom, admonishing him in a variety of accents. My litany of "dumb, stupid, idiotic," and other synonymous adjectives ran along under Joe's supercilious criticism and Jesse's low-voiced concern. Tom remained comatose and unresponsive throughout, but when we decided to drag him back to his room, he came alive with a vengeance.

"Oh, no, you don't. I'm going to the study. I was on my way there when one of the servants told me about this obscene performance. I cannot imagine how you could have the bad taste—"

"Never mind, you said that before," I said. "The study it is. I've been thinking we ought to have a council of war."

So we adjourned to that room, with Jesse and Joe supporting Tom, and Tom insisting he could walk perfectly well by himself. They dumped him on a couch and let him mumble to himself.

The room looked comfortable and cozy—and horribly empty, without Hank's tall body bent over the desk. All day I had been rushing around and arguing and expressing concern and worry; but I don't think it really hit me emotionally until that moment—that he was gone, and might not ever come back. . . . And how much I thought of him. Tears pricked my eyes, and I turned quickly toward the window, pretending to admire the view.

When I turned back, Tom was watching me. If he had noticed my momentary weakness he did not comment on it. His expression was not particularly sympathetic. It might, in fact, be described as highly critical.

The others had settled themselves in characteristic fashion. Edna was sitting in a chair in a shadowy corner, bolt upright, her hands tightly clasped on her knee. Jesse was slouched on a couch nearby, looking thoughtful. Joe wandered around, touching things—taking books off the shelf and putting them back, peering at the papers on the desk. Debbie stood with one hand on the back of the swivel chair. Her fingers rested caressingly on the worn leather.

"Well," I said brightly. "Here we all are. We're the only able-bodied, relatively sane people in the house, so if anything is going to be done, it's up to us."

"I presume that nothing has been done," Tom said. "That the entire day has been wasted."

"Jesse was out searching all day," I said indignantly. "He's exhausted."

Still prone, Tom turned on his side so he could see the others.

"Where did you look?" he asked Jesse.

"I covered about ten square miles of a sector northwest of the Devil's Thumb," Jesse answered. He went on to give specific dimensions that meant nothing to me, but Tom seemed to understand what he was talking about.

"It's a hopeless job, of course," Jesse went on. "Tire tracks don't show on that terrain."

"What made you pick that area?" Tom asked.

Jesse threw out his hands.

"I stuck a pin in a map—what else? We've no idea where to look or what to look for. I might just as well have asked Sid to use his pendulum."

"Sid claims the place is near Dead Man's Gulch," I remarked.

"Oh, no." Tom sat up and glared at me. "Don't tell me you had that jackass playing tricks too, in addition to Fortunata! Why didn't you all dress up in masks and costumes and dance around invoking the Great Spirit of the Comanches?"

"I thought one of them might make a mistake," I snapped. "A slip of the tongue. It does happen."

Tom lay back.

"I see," he said, in a more moderate voice. "You don't think one of those idiots is responsible for this, do you?"

"It's possible," I argued. "Suppose—just as a working theory—suppose Hank had decided to clean house on one or all of the crowd. Suppose, even, that he had detected out-and-out fraud. I mean, I know he is Mr. Sucker and a good-natured man ordinarily, but he can be pretty ruthless when he makes up his mind. And nothing would enrage him more than being made a fool of."

"That's bright of you, D.J.," Jesse said. "I hadn't thought of that possibility, but it certainly makes sense."

Even Tom looked mildly impressed for a moment. Then he shook his head.

"I'd know about any such decision. He'd have told me."

"Not necessarily. He didn't tell you about the great discovery, did he? I think he's become self-conscious about his wild theories. I also started to wonder how he has disposed of his money. Do any of the crackpots, or their phony foundations, get a share of the estate?"

"Good heavens, he wouldn't do anything so foolish," Joe exclaimed. "When so many universities and museums badly need funds—"

"He might have done," Tom said, ignoring this naive comment. "I don't know the terms of his will, D.J. His lawyers would know."

"Can you find out?"

"I can try." Tom frowned. "Actually, I have no authority to do such a thing. The police could, but only if. . . ."

"If Hank is dead, or presumed dead." Debbie supplied the words he was reluctant to utter. She sounded quite calm, but her hand had clenched tightly on the back of the chair. "They are a long way from that, Tom. They don't even admit that he's officially missing."

"I'll try," Tom said again. "I don't know, D.J. You've made out an interesting case, but I can't see any of those ineffectual old fools acting so positively. Where would they hide him—dead or alive? They don't know this country, or how to move around in it."

"They might have had local help," I said. "What about Jake?"

"You are more than just a pretty face," Jesse said, smiling approvingly at me.

"She is also an evil mind," Tom growled.

"That's what we need right now," Debbie said. "My mind is just as evil as D.J.'s, but I'm not as smart as she is. She is absolutely right. While you are trying to reach the lawyers, Tom, I'll find out what has become of Jake. He's a fool and a drunk. He may have babbled to some of his loathsome friends."

204

"Don't go looking for him yourself," I warned. "Send Juan. It makes sense for him to track down the guy who has been annoying his sister. I don't think we want to spread the word about Hank's being kidnapped, not yet anyway."

"Good point," Tom said grudgingly. He was looking a little more cheerful.

Joe had been looking from one of us to the other as we spoke. It was obviously a strain on his brain to follow the discussion. Now he pushed his glasses firmly onto the bridge of his nose and said, "Honestly, I think you are jumping to unwarranted conclusions. Plots like the ones you envision only happen in films or books."

"Who cares what you think?" Tom said rudely.

"Well, really!" Edna exclaimed.

She had been so quiet I had almost forgotten she was there. Tom didn't even look at her, but Jesse gave her a quick apologetic smile and said, "Come on, Tom, relax. We're all willing to cooperate, whatever our reservations. I've got a few myself. Not that I doubt your word as to what happened last night; but have you got any definite, positive proof that Hank didn't go off on his own?"

"I don't know what you consider proof," Tom answered.

"How about the note?" I asked. "None of you saw it, but I did, before the sheriff carried it off. It was typewritten—no handwriting at all, not even a signature."

"That does it," Tom said triumphantly. "Hank hated the typewriter. He's left me a number of notes—all scrawled in his atrocious handwriting, signed with his initials. Doesn't that prove the note was a fake?"

"It is a point," Joe admitted. "Very well. I suppose we

can spare a day from our work. Edna and I will search tomorrow."

"Thanks," Tom said. "That will help. You and Edna take one area, I'll take a second, and Jesse—"

"Not you, Tom," Debbie said. "A day out in that heat and you'll be flat on your back again."

"I'll go," I offered. "I can't stand another day of sitting around here."

This generous suggestion produced a general outcry from everybody except Edna. The gist of it was that a tenderfoot like me hadn't a chance in the mountains.

"We don't want to have to look for you too," Tom said.

"Come with me," Jesse offered.

"No," Tom said. He flushed slightly when I turned to look at him, but insisted stubbornly, "You'd just be in the way. He can go farther—"

"He travels the fastest who travels alone," I declaimed. "White hands cling where the bridle . . . something or other. . . . You male chauvinists can go jump in the nearest lake. I've got to do something; if I can't go alone, I'll go with Jesse. I promise I won't interfere with him."

"That's ridiculous," Tom growled. "You stay here. I can use you. We'll look through Hank's papers and—"

"We can do that right now," I said. "Though I don't see the purpose of it."

"Well, it would help if we had some direction in mind," Jesse said. "We'd need a search party of a hundred men to cover this area thoroughly, and even then it would take days."

Tom was silent for a moment. He was obviously thinking furiously, but his face gave no hint as to the nature of his thoughts. Yet for some reason I could not explain, I began to suspect he wasn't being entirely candid with us.

206

Finally he said, "All we can do is search the most obvious places. Caves, abandoned houses—"

"Wait a minute," I interrupted. "We just might find a clue in Hank's papers as to the location of his great discovery. If he *has* gone off on his own—which I don't believe—that is where he's gone. Even if he isn't there, if we can find out *what* it was he discovered, we might get a hint as to the motive behind this—and the identity of the kidnapper."

"I don't follow that," Joe complained. "What possible connection—"

"Never mind," I said kindly. "Well, Tom?"

Tom gave me a very dirty look, but he said mildly, "That's what I was thinking. Tomorrow you and I will—"

"What do you mean, tomorrow? We'll look right now. Where do we start?"

"Oh, all right," Tom said. "I need something from my room."

He started to get up, turned green, and sat down again.

"I'll get it," Debbie said. "Where is it, Tom?"

"On the top shelf of the closet," Tom mumbled. "An attaché case. Brown leather. It's got one of those combination locks."

"I'll be right back."

Debbie ran out. A muffling sort of silence descended on the rest of us. Jesse started to whistle softly through his teeth. I recognized the tune; it was an old Spanish song, "La Paloma."

"I could use some coffee," Tom said. "Anybody else?"

"You're looking at me," I said. "I refuse to make coffee. It's a symbol of male oppression, making coffee. Besides, I can't work that espresso maker."

"I wouldn't dream of asking you to task your feeble

mind," Tom answered. He sat up cautiously; waited a minute; then got to his feet. I sat down and watched with critical interest. There was a thick Navaho rug on the floor by the couch; if he fell, he wouldn't hurt himself . . . much.

He managed all right: a little shaky, but not bad. Under his hands the big gleaming machine began to gurgle and shake and make what I assumed were the proper noises. Finally it exploded, with a whoosh of steam, and Tom got out cups and spoons and things. Debbie came back, clucked at him maternally, and took over. Clutching the attaché case like a mother hugging a long-lost child, Tom shuffled back to the couch.

We watched with unconcealed interest while he opened the case, holding it so that the lid hid the contents. After fumbling for a few minutes, he shook his head and said in disgust, "Stupid of me. I had the keys in my pocket all the time."

As I watched him going through the complex process of getting into Hank's desk, I decided the amiable rich man wasn't quite as naive as I had thought. Everything was locked up tighter than a bank vault. A master key on Tom's ring opened a drawer which yielded other keys that fit the locks of the remaining drawers. Tom sat down in the chair and started searching through the drawers.

"I shouldn't do this," he grumbled. "This material is all private."

"You're in charge," I pointed out. "We won't see anything unless you choose to show it to us."

"Some of this is private even from me," Tom said. "I know, I have the keys; but I only use them when Hank tells me to. There are a couple of drawers I've never looked into."

In spite of his gentlemanly disclaimers, he was as curious as the rest of us. He also displayed a streak of sheer bitchiness I hadn't noticed before; he tantalized us by chuckling and raising his eyebrows as he looked through the material, stroking his mustache and muttering, "Well, well," every now and then. But when he tried to open the lowest right-hand drawer, he got what was coming to him. An expression of genuine amazement crossed his face.

"None of the keys work," he said.

"They must." Joe forgot to be sophisticated. He put his coffee cup down and trotted around to the other side of the desk. "Let me try."

"Nobody touches these keys except me," Tom said firmly. "I tell you, none of them work. This must be Hank's most private collection. The old son of a gun. I could have sworn he trusted me."

"We've got to get into it," I said. "It must be important, or Hank wouldn't have kept it a secret. Unless. . . . You don't think it's business papers, or anything that dull?"

"He doesn't keep documents like that in the desk," Tom answered. "When he brings work home, the papers are always kept in the safe." He thought for a minute, tugging at his mustache. "We'll break it open," he said finally. "It's a rotten thing to do, but I think the situation justifies it. Jesse, you wouldn't happen to have a chisel in your gear, would you?"

"Sure." Jesse jumped up. We were all keen now; there is nothing more suggestive than a locked drawer.

Jesse didn't fool around. His chisel was a foot and a half long. When he inserted it and heaved, the whole front of the drawer came off. Tom pounced, and Jesse stepped back.

"There's nothing in here but some snapshots," Tom said.

There was a general sigh of disappointment.

"Maybe they are photographs of the great discovery," I said hopefully.

"They might just as well be photographs of a mud pie," Tom said, scowling, as he shuffled through the photos. "Hank is the world's worst photographer. Look at this."

He handed me one of the snapshots. It was in black and white, and it did look a little like a close-up of a mud pie. I turned it upside down. Then it looked like an inverted mudpie.

"Are all the rest of them this bad?" I asked.

"Almost." Tom passed them around. We studied them in gloomy silence. Some were close-ups, but of what object, God and Hank only knew. Others were studies of desert scenery. The rocks and scrubby bushes were out of focus, but you could make out what they were supposed to be. They looked just like all the millions of other rocks and bushes I had seen since I arrived in Arizona.

"That could be a cave," I said.

"Or a shadow," Jesse said, looking over my shoulder. "Do you think this is supposed to be a cattle skull?"

I examined the photograph he was holding.

"It looks more like an ancient Aztec statue. This is hopeless. Maybe these are just practice shots, not meant to show anything specific."

"Then why lock them up?" Jesse asked.

"Hey, you dropped one," Joe said. He bent over and came up with another photograph. "You were standing on it," he said to Tom.

"So I was," Tom said.

We crowded around to look at the photo, which Joe

was holding as gingerly as if it might go off. This one was also blurry and out of focus, but compared to the others it was a miracle of clarity. And it showed something that might be a landmark—a tall pinnacle of rock that split at the top into twin horns.

"I've seen that before someplace," Jesse exclaimed.

"So have I," Tom said. "But where? It's off the beaten track, that's certain, or I'd recognize it immediately."

"You mean you know every funny-shaped rock in these parts?" I asked skeptically.

"Most of them," Tom answered.

Jesse nodded agreement. "You have to memorize landmarks, D.J. Yes, I've run into this one before. It certainly isn't in the area I searched today. I've got a hunch it may be near Dead Man's Gulch."

Tom put his head in his hands.

"Let's sleep on it, shall we? Lost memories are more apt to come back when you don't push them. I'm bushed."

"Me, too." Jesse yawned. "It's been a long day for all of us, and tomorrow looks like another tough one."

"What time do you want to start?" I asked.

"I'll wake you about six, okay?"

"Fine."

I glanced at Tom, to see if he was going to object. He said nothing, just busied himself relocking drawers and tidying up. He put the photographs in his attaché case.

"We'll all meet for breakfast at six thirty," Joe said brightly.

So we parted for the night. I was yawning myself, and everyone seemed tired; but I was conscious of a surge of optimism. At least I would be doing something, not sitting around.

Chapter Eleven

Wrong again.

I woke up next morning with an awful feeling of déjà vu. It had happened again, and I knew when—the previous morning. My clock showed almost eight.

This time I grabbed my robe before I left the room. I had a feeling I might not be getting dressed for some time.

Right, for once. I claim no credit for clairvoyance. It was obvious that something had happened, and it didn't take much imagination to figure out what it was. Sure enough, when I opened Jesse's door, he was still in bed. He was a neat sleeper; he lay perfectly flat, on his back, his arms folded; and I knew from the way he was breathing, even before my shaking failed to rouse him, that he was the latest victim of . . . well, what would you call him? Drugger? Druggist? The unknown person with the unlimited supply of pills, let's say.

There was no bump on Jesse's well-shaped skull. He was doped, that was all, and from the look of him he wasn't going to wake up for quite some time.

I stood there for a while looking down on him, my mind a blend of bewilderment and frustration. The first question I asked myself was: Why Jesse? The answer came pat: Somebody didn't want him to look for Hank. With the possible exception of Tom, who was hors de combat for the moment, he was the most experienced of us all, the most likely to succeed in the search.

So why not put him out of commission earlier, before he had time to search at all? Again the answer was obvious. Last night he had seemed to recognize the peculiar rock in the photograph. He had planned to look in a certain area. The fact that the unknown had struck so promptly implied that his hunch had been correct.

I started to rush off to tell Joe and Edna, the only other competent searchers available, and then stopped as I realized they must have left long ago. Why the Hades hadn't they come to see what had happened to me and Jesse? Well, but it would be just like them to go off and leave us. They thought everybody in the world was incompetent except themselves anyway. It would never occur to them to lend a hand to the feeble. No doubt they had exchanged smug criticisms of our laziness, and had gone on about their business feeling comfortably superior.

I tied the belt of my robe tightly around my waist and

marched down the hall to Tom's room. He was sound asleep, and so was Debbie, curled up in a ball on the couch. I shook her. She didn't respond immediately, and my heart did a flip-flop; was everybody in the house drugged? Then she stirred and yawned and opened her eyes.

"Sorry," she mumbled. "Took a sleeping pill . . . couldn't sleep. . . ."

There were too many damned sleeping pills lying around loose for my taste. I couldn't blame her, though; my own worry was only a faint echo of the nervous horrors that must haunt her mind.

However, this was a crisis, and I couldn't be sentimental. I shook her again. This time she woke up long enough to recognize me, and eventually the cogs slid into place.

"It's late," she murmured drowsily. "I thought you were going out with Jesse."

"Jesse is out cold," I said. "Somebody slipped him a Mickey last night."

That got her on her feet. She stumbled into the bathroom, to see what cold water could do, and I went to awaken Tom. At least he was not drugged. He was just nasty and mean and slow to wake up. I wondered if he was always like that in the morning.

He received my news with no more than mild interest.

"Is Jesse all right?" he asked politely.

"Sleeping the sleep of the just," I said. "If I'm boring you, just say so and I'll leave."

"Go get dressed," Tom said.

"What?"

"If you can think of anything more sensible to do at this moment, do it. Personally, I can't. I'll meet you in Jesse's room."

214

When I got back to the scene of the latest crime, Tom and Debbie were already there. So was Juan, playing doctor.

"I refuse to drag this guy around the room all day," he announced. "Once was enough."

"No need," Tom said. "He can't tell us a thing we don't already know. How long will he be out?"

"How the hell should I know? I wouldn't count on him for anything today, though."

Tom appeared to be remarkably cheerful under the circumstances.

"I just might do a little exploring myself," he said.

"Go ahead," Juan said sourly. "Don't bother coming home, just go straight to the hospital. A few hours in that sun is all you need."

"I feel fine."

"Sure you do. You had a nice long rest, and the drug has worn off; but I suspect you have a slight concussion as well. Tearing around in that heat is not going to do it any good. But suit yourself."

"Are you going to town?" Debbie asked.

"I said I would, didn't I? Frankly, I think you're all crazy. Insanity must be catching around this house. But I don't mind looking for good old Jake. I'd like to have a word with him."

"Be careful," I said.

"Don't worry, I know that cruddy character well. I can take care of myself."

I was inclined to believe him. He was a stockily built, muscular young man with steady brown eyes.

"Remember," Debbie said. "The point of the exercise is not to beat Jake up, but to question him."

"Don't worry," Juan repeated. "Just you keep out of

trouble. I don't want to come back and find another unconscious body. I ought to start charging you."

When he had gone, Tom rubbed his hands together and
said briskly, "How about a little breakfast?"

"Why not?" I followed him to the door. "Coming, Debbie?"

"No."

"What's the matter?" Tom asked.

"Oh, nothing. Not a thing. You two sit down and have
a nice, long, relaxing meal. You could take a swim after
that, or play a game of tennis—if that isn't too tiring for
the invalid."

Her name should have been Storm Cloud instead of
Sunshine. There were pent-up tears behind her anger.

Tom's mouth dropped open. I mean, we were all worried about Hank, but her concern must have seemed ex-
cessive to him. I don't know whether he caught on or not,
but his response was perfect.

"Believe me, Deb, I'm as worried as you are, and I feel
a lot guiltier than you ever could. If I had been a little
sharper the other night. . . . But I'm not going to wallow
in guilt feelings, or go riding off in all directions without
a plan. We've wasted enough time already, thanks to me.
Besides," he added, with a glance in my direction, "we
have to spend some time fueling D.J. She can't move,
much less think, without enormous quantities of food."

I hammed up my outraged response to this, and won a
feeble smile from Debbie.

Since we wanted to talk without being interrupted or
overheard, Tom ordered food sent to the study, and we
adjourned there. He waited until after the waiter had left,
and then said, "First of all—most important—I think we
can safely assume Hank is still alive. If they had wanted

to kill him, they would have done it on the spot. If they didn't kill him then, there's no reason why they should do it at a later time. So relax, both of you; this is not one of those 'every minute counts' situations."

I glanced at Debbie. Tom's argument was fine as far as it went, but it did not cover the ghastly possibility Debbie had suggested. However, she had brightened up, so I saw no reason to remind her of her nightmare.

"What we're looking for is a prisoner, not a dead body," Tom went on. "That makes it easier. You could never locate a grave out in that wasteland, but a prisoner implies a prison—an enclosed space that can be locked and/or guarded. Debbie, how thorough was that half-hearted search yesterday morning? Did they investigate all the abandoned outbuildings, and the ruins—places like that?"

"I'm not sure. But, Tom, you don't think they would try to hide him that close to the house, do you?"

"Why not? It's the old Purloined Letter technique; you hide something in a place so obvious no one would think of looking there. Besides, if the kidnappers are guests in the house, they haven't had time to get him far away."

"You're right." Debbie's eyes sparkled. "I don't think anyone did investigate the ruins."

"What ruins?" I asked, helping myself to the last lonely spoonful of scrambled egg that nobody else seemed to want.

"I guess you'd call it a ghost town," Tom answered. "When the big copper boom was in full swing in Jerome and the Mingus Mountain area, somebody found a vein a couple of miles north of here. The vein petered out before long, and so did the town. But it would be a good place to hide a missing person."

217

"That's a great idea." Debbie jumped up. "I'll change and be ready to go in ten minutes."

She ran out of the room. I stayed where I was.

"How much of that optimistic lecture was for real?" I asked.

Tom picked up a pen and began to doodle on the clean desk blotter.

"About half."

I hated to mention the subject, but I had to; it had been haunting me. "Debbie suggested something yesterday . . . about leaving a person out in the desert till he died of dehydration."

"That theory, and all its nastier corollaries, has already occurred to me," Tom said. He looked up from his scribbling, and at the sight of my face his own grim look relaxed a little. "Honestly, D.J., I don't think it's likely. All the action so far has been designed to keep you from visiting Hank's find."

"Me? Why me?"

"If we knew the answer to that, we'd know a lot of other things. Think it through, D.J. There were a couple of feeble attacks on Hank before you got here, but the campaign intensified after you arrived. Hank already knows where the place is. The only way to destroy that knowledge is to destroy him, and they've had God knows how many chances to do that. Why should they do it now?"

"Then you really do believe he's being held prisoner somewhere nearby?"

"I think it's the most likely theory. Why the dubious look? We can't just sit here and wait for the kidnappers to finish . . . well, whatever it is they want to finish. We've got to search for Hank."

"Granted. But I don't see what you can hope to accomplish without a hundred-man search party. And if you do find Hank, he may not be alone."

"I thought of that."

"Oh, you did, did you? What are you going to do if you run into a band of desperate kidnappers? Shoot to kill?"

Tom's face didn't actually change expression, but his eyes took on a funny blank glaze; and it was at that moment I got a flash of what could only have been ESP. "What happened to your gun?" I inquired gently. "No, don't tell me; you had it on you the night Hank was kidnapped. Sure you did, you big hero. They took it, didn't they?"

Tom squirmed uncomfortably.

"Referring to them as 'they' is so impersonal," he complained. "Why don't we think of a name for them? The Gang, or the Mob, or—"

"They took it," I repeated, "didn't they? Swiped it right out of your hip pocket, or wherever you had it cunningly concealed."

"Why harp on that?" Tom demanded huffily. "I owe my ex-roommate fifty bucks; that's my problem."

"Uh-huh. So you're going to march out into the desert, with a concussion and without a gun, and try to find one man in the middle of a howling wilderness, and if you do find him, you are going to steal him back from a bunch of criminals who—"

"You ought to be writing horror stories," Tom snapped. "I have never met a woman with such an uncontrolled imagination—and that includes Frieda von Stumm. Listen to me, D.J. I am going out to look for Hank, because if I sit still any longer, I'll lose what is left of my mind. And I'm taking Debbie with me, because she is even nearer the ragged edge of hysteria than I am. I am not taking you. Wait." He leveled a long peremptory finger at me as I started to protest. "The search itself is not my primary aim—though you never can tell what we'll find. I've got a couple of other things in mind—including the hope that my activities may stimulate the Mob to take action. If the kidnappers do have Hank stashed away someplace, they'll have to visit him periodically, if only to bring him food. That's where you come in. You are going to stay here, near the telephone. I've given orders that if anybody tries to take out a car, or a horse, the boys are to ring you. If you get a call from the garage or the stable—"

"I rush out, disguised as a cactus, and follow the suspect," I said. "How far do you think I'd get before the suspect got suspicious?"

"The men will cooperate," Tom said. "One of them will go with you—for God's sake, don't go alone. At the very least we may be able to narrow down our suspicions."

I pondered this scheme for a few moments. Wild as it was, it did offer possibilities—better ones than any I had thought of.

"If you're looking for suspects, I can think of a few," I said. "Joe and Edna were roaming around all day yesterday—and they went out again today."

"I'm not as stupid as I look. Joe and Edna are on my schedule—after I've searched the ruins."

Before I had time to comment, Debbie returned.

"I'm ready," she announced. "Hurry up, will you, D.J.? You'll need boots and a hat—"

"She's staying here," Tom said. He outlined his crazy idea to Debbie, and she nodded approvingly—which only proved that she was too worried to think straight. Then the two of them departed. As he left, Tom tossed me a bunch of keys.

"While away the time by continuing to look for clues," he said smugly. "Maybe you'll find something we missed last night."

This gesture of confidence took a little of the edge off my annoyance. Last night he had implied that those keys could only be removed from his dead body. He must trust me a little, I thought.

I have passed more boring days than that one, but I have never experienced such a combination of boredom and nerve-racking tension. The hours dragged on into eternities. I was afraid to leave the room. I didn't even dare look in on Jesse, for fear the telephone would ring while I was gone. By noon I had searched every drawer in the room three times, and was pacing the floor. One of the servants came in about then with a tray. Tom must have ordered it because, believe it or not, I had not thought of food. There was enough for five people, including three desserts. I cursed Tom—and ate every scrap. Then I searched the drawers again. By that time I wasn't looking for clues, I was looking for a gun—or a knife, or a club—something I could use on Tom when he got back. Knowing Hank's views on violence and the unnecessary taking of life, I didn't really expect to find anything lethal, and I didn't. But it served to pass the time. The phone squatted on the desk like a mute black imp.

By two o'clock I had a nervous headache and a full-blown ulcer. Or maybe it was indigestion. I sat down and repeated my mantra to myself and discovered, as I had always suspected, that meditation is only effective when you aren't worried about anything. After that I just sat.

It must have been a little after three when Debbie returned. I hardly recognized her. She slumped into a chair and removed her hat. It was coated with dust or fine sand, and so was she.

"What happened?" I asked, after a while.

"We searched the ruins," she said, in a flat, dead voice. "Every corner."

"At least you eliminated one possibility," I said.

She went on as if I had not spoken.

"Then we went out to Joe's dig. He and Edna weren't there."

"They wouldn't be there," I said. "They planned to search—"

"We met them on the way back," Debbie said. "They said it was getting too hot to stay out any longer. I slapped Edna—"

"What for? Not that I blame you for slapping her, just on general principles, but—"

"She was so damned smug," Debbie muttered. "She laughed at me when I said Hank was in danger, and that we couldn't waste time. After I hit her, Joe hit Tom, and he keeled over. I guess he had a little too much sun."

"Joe hit Tom?"

"That was after Tom grabbed Edna when she tried to hit me back," Debbie explained.

It would have been funny if it hadn't been so awful—the four of them scuffling like quarrelsome children. I couldn't blame Debbie, though; we were all strung tight as guitar strings. I didn't say anything, and after a minute or two Debbie's dry, dusty face cracked along the seams and two tears plowed muddy tracks down her cheeks.

"I'm sorry," she whispered.

"What about? Don't apologize for slugging Edna, I think it was a super idea. And if you want to cry, go ahead."

She did. She put her head down on the desk and wept mud all over Hank's papers. I didn't think he'd mind.

II

I left Debbie to recover herself and went off to check on the casualties. Tom was in his bathroom and refused to come out, even when I kicked the door.

"I just wanted to see if you are all right," I shouted. "Do you want an icepack, or a raw steak, or—"

"I've got everything I want except privacy," was the muffled reply. "Get lost, will you?"

It is impossible to express tender sympathy screaming through a door two inches thick. So I left.

Jesse was a lot more appreciative. He was beginning to show faint signs of life when I arrived, so I called down for coffee and fed him a couple of quarts. Another of those spectacular Arizona sunsets was reddening the window by the time I got him on his feet. I viewed it without my usual appreciation. I was wondering how many more times I was going to have to spend the day doing this sort of thing. It was already getting boring.

"So we've lost another day," Jesse said disspiritedly. "Who the hell is doing this, D.J.? I can't figure out how they slipped me the stuff."

"There are a dozen different ways," I said. "In your food at dinner—your thermos and water bottle here— coffee. . . ."

"Ah." He nodded. "You thought of the coffee too?"

"The time interval would be about right. But if it was

in your coffee, someone in the study must have put it in your cup. We were all drinking the stuff, and you were the only one affected."

"It wasn't you, was it?" He smiled, but I'm not sure he was joking.

"No. If Tom's theories are correct, I'm the person all this is aimed at—indirectly. Someone is trying to keep me from seeing Hank's find."

"An unnecessarily oblique method, surely? Why not drug you?"

"That would be too obvious, I guess. Tom would probably say I eat so fast it's impossible for anyone to slip a Mickey into my food before it goes into my mouth. But seriously, Jesse, if you eliminate the people who have been victims, there is only one suspect left."

"Whom do you mean?"

"Joe and Edna. I consider them a single entity because she has no mind of her own."

"You're eliminating Madame, and Sid, and that crowd, then? I'm not sure you can do that, D.J. Tom's theory is only a theory; there's no real proof of the motive behind all this. In fact, it seems to be developing into an almost random vendetta—a vague malice directed at nobody in particular. Just the sort of thing you could expect from those paranoid types."

I put my head in my hands and groaned.

"I can't think sensibly. We just seem to go around and around in circles, getting nowhere."

Jesse made sympathetic noises, but there was really nothing he could say. We were sitting in gloomy silence when the door burst open and Tom came in.

"Excuse *me,*" I said. "I'm afraid I didn't hear you knock."

"I didn't know you were here, and I expected to find Jesse still asleep," Tom answered smoothly. It was a reasonable explanation. I didn't believe it. "Feeling better?" Tom went on, looking at Jesse.

"Better than unconscious, I guess," Jesse said, with a faint smile. "I'll be okay tomorrow. I suppose you still plan to continue searching?"

"Yes." Tom moved toward the window. "I also plan to go on an orange and boiled-egg diet, with water from the bathroom tap."

I thought he had flipped for a minute. Jesse caught on before I did, perhaps because he had similar thoughts.

"It might be a good idea if we all watch what we eat and drink," he agreed. "This character seems to have an endless supply of drugs."

Tom nodded. His face was turned toward the light, and sunset gave his skin a healthy pink glow, but he looked awfully tired. I could see the scraped, swollen spot on his jaw where Joe's fist had landed.

"Have you talked to Joe and Edna?" I asked. Then I bit my tongue, but it was too late. My big mouth had done it again.

Tom's hand went up, reflexively, to touch the bruise. I think he blushed, but it was hard to tell in that light.

"Yes," he said shortly. "Joe says he's had enough of this nonsense. He and Edna are going back to work tomorrow."

"That just leaves us, then," I said.

"What are your plans?" Jesse asked.

"Debbie and I searched most of the area near the ranch," Tom answered. "From here on it's pure guesswork."

"I may have a suggestion," Jesse said quietly. I turned

225

toward him hopefully; he raised his hand, smiling and shaking his head. "Don't get your hopes up, D.J. But I've been thinking about that photograph, and I'm almost sure I know where the horned rock is. If you agree, Tom, I'll head out that way first thing in the morning."

III

I considered Tom's suggestion of boiled eggs and oranges and came to the conclusion that it was unnecessary to go to those lengths. Anything that came off the buffet table was bound to be safe so long as I ate it quickly and never took my eyes off it. I guess the technique looked a little strange, though. Madame tried to strike up a conversation while I was eating. I never once looked her in the face, and after a while she gave up and left. I heard her say in a very audible voice, "I knew that girl wasn't normal. She is behaving *very* oddly tonight." The answering rumble of agreement came from Frieda von Stumm.

I escaped to my room right after dinner, bolted everything that could be bolted, and crawled into bed. Tom had promised to wake me. I found it difficult to get to sleep. If I believed in premonitions I would claim that I knew the next day was going to see some sort of climax. Since I don't believe in them, I will only claim I was nervous.

I finally dropped off to sleep, but I woke the instant I heard the first tap on the door, and shot out of bed as if I had been propelled by a spring. It was just beginning to get light. I unlocked the door and opened it.

When I saw Tom standing there, fully dressed and presumably in his right mind and body, I felt sick with relief. We both said simultaneously, "Are you all right?"

"All right so far," Tom said pessimistically. "We seem to have weathered the night, anyhow."

226

"Jesse?"

"Getting dressed. Debbie woke me. It's going to be a long, hot day, D.J. Snap it up, will you?"

I was the last one down. Tom was pacing, staring at his wristwatch. "Try to control your appetite this morning, please," he said, as I selected a plate. "We haven't time for you to eat one of your usual meals."

I had already decided I was not going to succumb to the sort of childish bad temper that had marred the previous day for the others, so I did not reply. Joe and Edna were eating their breakfast ostentatiously removed from the rest of us. They weren't even speaking to each other. Joe looked even smugger than usual, no doubt rejoicing in his prowess in flattening a man who was still convalescent. Edna looked miserable. She kept glancing in our direction as if she wanted to make up, but was afraid to do anything without Joe's permission.

I sat down at the table. Jesse was drinking coffee. He gave me a smile and a soft "Good morning." Debbie's plate had not been touched.

"What's the plan?" I asked.

"We're killing two birds with one stone," Tom answered; and then winced visibly at the ominous sound of the metaphor. "I mean, we're looking for traces of Hank, naturally, but we are also going to try to locate his mysterious site. I sent one of the men into Sedona last night to have rush copies made of those god-awful photographs of Hank's. Here they are." He distributed the copies. Looking at them didn't raise my hopes any. The copies were even dimmer than the originals. "Jesse thinks he knows where the horned rock is," Tom went on. "I've got a hunch of my own. So, in order to cover as much territory as possible, we're going to split up. Jesse will test his theory, and I'll go northeast. I have a vague recollection of having seen some such formation in that direction. You'll come with me, D.J."

He was awfully bossy. I would have objected except for two rather important facts: one, as Hank's secretary, he had more authority than the rest of us; two, he needed a companion more than Jesse did. I suspected Juan was in the very early stages of med school, and that he had underestimated the severity of the blow Tom had received. If I had been his mother, or his girl friend, or something like that, and if the situation had been a few degrees less serious, I would have suggested he go back to bed for a few days.

Since I was none of those things, and since the situation was serious, verging on critical, I simply nodded.

"What about Debbie?" I asked, scraping up the last of my blackberry jam with a piece of English muffin. "Does she go with Jesse?"

"She and Juan are taking off on their own," Tom answered. "As I said, we want to cover as much territory as possible."

"Did Juan find out anything about Jake?"

"He's left the area," Debbie said. "One of his crummy friends told Juan nobody had seen him for a couple of days. Which means—"

"Nothing," Tom finished. "He may be involved, and he may not. If Hank terrorized him sufficiently, he could have taken off for healthier parts. For God's sake, D.J., haven't you had enough food?"

"No. But I'll stop eating."

It must be nice to be rich. I don't know how many vehicles Hank owned, but I don't suppose even a millionaire rancher needs more than two or three jeeps, providing he also has a silver-trimmed Rolls Royce and a dozen assorted cars of other species. Joe and Edna were using one jeep; another had disappeared when Hank did; but there were three jeeps gassed up and ready when we reached the garage. Jesse climbed into one, with a wave at me. Tom and I took the second one, and Debbie got behind the wheel of the third and began honking the horn.

"Take it easy, Debbie," Tom said. "He'll be along."

"I'll leave without him if he doesn't hurry up," Debbie said.

"Remember what I told you," Tom said, giving her a long, meaningful look.

"You, too."

"What was that all about?" I asked, grabbing my hat as the jeep started.

"A general warning. No heroics; return and report if they find the slightest trace."

That was the last statement he made for some time. We were off in a cloud of dust, not to mention fair-sized rocks. The gates were the only things that slowed us down. Tom would come to a crashing halt, I would leap out and open the gates, Tom would drive through, I would close the gates and try to get back in the jeep before he took off again. . . . We did that three times before we were out on the open desert. I held on to my hat and tried not to breathe.

It was still quite early. The round red ball of the sun brightened from copper to gold as it climbed the sky. Even a tenderfoot could tell where the east was, but at first I was too busy staying in my seat to think. Then I put a couple of facts together.

"We're going northwest," I shouted.

"Clever girl," Tom yelled, hunching over the wheel. "You told the others we were going northeast."

"I lied."

That awful ride seemed to go on for hours, but I guess it couldn't have lasted for more than forty or fifty minutes before Tom slowed to a comparatively reasonable pace. I tested my back teeth experimentally. They were still there.

Tom had not slowed down because he was concerned about my comfort. No longer bowed over the wheel, he gawked like any tourist, searching the rocky slopes ahead.

I had never seen wilder country. Of course I don't get around a lot, but I imagine that even for the Wild West this terrain was considered rough. We had long since left the faintest semblance of a track, never mind a real road, and the only reason why we had not had half a dozen flat tires was because these were the kind of tires that don't go flat. I knew we couldn't be more than twenty miles from a town or a state highway, and yet this country looked as if it had never seen the presence of man.

The view ahead, which had been dominated by the graceful snowcapped peaks of the San Francisco mountains, had narrowed as we approached the rocky slopes of the Rim. Up ahead I caught a flash of green. It wasn't vivid, wetly shining emerald-green, but a dusty grayish shade; even so, it looked as beautiful and unexpected as genuine emeralds in that desolation. As we came closer I saw the mouth of a small canyon, with a stream running through it. Cottonwoods and willows leaned over the bank, trailing yellowing leaves in the brown water. Tom turned into the mouth of the canyon and stopped. He had to; there wasn't enough flat space inside to park a Vespa. But it was lovely—a ribbon of green, moist life, like Oak Creek Canyon farther east, but miniaturized, as tiny and perfect as a model in a museum. Sun and shadow made flickering patterns on the pebbly surface of the stream.

Tom got out of the car and reached in the back seat. I had noticed a couple of canvas bags there, and had assumed they contained supplies. Now, with a sinking heart, I recognized a pair of backpacks. Tom slung one over his shoulders and gestured toward the other.

"From here on we walk," he said.

I hoisted the second pack.

"What's in here? Rock samples?"

"Water, binoculars, first-aid kit. . . ." Tom gave me a mean smile. "And food, of course. The food is in your pack, so if you want to eat, you'll have to work."

I might have known we wouldn't stay in that pretty little canyon. It was only an entranceway to worse places. The slope down which the little stream ran so merrily was about thirty degrees, and the broken surface on either side of the water served as a natural staircase. I followed Tom, trying to put my feet where he put his, and increasingly grateful for my boots. This was snake country if I'd ever seen any, and the stiff leather was some help in keeping my ankles from turning. But by the time we reached the top of the slope I was very conscious of the fact that this place was a couple of thousand feet higher than Cleveland.

Little did I know that the first half hour was the easiest part of the hike, and that by noon I would be looking back on it with fond nostalgia. The stream turned in one direction and we turned in another; don't ask me what directions, I hadn't the vaguest notion of where we were going. For the next thousand years we climbed over boulders and squeezed through the mouths of narrow arroyos and clung by our fingertips to barren cliffs.

Actually, to be honest, we didn't do much climbing. As Tom pointed out in one of his rare conversational moments, I was in no shape to be a mountaineer. I wheezed at him; I didn't have enough breath to spare for repartee. Most of the terrain was so weathered and tumbled that there were plenty of foot- and handholds, but in one place we did have to take to the cliff face. The drop was no more than ten or fifteen feet, but that's five or ten feet too high for me, and I was sweating like a steelworker by the time I got down. Tom grabbed my hips and lowered me the last few feet. For some reason, perhaps because my knees were like jelly, I almost folded when my feet touched ground. He put his arms around me and I leaned back against him, while I struggled to catch my breath.

My breathlessness was partly due to height and exertion, but it was mostly due to terror. Tom didn't say anything; he just held me till I stopped gasping. Then his hands shifted position and he spoke. His breath stirred my damp hair.

"I take back what I said about your shape. It may not be right for mountaineering, but there's nothing wrong with it otherwise."

"I've gained five pounds," I mumbled, letting myself go even limper. "Wow. That feels good. . . ."

"I can't understand why you haven't gained fifty. How can you eat the way you do and get no more than—er—"

"Pleasingly plump?"

"Pleasingly is about right. . . ."

For a while neither of us moved, or spoke. I can't describe my sensations without resorting to hackneyed words, but there really was a feeling of timelessness about

232

that moment. I felt so comfortable. My head fit just right into the hollow of his shoulder, and the hard warmth of his body against my back was supportive emotionally as well as physically. I sensed that the feeling was mutual—that we were both giving, as well as receiving, comfort, and there was no need to do anything more because we were as close as two people could be. It was just like a page out of Mother's favorite author.

Not that Barbara Cartland would have accepted us as her leading characters. Her people are neat and clean. They don't drip sweat or get dusty, and when her heroes are wounded, they ooze blood prettily from their shoulders or their arms—nothing vulgar. Her heroines don't wear big clumpy boots or jeans that are too tight because they have eaten too many cream puffs. She doesn't have the faintest idea what it's all about.

After a while Tom's arms relaxed. I slid gently down, between them, to the ground, and looked up at him expectantly. He turned and reached for one of the packs.

"We'll rest for a few minutes," he said. "Relax."

"I was relaxed," I said, shifting position in an attempt to find a place where sharp rocks didn't dig into my posterior. There was no such place.

Tom didn't answer, but busied himself with the pack. I knew what was bugging him. He was feeling guilty for letting himself be distracted, when Hank might be withering away into a mummy out in the sun. His cynicism was a thin veneer over an exaggerated sense of responsibility. Don't they say a cynic is only a frustrated idealist?

A real cynic is also cynical about himself. He is his own worst critic. When Tom started working for Hank, his motives might have been as selfish and self-seeking as he had claimed, but that was no longer the case, if it ever had been. Not only did he earn his keep, but he had spent his spare time learning as much as he could about Hank's interests—everything from turquoise to poor old crazy Le Plongeon. Barbara C. would probably say that love had worked its magic. Maybe it had. People are so frightened of that word; it's only acceptable when it applies to mothers and children, or two beautiful young people having an affair. It's a much bigger word than that. If the emotion Tom felt for his employer was not love, it was close enough to it. Hank inspired that feeling in people if they had the capacity to feel it. Not everyone does.

"I'm ready to go on as soon as you are," I said.

"We both need a rest," Tom answered, without looking at me. "You've kept up pretty well for an amateur."

Actually, I wanted to lie down and die. I had not had time to notice my discomfort while I was moving; but as soon as I sat, sweat began running all over me and every muscle started to ache. It was hot and airless in the cleft in the rocks where our last descent had taken us. The narrow walls made a little shade, so I shifted into a patch of it with my back against a boulder.

Tom handed me a canteen and applied himself to a second one. His Adam's apple bobbed up and down as he drank. His mustache dripped sweat and his shirt was stuck to his body. I wondered which of us would give out first. If he collapsed, I couldn't find my way back to the car, much less carry him.

"I'm exhausted," I said. "How much farther are we going?"

"I wish I knew. I'm lost. . . . Hey, don't look so horrified; I know how to get back; I just can't find that damned rock. I could have sworn it was within a couple of miles of the creek where we left the car. We'll try another direction after we've rested."

"We might as well eat something," I suggested, reaching for my pack.

Tom grinned. "You're feeling better, I see."

I doubted that he was. He looked terrible. All morning I had been following that white patch of bandage on the back of his head, like a rabbit's tail. Isn't that how Peter Cottontail's mother got him away from Mr. MacGregor? Well, anyway; I started feeling soft and sentimental, and so I said briskly, "Here, have a sandwich. Ham and cheese. Or would you rather have pâté?"

Tom caught the foil-wrapped packet I tossed him.

"I ordered those for you," he said.

"Only three with pâté? You know that won't hold me for very long."

I must admit the sandwiches tasted good. There's nothing like fresh air and exercise to give a person an appetite.

We munched away in companionable silence, broken only by a faint far-off rattle of rock, as if some small invisible entity were climbing around the cliffs. I suppose there was life out there—rodents and lizards and other small fauna. That reminded me of Hank and his passionate concern for living things; and suddenly my sandwich didn't taste so good.

"Suppose we do find the rock, and the site," I said. "Do you think it will give us any clue as to where Hank might be? Surely they wouldn't take him there."

"Not unless there's an easier route to the place. Which is possible; I'm wandering around in circles at the moment. But what I'm hoping to find is the motive for all this. If I can convince the sheriff that someone had a practical, comprehensible reason for wanting Hank out of the way, he'll cooperate. The motive has to be out there somewhere. If it isn't, we're sunk."

"You've got a theory, haven't you? What is it?"

"It's not a theory, it's just a crazy hunch. I'm not going to tell you what it is; if I'm wrong, I'll look like a fool and you'll think I was. . . ."

"Was what?"

"Never mind. If you can't see it, maybe I'm all wrong. It seems so obvious to me, but. . . ."

"You're full of vague hints and dire suggestions," I said grumpily. "Well, let's get on with it. If I sit any longer, my muscles are going to petrify."

I stood up, suppressing a groan, and stretched. Then I stooped to pick up my pack. It was a few feet away, and behind me; when I straightened up again I let out a gasp.

"Tom—look! Over there. Isn't that—"

It was only visible from one place. The walls of the narrow canyon hid it otherwise. I couldn't be sure that the outline was the one we had been searching for, but as soon as I had guided Tom into position, and pointed, he gasped too.

"I think so. It could be. Come on, let's move."

I lost track of the damned rock as soon as we started walking. I can get lost going around the block. Fortunately Tom's sense of direction was as good as mine was rotten. As we followed the tortuous, bewildering maze of the canyon, he bore to the left whenever possible, and then we saw it again—two jagged twin peaks, reddish brown against the turquoise sky. Tom got out the photograph and we put our heads together.

"It doesn't look quite right," I said.

"We're on the wrong side of it. Almost a hundred and

eighty degrees off. Lucky you caught it; at any other angle the twin peaks blend into one."

Would you believe it took us almost two hours to get around to the other side of that wretched spire of rock? We caught occasional glimpses of it as we climbed, up and down, back and forth; as Tom had suggested, the silhouette changed with differing points of view. It gave me the cold shivers to think how close we had come to missing it altogether.

A few other thoughts gave me the shivers too. For instance—time was passing, and we were a long way from the jeep. I wondered if Tom could find his way back in the dark. Yet it never occurred to me to suggest we turn back and try again next day; an illogical but overwhelming optimism kept my stiff muscles moving and supplied breath when I thought my last one had been taken. Even if we found the site, there was no guarantee that we would discover a clue as to Hank's whereabouts—and he was the treasure at the end of the rainbow, no question about that; the golden regalia of Montezuma wouldn't have seemed more beautiful than his craggy, wrinkled face.

The sun had passed the zenith and reached boiling point as we stumbled across a rocky plateau and saw the twin peaks slide into a familiar perspective. I realized then that the landmark was not a mountain, or anything that high. It's hard to gauge the sizes of natural objects unless you have something whose dimensions are known for comparison. That's why archaeologists put rulers or meter sticks in their photographs of antiquities—so you can tell how large they are. I had had nothing with which to compare our twin-topped rock until we got fairly close to it. Then I saw that it was only about forty feet high.

It marked the entrance to another of those cursed arroyos. I had seen at least a hundred and fifty of them that day, and the sight of another did not particularly thrill me. The rock did. It was such a delight to find something we had been looking for. In my rapture I forgot the first rule of hiking, which is, keep your eyes on where you are going. While gaping at the peak I stumbled and hit the ground with a bone-wrenching smack.

Tom turned. Our success had wiped out any lingering traces of sentimentality about round, well-shaped young women. "Get up," he said irritably. "What the hell are you doing?"

I didn't answer, partly because the fall had knocked the wind out of me, and partly because I had just seen something. It stood out against the brownish-gray dirt like a piece of fallen sky—a spot of heavenly, exquisite blue.

I slithered forward on my stomach and picked it up. It was turquoise, all right—a polished oval piece several inches long, with the sensuous glow I had learned to recognize as Bisbee Blue.

"Look," I croaked, holding it out to Tom. Even at that moment I was conscious of the lure of the gleaming azure.

"It's Hank's!" Tom grabbed it. "He lost a stone out of a concha belt a couple of weeks ago. . . . Yes, this is the same turquoise. He's been here. D.J., we've found it!"

Dragging me to my feet, he grabbed me and swung me around, yelling like a—Comanche, I believe, is the conventional simile. I found enough breath to yell too, though it wasn't easy. After we had worked off a little steam, he put me down and grabbed my hand and we started to run toward the arroyo.

High above our heads, ponderosa pine and Douglas fir raised green fingers toward the clouds; but if there had ever been water in this narrow canyon it had dried up long ago. The spiny leaves of yucca and cholla cactus jutted out from ledges on the rocky walls. At first that was all I could see. I was looking for a pueblo, like the one Joe and Edna had found, or perhaps for a cave. I was convinced that Hank's great disovery must be an archaeological site of some sort, and a cave was a good bet; the Anasazi didn't live in caves, but their remote ancestors did. Sandia Cave, in New Mexico, was one of the first places to yield the sequence of early prehistoric hunting cultures.

I saw no caves, and no pueblos; only ragged rocks. We had slowed to a walk; like me, Tom was staring from one side to the other, as if he expected to see a Martian pop its head out of a hole. There was not the slightest trace of a human presence, not even a beer can.

Then I saw it. I don't think I would have noticed it if I had not seen so many other similar shapes, many of them embedded, as this was, in rock that was virtually the same shade of brownish tan. That's what fossils are— rocks. Once-living tissue, turned to stone by the slow passage of millennia.

Tom and I were still holding hands. I dug in my heels and dragged him to a stop.

"Lift me," I said.

"What?"

"Lift me! No, wait. Kneel down. I want to stand on your shoulders."

No wonder I was beginning to like that man. He could exchange insults and wisecracks with the best of them, but when action was necessary, he moved. After one look at my intent face, he dropped to one knee and helped me climb onto his shoulders. I clutched his hair as he rose

239

carefully to his feet; then he held my ankles and I stood up, steadying myself against the canyon wall.

Even then the bones were several feet above my upraised hands. But they were bones, all right—the biggest bones I had ever seen, considerably larger than any of the fossils I had studied. Mammoth bones. . . . All mammalian bones have certain features in common. Unless I had wasted my hours of study, these were leg bones —femurs. Lying right next to one of them, still partially embedded, was a beautifully fluted stone point.

The find was exciting enough right there. Prehistorians have found several sites with mammoth bones and the hunting points of early man, but they aren't common. Any university in the country would consider this find worth investigating. Mammoths have been extinct for a good many centuries; according to the carbon-14 dating method, the mammoths slaughtered by Folsom man go back to about 10,000 B.C.

No wonder Hank had been so amused at the mention of dragons. When the first fossils of giant extinct animals were discovered, learned European scholars had solemnly declared them to be the remains of mythological monsters. They were dinosaur bones, reptiles, not mammals, and millions of years older than the hairy mammoths contemporary with prehistoric man; but all the giant extinct animals have formed the matter of legends.

I was about to direct my human ladder to let me down when I saw something else. It was just a dusty curve of rock, a little rounder and smoother than the rocks around it; and if I had not spent months looking at and touching similar curves, I might not have seen it.

My breath literally stopped. I told myself my eyes must be playing tricks on me, but when I stretched as high as

I could—producing a grunt of protest from Tom—the shape did not change. It looked like a skull—a human skull.

I don't know whether I can explain in a few words what that meant. I know I can't possibly convey the surge of wonder that gripped me.

As I have said, we have found a number of the sites where the American hunters of the Pleistocene Era slaughtered their prey. Scholars call this the "Big-Game Hunting tradition," and it's a good name; the animals these men killed with their fluted flint blades were mammoths and camels and giant bison. It wasn't quite like the mental pictures you might have, though—the great hairy beast, bigger than the largest elephant, trumpeting and stamping as the intrepid warriors rush in to stab it with their puny stone weapons. Probably the beasts which were slaughtered and eaten on the spot were old and weak, or young and weak, or disabled in some way. Even so, it took courage for naked men to attack a wandering mountain of steaks and roasts. Before the 1920's American prehistorians would have denied it ever happened. In fact, they would have denied that men lived in the Americas as early as the era of the mammoths. Then a wandering cowboy spotted some fossil bones with a lance point right in among them. American prehistory had to be revised. Other finds followed.

But—and this is the reason why my breath was still coming quickly, why I doubted the evidence of my own eyes—nowhere had excavators found human bones to go with the lance points of Clovis and Folsom man. It's not surprising that they would fail to do so; ancient men hunted in packs, like dogs. If one of them fell under the tusks or the trampling feet, his comrades would probably carry his body away for burial. Yet if my eyes were not playing tricks on me, some Paleolithic warrior had never found a proper grave. There was the rounded curve of his stony skull.

Hank had made a find, all right. Scholars jeered at him, but he knew enough to realize what he had found, and to know he needed a certified "bone man"—me. Dragons couldn't have been more exciting.

Chapter Twelve

I was brought back to reality by a groan from Tom.

"Aren't you about through up there?"

"What? Oh. Yes, you can let me down."

He returned me to terra firma and then stepped back to have a look himself.

"Looks like bones," he said. "Mammoth?"

"Tom," I said. "I think there's a human skull up there."

For a classical archaeologist he caught on quickly. As I had recently realized, he had been studying on his own;

he probably knew as much about the subject as I did. It's marvelous to communicate with someone who shares your field, who doesn't require long laborious explanations. When I mentioned the skull, Tom's face took on the same look of wonder I felt on my own.

"Are you sure?"

"Not absolutely. But I definitely saw a flint point among the mammoth bones. Brace yourself for company. When I report to Bancroft, this place will be swarming with anthropologists."

Tom nodded. We stood staring up at the insignificant-looking gray lumps that held so much promise; and finally Tom said in a peculiar voice, "Then this is Hank's great discovery."

"It's as great as a discovery can get," I said, in surprise. "And I don't blame him for wanting to keep quiet about it until someone verified it. If he had announced he had discovered the bones of Folsom or Clovis man, scholars like Bancroft would have laughed it off as another of Hank's hoaxes. The only thing I don't get is why he wanted that damned magnetometer. The bones are right there in plain sight; wind and rain and running water must have uncovered them. . . ."

"Forget the magnetometer. Hank is gadget happy; he'll snatch at any excuse to play with a new machine. The thing I don't understand is why anyone would commit mayhem to keep this site from being investigated."

"Oh." I was still excited, but as the first feeling of awe subsided I realized, with shame, that I had forgotten our major purpose in coming here. Then I said, "Oh!" again, in another tone, and grabbed Tom's arm. "Tom, this does provide a motive. What wouldn't Joe more rare. These pieces have additional value because of their age. I figure some tribe hid its entire collection up there when they were under attack, by Spaniards or by later white predators. Or maybe it was a ceremonial deposit. Turquoise was sacred, and it was sometimes buried in the kivas as offerings to the gods."

"So this is why Hank was kidnapped," I said. "Why I wasn't supposed to find the mammoth bones. Why, this whole area will be swarming with people before long; they'll explore every crack in the cliffs looking for more fossils—"

"You're slow, but you're sure," Tom said. "Damn it, I knew there must be something else out here besides archaeological remains. The kidnappers needed time to clear out the cache. It's impossible to work for long in that hole. It's filled with stinking dust that billows up at the slightest touch and makes breathing very hard. The ceiling is low and unstable; looks as if part of it had collapsed recently. We won't be able to get to the far end without doing some extensive digging and shoring up."

I held out my hand. Tom opened his fingers and poured a stream of moving blue into my palm.

"Talk about dragons," I said. "Traditionally the guardians of buried treasure. . . ."

"That's not the half of it," Tom said. "I know turquoise fairly well, and I don't recognize this variety. There may be a mine around here somewhere. If the rest of the ore is of this quality. . . ."

"You are too smart to live," said a voice.

I spun around, dropping the beads. Tom grabbed me by the shoulders.

"Stand still," he said. "He'll shoot if you move. What

248

Stockwell give to announce a find like this, and claim it for his own discovery?"

Again I was glad of Tom's quick, trained mind. Some people, like Sheriff Walsh, might find it hard to believe a man would commit assault and battery and kidnapping over a pile of brown bones. I didn't have to convince Tom. He knew that a lure like this one could twist some peoples' moral sense faster than gold.

"We keep coming back to Joe and Edna," he muttered. "First opportunity, and now motive. . . . Damn it, D.J., some part of my mind just doesn't believe it."

"If we rule out the crackpots, they are the only people in the house who did have the opportunity. Yesterday and the day before they vanished early in the morning and were gone the whole day. Together they could handle Hank; Edna is a lot stronger than she looks, she's spent her whole life acting as a pack mule for Joe. People like that, who have practically no imagination, and no sense of humor, are able to justify any terrible action to themselves. I can just see Joe pointing out to Edna that Hank doesn't deserve to find a prize like this."

"I don't doubt his callousness; I doubt his guts," Tom said.

I didn't mean to, but I couldn't help glancing at his bruised jaw, which had assumed a pretty purple shade by this time. A wave of angry red went over his face. "I owe him one," he said. "I wasn't ready for that, and besides—"

"You weren't yourself," I agreed. "I think Joe and Edna are prime suspects, and I suggest we get back to the house and give them the third degree. I will guarantee to break Edna in fifteen minutes. I can always hypnotize her."

"I guess you're right. We'll rest for a few minutes before we start back; it's going to be a long walk." He added

245

sarcastically, "Have a bite to keep your strength up. Unless you've eaten all the food."

I hadn't, of course. There was still half a sandwich and a cherry tart left.

I applied myself to this scanty snack and to the canteen, still bemused by the discovery and by our prospects of locating Hank. Instead of sitting down, as he had suggested I do, Tom prowled like a big cat, peering into cracks in the rock and pushing bushes aside. I couldn't imagine what he was looking for. It seemed to me that we had already succeeded beyond our wildest hopes.

I was eating the cherry tart when I looked up and realized he had disappeared.

I leaped to my feet, scattering cherries in all directions. "Tom!"

"Here." His voice came rumbling back, weirdly amplified and distorted.

"Where are you?" I screamed.

"Here."

That wasn't much help, since he didn't show himself. I started running in the only possible direction—toward the end of the arroyo we had not yet explored.

A smaller side canyon opened out of the first one—a baby, miniature canyon. The first interesting sight I beheld were Tom's boots sticking out of the side of the cliff, rather like the mammoth bones, only lower down.

"What the hell are you doing?" I shouted angrily.

The boots kicked, groping for a foothold. They were eventually followed by the rest of Tom. He slid down to the floor of the canyon, accompanied by a regular hail of loose rock. I threw up my arm to protect my face.

"For God's sake stop yelling," he said, as I opened my mouth to expostulate with him. "There's material for a

246

dozen avalanches up there, and the rock is dang[...] loose."

"So I noticed. I suppose that's why you were c[...] into holes—such convenient places to be buried [...] there was a rock fall."

Tom's reply was an imbecilic grin. He was, if pos[...] even dirtier than he had been, and a pungent, pe[...] smell had been added to his other charms. Sweat tra[...] runnels through the caked dust on his face; his arms [...] bleeding from innumerable small scratches; and he [...] grinning like a happy idiot. He held out a clenched fist [...] slowly folded his fingers back.

For a moment I thought he was showing me Han[...] turquoise. Then I realized that this one was bigger a[...] rougher, and that the color was subtly different. But it ha[...] the same sensuous glow—that elusive quality calle[...] "zat."

"Up there?" I gurgled, pointing.

Tom opened his other hand. The cupped palm was [...] filled with small beads of the same glowing blue. They [...] had been pierced, as if for stringing.

"I spotted the big one halfway up, as if it had fallen from somebody's pocket," Tom said. "The beads were loose, on the floor of the cave. There used to be bats in there; the floor is knee deep in droppings."

"But what are they?" I stirred the handful of beads with a respectful finger. "They aren't just nuggets; they've been worked. How did they get there?"

"Buried treasure, my girl." Tom's breathing was fast and ragged. He inhaled deeply, trying to calm himself. "People think of gold and silver when they talk of treasure, sure. Do you know how much turquoise is worth today, even the raw ore? The top quality is getting more and

247

a damn-fool stupid jackass I am! I should have known he wouldn't believe me . . . that he'd follow. . . ."

He had Tom's gun. Tom told me that later; you couldn't have proved it by me at the time since, one, I had never seen the weapon the kidnapper had stolen from Tom, and, two, when a gun is pointing at me I do not notice details, only that round black hole. I was surprised to see him, but I wasn't surprised to see who he was, if you follow that distinction. I had been too bemused to think logically, but my mind had begun working on that term "buried treasure" as soon as Tom pronounced it. He had suspected for some time, apparently.

"I hadn't planned to commit murder," Jesse went on in an irritated voice. "It's stupid and inefficient. But you leave me no choice. If you hadn't figured out about the mine, I might have been able to clear out this cache tonight and tomorrow. However, I can't persuade Hank to lease me a piece of his property if he knows there is turquoise on it. So you two will have to go."

"I'm not ready to go," I protested.

Jesse smiled, flashing those pretty white teeth. For a moment my mind reeled with disbelief. He looked so normal and handsome and pleasant standing there, lightly balanced on top of one of the big boulders at the base of the cliff. He hadn't followed us, he had been here all along. He didn't care where we went so long as we didn't find this place.

During all the hours when I had assumed he had been searching for Hank he had been working to remove the treasure. No doubt he had been delayed by the conditions Tom had described, and by the inaccessibility of the site; it would take him hours to get here, and his actual working time wouldn't be very long. He had probably been working when he heard us coming; we had not bothered to lower our voices. Scrambling out of the cave into a place of concealment, he had dropped the stone that had alerted Tom to the location of the cave. If we had left well enough alone, and had been satisfied with the mammoth bones, he would have let us go.

"You would have to be so smart," I said bitterly to Tom.

"My sentiments exactly," Jesse said. "I'm really sorry, D.J. I did my best to keep you away from this place. It's your own fault. If Tom hadn't put me out of action yesterday, I might have finished my work before you found it."

"You drugged Jesse?" I turned my head to glare at Tom. His hard grip on my shoulders kept me from moving anything except my head.

"I used his own sleeping pills," Tom said. "Found them in his room when I searched it a few days ago. He had all sorts of goodies stashed away."

"Like the uppers he put in my drink." Now that I looked back, I could have kicked myself for being so obtuse. So many little things should have told me the truth. Jesse had been the obvious suspect all along.

"I thought if I put him out of the way for a while, we could at least be sure he wasn't committing any murders," Tom said.

"Like so many good ideas, it backfired," Jesse said.

"You've been awfully slow about this," I complained. "Why has it taken you so long to get the treasure out?"

"Obviously because I didn't find it until a few days ago. I followed Hank here on his last trip. I thought maybe he had really found something valuable. Was I disgusted when I saw him drooling over those damned bones! After he left, it struck me that the fanged rock was similar to

250

one that is mentioned in an old legend. The story of the Sinagua turquoise has been dismissed as fiction, like so many of the treasure stories of the Southwest. Most modern students of the subject have forgotten it, but I had come across an old book published in 1746 which referred to it. So I started poking around."

He went on talking, getting more and more interested in his story, and more and more pleased with his own cleverness. I had noticed that trait of his before.

As I listened, feigning fascinated interest in order to postpone the moment when he would turn his attention to more practical issues, I realized that Tom's fingers were trying to tell me something, squeezing my shoulders in a slow rhythmic pattern. I hoped it wasn't Morse code. I do not know Morse code—except for SOS, of course, and while that phrase was appropriate, it wasn't a particularly pertinent message for Tom to be sending me.

His left hand pressed harder on me than his right. I thought I understood what that meant. Maybe it was ESP again, but probably it was just common sense. If Jesse was going to shoot us, there was no reason for us to stand still and make it easy for him. If Tom jumped in one direction and I went the other way. . . . There were lots of rocks to hide behind. It wasn't a very good idea, but it was the only chance we had.

I nodded vigorously, to show I understood. That was a mistake; the back of my head hit Tom's chin, so that he bit his tongue and squawked with pain. Jesse stopped talking about the lost mine of the Sinaguans.

"I am wasting time, aren't I?" he said. "Thanks for reminding me. I guess you get it first, D.J., unless you want to change places. No use hiding behind a woman's skirts, Tom; when she falls I'll have a clear shot at you."

"I wouldn't risk it," Tom said. "If they find our bodies, with bullet holes—"

"They'll never find your bodies. There are a million ready-made graves around here." Jesse jumped lightly down off the rock and started toward us. It occurred to me that we ought to make our move before he got any closer, and the same thought must have occurred to Tom. His left hand grabbed my shoulder and shoved.

I staggered off to the side, not trying too hard to keep my balance; it is natural instinct to hug the ground if something is coming at you, such as bullets, and I figured I could crawl as fast as I could run in that terrain. I was vaguely aware of a moving brown blur—Tom—going fast in the opposite direction. Then the gun went off. My God, what a noise! I almost died of sheer terror, but I kept moving, scuttling like a crab toward the nearest crevice and expecting at any second to feel pain, blood. . . .

Two more shots reverberated, ricocheting back and forth between the narrow walls. I was in my crevice by then, rather wishing I were not, since there didn't seem to be any way out of it. I wondered if my ears had gone bad. The echoes of the last shot didn't die away; instead they seemed to be increasing. As they rose in volume, they were challenged by a couple of loud, human cries. One voice sounded like Tom's. I concluded that he had been hit, and like the fool that I sometimes am, I started to crawl out of my hole. I didn't get far. A boulder the size of my head bounced and splattered, not three feet from my inquiring nose. I ducked and closed my eyes. Fragments stung my forehead and grazed my cheek. Then the heavens fell. I crouched back, my arms folded over my face, my knees bent, trying to retreat into the womb of the rock, while the cliffs rained down.

252

It seemed an eternity before the echoes finally faded into silence. I lifted my head and looked out over my forearms. Then I heard Tom's voice. He was whispering. I could see his point; one landslide a day is enough.

"D.J. Where are you? Answer me—darling, it's all right, he's gone. . . . For God's sake, D.J., if you can speak. . . . Just groan, or curse, or—"

I wasn't unaware of what he was saying, but I was in no state to be particularly moved by it. I had other things on my mind.

"I'm here," I said, in a squeak.

"Where?" Tom came trotting into the range of my vision. His shirt was torn to ribbons and blood streamed down his face.

"Here," I said, not moving. "Hi, there."

"What an idiotic thing to say." Tom caught sight of me curled in my shell; he extended a long arm and dragged me out. "There's blood on your face," he said.

It was just a trickle, from a cut over my eye, but he made it worse by smearing it with his dirty fingers, mumbling agitatedly as he did so; then he wrapped his arms around me and kissed me.

It wasn't one of the world's greatest kisses. Barbara C. wouldn't have thought it worth mentioning. But I liked it, even if it did taste like mud and smell like bats. I dissolved into a limp mass of acquiescent protoplasm, and Tom had to shake me a couple of times to start my lungs working again.

"Brace up," he said briskly. "We've got to get the hell out of here."

I guess it hadn't been much of an avalanche. I had expected to find the landscape transformed, unrecognizable. It looked pretty much the same except that there were a lot more rocks lying around.

"Where's Jesse?" I asked, hoping to see a boot or a hand sticking out from under a pile of rock.

"Gone. The rocks knocked the gun out of his hand; probably damaged him some, he was favoring one arm and limping when he took off. I tried to get to him, but he's not so stupid; he knew he couldn't take me barehanded."

I allowed him the boast; he was entitled to it. No wonder he was so banged up. While I was trying to burrow into the ground, he was charging through a rain of boulders trying to catch a killer. I was very moved. As usual in those situations, my brain and my mouth lost touch with each other, and I said something stupid.

"Is there anything left to eat?"

Tom turned me around and swatted me on the behind. It was a good, solid smack, so I concluded that he didn't feel as bad as he looked.

"Feeding time for the animals comes later. Jesse's little scheme has blown up in his face, and God knows what he'll do now. We've got to head him off and find Hank."

Well, I didn't see how we could, since we didn't know where he was going, but I could not argue with Super-Archaeologist, the scourge of criminals. I was so worked up I would have headed straight out of there without even stopping to collect our gear. Tom had better sense. The remnants of the food and drink went into one backpack now. He kicked the empty one aside and started to heave the full one onto his shoulders.

While he had been working I had gotten a good look at him, and I realized that his version of the avalanche had not been entirely accurate. At some point in the proceedings he must have fallen, because his back looked as if it had passed through a grater. I grabbed the pack from him and slipped into it.

"You don't need this," I said. "Get moving. I'll try to keep up."

If the journey out had been a nightmare, the return trip was indescribable. It couldn't have taken nearly as long; Tom had a compass and apparently knew how to use it, so we went by the straightest possible route. But that word "straight" has no meaning out there, unless it is used in phrases like "straight up and down." Twice we had to retrace our steps when we found ourselves in cul de sacs of natural rock, and we did more climbing than I would ordinarily have permitted. It wouldn't have been quite so bad if we had not been in such a frantic hurry. Jesse had had several minutes' start, and he knew the way. He was gaining on us every moment. The need for haste was like a sickness, churning in my stomach, weakening my muscles. Tom must have felt it too, but he moved with a deliberation that made me want to scream with impatience. This was a case of make haste slowly, though, and under my panic, I knew it. A single misstep could have resulted in a fall, broken bones, and further delay. I don't ever want to do anything like that again.

By the time we reached the top of the canyon with the stream running through it we had finished all our water, drinking on the run, and my throat felt like one of the dustier arroyos. We stopped just long enough to drink from the stream; then we plunged down the slope, pebbles rolling away from under our boots.

I threw myself across the fender of the jeep and patted the rough, hot surface fondly. All during that awful hike I had been tormented by the fear that it wouldn't be there.

Tom had been suspicious too. He took time to check the tires and look under the hood before he started the engine.

"Brakes?" I suggested, settling myself in the front seat. I have never been able to understand why the heroes in those chase stories don't notice there is something wrong with the brakes until they hit the steepest part of the mountain road. Don't they ever stop at stop signs, or before they pull out onto the highway?

The brakes were all right. Evidently Jesse had taken another route out of the canyon. If he had passed this way, he wouldn't have left us a serviceable vehicle.

At least now we could call the police. Hank had been missing for several days, and Walsh must be getting a little uneasy. He would be in trouble if he interfered with Hank when Hank didn't need help, but he would be in worse trouble if disaster resulted from his failure to take action. Our story should convince him; Jesse had made a flat-out confession, and we had both heard him. Even if Jesse got away this time, they would probably catch up with him sooner or later. He wasn't the type to turn over a new leaf and hide himself in a life of honest labor.

But we couldn't let him get away. The crux of the problem was not catching Jesse, it was finding Hank, and we couldn't do one without the other. I could have cursed myself for letting Jesse ramble on about his treasure hunt, when a carefully aimed question might have prompted him to brag about what he had done with Hank. He had said he hadn't planned to commit murder. That must mean Hank was still alive. But where? Jesse might just run off and leave him, in which case he wouldn't be alive long —hidden somewhere, drugged or tied up, without food or water. . . .

256

Or Jesse might head straight for the place where he had concealed Hank, hoping to use him as a hostage to buy his freedom. Nasty as that situation could be, it was one I hoped would ensue. Otherwise our chances of locating Hank in time were slim indeed. We could probably talk the sheriff into forming a search party now. Juan and Debbie would help; even Joe and Edna would lend a hand —they couldn't refuse, not after what had happened. They should be back at the ranch by now. The working day was long over. The sinking sun sent long purple shadows across the ground and lit the eastern mountains with a coppery glow. It would be dark in a few more hours. Getting an official search underway would take time, and you can't search in the dark. . . .

I turned toward Tom, meaning to ask him if he couldn't go a little faster. When I saw the way his jaw was set I closed my mouth. He had more devils at his back than I did; I knew he was berating himself for muffing his guard duties, and for failing to get his hands on Jesse this last time. God knows he had done his best on both occasions, but guilt is usually the least logical of all emotions.

When we reached the house he rushed in, leaving the front door open. I set the brake, which he had neglected to do, and followed, more slowly. Now that we had reached our immediate goal, my mind had blanked out. I couldn't think what to do first. So I followed Tom. His footsteps thundered up the uncarpeted central stairs and along the corridor.

He was in Jesse's room when I caught up with him. He glanced at me over his shoulder.

"We did it," he said. "We beat him back. He hasn't been here. I'm going to call Walsh. See if you can locate Debbie."

Still enveloped in a web of fatigue and confusion, I watched him run off. I propped myself against the door-jamb and examined the room. The maids had straightened it; the bed was made, the wastepaper baskets were empty. Tom had left the closet door ajar, and I could see rows of shirts and coats hanging. He was probably right; Jesse might not have stopped to pack, but if he had returned to the house, to pick up belongings he felt he couldn't live without, he'd have left traces.

I couldn't share Tom's enthusiasm about this. Maybe I was suffering a reaction, but I felt limp and depressed. We had no reason to assume Jesse planned to come back here. He might have clothes and money stashed away else-where. Unless he chose to communicate with us, bartering Hank's life for immunity, I didn't think we had the ghost of a chance of catching up with him now.

Tears of fatigue and frustration filled my eyes. I thought of Hank greeting me that first time, his eyes as blue as the turquoise he wore with such innocent pleasure, and his anxious greeting: "No problems?" I thought of him hiding behind a pillar in the patio, fussed and embarrassed without his pants, and of the way he handled the sick animals. I thought of the bracelet he had tried to give me—one of his treasures. The tears spilled over and ran down my cheeks.

I didn't want anyone to catch me snuffling like a baby, so I went into Jesse's room and closed the door and stood there mopping my face on my sleeve till I got control of myself. My eyes were still tearing from all the sand I had rubbed into them; I went to the bathroom, hoping to remove the signs of woe so Tom wouldn't find out what a weakling I was.

The cold water was like a shot in the arm. I splashed it

over all the exposed parts of me and toweled myself dry. The towel was a mess by the time I finished, with an impression of my face in brown mud.

My mother did her best to bring me up right. One of the things she tried to teach me was not to put wet towels in hampers. I still do it, though. Everybody does, except mothers. Quite automatically I lifted the lid of Jesse's hamper. I was about to add my towel to the heap of clothes within when I realized that the stains on the topmost article—a crumpled khaki shirt—were bright red.

I lifted it out and held it up, like in one of those stupid soap commercials. "Greasy dirt. . . ." This wasn't grease. It was blood, and it was still wet.

So Jesse had been hurt in the landslide—and badly, or he wouldn't have bled all the way back to the house. The damage had not been bad enough to slow him up much, however; he had arrived before we did, and he had had sense enough to keep signs of his presence to a minimum.

There were bloodstained towels in the hamper too. I stood there holding them, my mind racing. He couldn't have been gone long, the stains were still fresh.

My first impulse was to rush out, shouting for Tom. My second impulse canceled the first; and I still maintain, in spite of what resulted, that it was a rational decision. All our senseless rushing around had led to a series of spectacular near misses. Now, of all times, it behooved me to think sensibly.

Jesse might simply have walked into the house and walked out again; no one had any reason to stop him. But he couldn't be sure of that. We might have reached the house before he did, and alerted the others. There must have been something in his room that he needed badly, or he wouldn't have risked coming. Surely he would minimize that risk by choosing a more inconspicuous route than the front door.

I dropped the towel on the floor and went to the window. It really wasn't a window, it was a set of French doors; like almost every other room in the house, this one had its own balcony. It was framed in wrought iron; the door handles and hinges were of the same metal. No traces showed against the black, but when I touched the outside handle, it felt sticky.

The courtyard below lay silent and peaceful in the evening light. The fountain in the center was formed of faded Mexican tiles in a pattern of blue and cream. Graveled paths shaped a hexagon around it, with flowering shrubs and flower beds. Jesse must have come through the arched gateway opposite and climbed up to his room . . . how?

A glance to the left gave me the answer. There were two other balconies on this side of the patio. From one of them, a charming little iron staircase twisted down to ground level. The balconies rested on the roof of the columned loggia that ran along this side of the courtyard. It would be a simple matter to step over the railing of one balcony onto the next.

All this speculation and investigation really had not taken much time—not more than a minute or two. I was about to go back and report, having learned as much as I could at the moment, when something hit me like a bolt of lightning. Why it should choose that moment to do so I can't imagine; I suppose the idea had been boiling around in my mind for days, and it suddenly came together.

The balcony next to Jesse's must be Edna's. The Stockwells had rooms on this corridor. I had always known that; if I have not mentioned it, it is because the fact didn't seem important. Now. . . .

Now I remembered the way Edna looked at Jesse, and his courteous, almost tender manner with her; her unaccountable tears and distress the night I had suggested Hank might be in danger, her vigorous denial of that self-evident fact. . . . Jesse had a helper. Two people had been involved in the attack on Tom.

I was over the balcony railing and onto Edna's balcony in less time than it takes to describe the act. I admit I wasn't thinking clearly. I was so enraged at the idea that the clue to Hank's whereabouts might have been so accessible all the time, in that brachycephalic skull of Edna's. I had no proof, of course, but I was in no mood to worry about a little thing like that. Time was of the essence now. At this very moment Jesse might be on his way to the place where Hank was hidden. If we could get there first. . . .

The draperies were shut and the French doors were closed. I threw myself against them, in the approved heroic style, fully expecting them to be locked. They weren't. The doors burst open and I plunged into the room.

They made a pretty tableau—the wounded man and his tender nurse. Jesse was seated in a chair, his arm extended, and Edna was wrapping bandages about it, just above the elbow.

I stood there clutching the desk that had stopped my impetuous forward progress and stared at them, and they stared back at me. I don't know which of us was more surprised, but I guess I was. I may not think sensibly all the time, but I assure you I would not have rushed into that room if I had had the slightest idea Jesse would still be there.

The mere fact that Edna was tending the wounded did

not prove her complicity. Jesse was an expert liar. But if I had had any doubts about her, her sudden pallor and cry of alarm would have removed them. I've seen pictures of convicted mass murderers who looked no guiltier.

I hesitated for a fatal instant, trying to decide which path of retreat to take. Not that it would have made any difference. They could have grabbed me while I was trying to climb the balcony rail, and the door to the hall was locked. And by the time I had made up my mind that neither method was going to work, Jesse had picked up a gun and pointed it at me.

That was what he had come back for—his weapon. He had lost Tom's in the landslide. Naturally he would have a gun of his own; he was as immersed in his own fantasies as were the other crazies. A rough-tough Western prospector has to be prepared for pesky redskins and coyotes and bushwhackers, doesn't he?

"You damned fool," Jesse said to his beloved, "I told you to lock the door."

"I did," Edna bleated, wringing her hands. She had dropped the roll of bandage; it trailed like a long white worm.

"I meant the balcony doors, too, you cretin. Finish what you were doing. I can't run around dragging bandages behind me."

Unfortunately, it was his left arm that had been hurt. His right was functioning perfectly; the muzzle of the gun was aimed straight at my stomach.

Edna obeyed him, though her hands were shaking so badly she could hardly use them.

I had thought of a few epithets too—for both of them —but I decided this was the time to be tactful.

"Why don't we make a deal?" I suggested, in my most

262

ingratiating voice. "You're stuck this time, Jesse. Tell me where Hank is and I'll let you get away."

"You'll let *me* get away?" For a moment his face was so ugly I thought my last moment had come. Then he laughed. "You're something, D.J."

I do not think too well with a gun pointing at me, but despite the panicky fluttering of sheer physical terror, I knew I was in no immediate danger. I had stupidly provided Jesse with a hostage. He wouldn't shoot me if he could help it because he needed me to get out of the house. At any moment Tom would realize I was gone, and he would come looking for me.

Even as the thought passed through my mind, I heard the uproar begin. Tom must have gone back to Jesse's room and found the bloodstained items I had scattered around the bathroom; even through that thick door I could hear the urgency in his voice as he shouted my name.

I debated briefly as to whether I should risk answering him. Jesse read my mind.

"Don't do it," he said. "I'd rather not kill you just yet, but I wouldn't mind blowing off a few of your fingers. I can do it. I'm an excellent shot."

So that settled that point. Jesse went on, "Tie her hands, Edna. Hurry up. They are starting to search the house."

Edna had finished tucking in the end of the bandage, and had risen to her feet. Jesse's suggestion made her shy back like a nervous horse.

"You come near me, Edna, and I'll give you such a crack," I said pleasantly.

Edna started to back toward the French doors. Jesse swore.

"Do what you're told, you stupid bitch. How can she

hurt you when I've got a gun on her? Use that roll of tape."

The noise outside was increasing. Tom was bellowing, feet were running up and down, doors were opening and slamming. . . . Edna sidled toward me. Then she jumped a good six inches as something banged against her door and the knob began to rattle.

"Edna, are you there?" Tom called. "Open the door. Have you seen D.J.? Answer me, damn it!"

Jesse let out a string of curses that would have curled my mother's silvery hair. He got up and advanced on me, shoving Edna out of the way as he passed her. She stumbled and fell to the floor, staring at him incredulously.

I looked from the door, which was quivering as Tom kicked it, to the big black hole at the end of the gun, which was getting closer and closer and. . . . I was so preoccupied with this particular sight I didn't even see Jesse's fist; but I felt it. It was the last thing I did feel for some time.

II

When I woke up I was staring straight up into a bank of fluorescent lights, bright as the sun. It was a better view than the last one I had seen, but it hurt my eyes. I closed them and lay still, trying to sort things out.

I didn't need my eyes to know where I was. The animal smell was pervasive. The animals were restless; a cacophony of howls and growls and barks and meows assaulted my ears. They say animals are aroused by the odor of human fear. If that is true, they had good cause. I was scared enough to rouse a whole zoo.

I was lying on my back, with a hard lump of discomfort localized in the middle of my spine—my own hands, tied behind me. The tile floor wasn't particularly comfortable either, and my jaw hurt. I turned my head away from the light and opened one eye.

As I had suspected, Jesse was close by. I could see his feet right next to my head. He was kneeling by a window, between two sets of cages, and as I opened the other eye, to get a better view, he called out to someone.

"Where's that car? You've got five more minutes before I blow D.J.'s right hand to splinters."

"Oh, Lord," I said involuntarily.

Jesse turned his head toward me. Over his left shoulder, I could see the animal in the cage beyond. It was a large brown rodent of some kind, with protruding teeth that were bared in an agitated snarl, and it looked a lot pleasanter than Jesse did. He bared his teeth at me too.

"Awake, are you? It's about time. If you didn't eat so damned much, I could have gotten out of here."

"Oh, really?" I said, delighted to hear it.

Ordinarily I resent insults about my weight, but this time I didn't mind. I only wished I weighed two hundred pounds instead of a mere. . . . Never mind. Jesse must have headed for the garage, with me draped over his shoulder, after dropping me off the balcony. . . . Yes, there was a sore spot, in just about the appropriate area. With my weight slowing him down, he was unable to make it to the garage before the hue and cry headed him off, so he had holed up in the animal hospital. Now they had him cornered and he was bargaining for an escape vehicle, with me as the means of barter. It was not the nicest situation to find oneself in, but I preferred it to being out in the desert alone with Jesse.

I rolled over on my side and tried to sit up. The rat growled at me and so did Jesse.

265

"Don't try any heroics," he said, waving the gun at me.

"Not me," I assured him.

It was dark night outside the window, but the dark was crisscrossed by beams of light and I could hear voices.

"Four minutes," Jesse shouted.

After a moment another voice replied.

"No deal until I see that D.J. is all right."

Jesse grabbed me by the hair and yanked me to my feet. I yelled.

"Did you hear that?" Jesse called. "You'll hear worse if that car isn't here in three minutes."

He pushed me in front of the window. A chorus of voices greeted my appearance. I heard Debbie call out, and a wordless shout from Tom; but one voice rose above the others and when I heard it I almost dropped.

"Hi, there, honey. Any problems?"

"Hank!" I screamed. "Hank, are you all right?"

Jesse put his hand on the top of my head and shoved me back down onto the floor. I didn't resist. It may sound absurd, but I was no longer afraid. The mere sound of that booming, confident voice, with its ridiculous question, removed all my fears. "Any problems?" Well, yes, I did have a few; but so long as Hank was okay, they were minor. Jesse must have abandoned poor old Edna, and of course she had talked the minute anyone pressured her. She would. She was a pitiful mess anyhow, and after the way Jesse had treated her, she had no reason to protect him. I wondered why he hadn't silenced her. He must have realized that he had lost the game anyway; the best thing he could hope for now was to get away himself.

I squirmed out from under his hand.

"You know," I said conversationally, "you aren't in

such bad shape, Jesse; you haven't killed anybody yet. Why spoil your record?"

Jesse mouthed something at me. His words were drowned by a yowl from the big cat at the other end of the room. I think he said "shut up." The words didn't matter. His expression conveyed his sentiments clearly enough.

I subsided into a squatting position, feeling considerably subdued. My first optimism had passed and I realized that my position was not too good. The look on Jesse's face had told me something I had not realized before. He really hated me. I guess he blamed me for his failure, which wasn't really fair; Tom had had a great deal to do with it too. But I was here and Tom was not. I reappraised my chances of survival in the light of this new knowledge, and the conclusion depressed me.

Jesse would take me with him, if and when he got the car he was demanding. I could count on staying alive, if not healthy, just so long as the pursuit kept up with us. But if he ever succeeded in losing the others, I became an encumbrance. I had a feeling Jesse would deal efficiently and ruthlessly with encumbrances. Besides, he obviously didn't like me very much. Even if he didn't kill me, there were a lot of other unpleasant things he could do to me while I was with him.

Obviously it would be nice if I could get away from him. I glanced longingly around the room, what I could see of it. We were tucked into an alcove between the cages; I could see only the animals next to us and the ones across the aisle. A raccoon, a skunk, a couple of rabbits, a squirrel. . . . Not much help there. The raccoon was pacing back and forth in the cage mumbling to itself—or whatever raccoons do.

267

I was sitting there racking my brain for an idea, any old idea, when there was a change in the quality of the noises in the room. The animals were obviously disturbed by the change in routine and by the presence of strangers. They were banging around in their cages and uttering their varied cries. Now a new sound blended with the others. It wasn't as loud as some of the growls and snarls, and it took me a few seconds to identify it. When I did, the hair on my neck started to rise. The sound was the rusty purr of the mountain lion.

From where I sat I couldn't see the lion's cage, or the door. I wondered why Jesse hadn't selected a spot from which he could watch the door, but I suppose he felt he didn't have to, with me as a hostage.

Jesse glanced at his watch and then rose cautiously to his feet, keeping to one side of the window.

"Time's up," he shouted, with a malevolent look at me. "Where's that car?"

"Here," was the response. "It's coming."

Jesse craned forward. I craned my neck in the opposite direction. Was it only my imagination, or did I hear the soft pad of big heavy furry feet?

It was not my imagination.

I said something like "Awk," and nudged Jesse with my shoulder, since my hands were not available. It was a dumb thing to do. He was so keyed up he would have shot at a shadow. But when he whirled around, with his little gun at the ready, he saw what I had seen—a brownish tan muzzle and a set of whiskers and one slitted eye.

He let off a shot—pure reflex, the target was only a couple of inches square and his hand was none too steady. He missed. The sound of the shot was answered by a bloodcurdling yowl. I tried to squeeze myself into the

268

corner next to a horrified squirrel. I think Jesse had forgotten about me momentarily. I don't care how brave you are, or how many guns you have, there is something about being face to face with a mountain lion. . . .

The lion had emerged from behind the row of cages and was standing squarely in front of the alcove. Its tail was lashing back and forth, and its teeth were bared. Standing beside it, his hand on its neck, was Hank.

Admittedly, he was a magician with animals. But I don't think he would have tried this particular stunt except for one thing. He was stoned. High is not the word for what he was. No wonder his voice had sounded so confident. He was in that brief and blissful state where difficulties fade away and you see only the straight primrose path to your goal. Jesse must have kept him drugged the entire time. There is something to be said for using amphetamines instead of sedatives; the victim is so happy he doesn't want to move.

Hank was still happy. Irrational and happy and also filled with righteous indignation.

"Don't worry, D.J.," he said cheerfully. "He won't hurt you."

The lion growled.

"Get that animal out of here," Jesse said hoarsely. "I'll shoot. I'll shoot it, and D.J., and. . . ." The gun moved as he spoke, from one prospective target to the other. I didn't protest when it swung toward me; it is a moot point as to whether it is better to be shot or eaten by a lion.

"No, no, no," Hank said. "You can't shoot everybody, you know. Not all at once. I doubt if one of those little bullets would stop Albert here. He moves pretty fast. If I take my hand off his neck. . . . Drop the gun, Jesse. Drop it and step out here."

Jesse hesitated. Hank added, in the same soft, sweet voice, "If you made the mistake of hurting D.J., I'd just let go of old Albert. And then I'd stand here and watch."

There was a moment I'll never forget, while Jesse tried to make up his mind. Albert's hindquarters wriggled, the way a cat's does just before it jumps on a mouse. I tried to get in the cage with the squirrel.

Then the gun hit the floor, and Albert settled back on his haunches with a human-sounding sigh of disappointment, and Hank said, "All right, boys, come on in. He's all yours."

III

We were together in the small parlor next to the dining room—Hank and me and Debbie and Tom. I was drinking. I had been drinking ever since they carried me out of the animal house, and my teeth still had a tendency to chatter on the rim of the glass. Doc Parsons had come and gone, the posse had dispersed, the sheriff had gone back to town with his prisoner. The wounded had been tended, and Hank had received an injection to counteract the drugs he had been given. Not that it was easy to tell, with him.

"What I can't understand," he said in mild surprise, "is why you were so scared, D.J. Albert wouldn't hurt a fly unless I told him to."

The rest of us exchanged glances, and Tom tactfully changed the subject.

"What are you going to do about Edna?"

"Why, nothing. That poor girl has gone through enough already. And she did tell you where I was, didn't she?"

"After I slugged her," Debbie said.

"You have all the fun," I complained. "I was so looking forward to hitting Edna."

"She never meant any harm to come to me," Hank insisted. "Jesse told her he just wanted to keep me locked up till he got the turquoise. I never saw his face, you know; never knew, till you guys came for me, who the kidnapper was. There wouldn't have been any trouble getting me to lease him the land where the mine is located. It's wasteland, worthless. I'd have figured he was following up some fool treasure story."

"Is the mine all that valuable?" I asked.

"I guess so," Hank said placidly. "I never knew any of the turquoise was there. I was too interested in the bones. D.J., you aren't mad at me for keeping it a secret, are you? I was afraid you'd laugh and think it was another of my crazy ideas."

"I'm not mad at you for *that*," I said.

"It really is something, isn't it?" Hank said. He looked at me with his big blue eyes, and I relented.

"It is really something," I agreed. "Wait till I tell Bancroft. We'll have him eating crow for the rest of his life."

"That will be great. I owe that guy. I want you to take care of the dig, D.J. Tom has done a little studying these last couple of years; maybe he's learned enough to help you."

I started to object. I mean, modesty is not my strong point, but to handle a dig like that. . . . Then I saw the familiar glint in Hank's eye, and decided this was not the time to argue. It would all work out.

"He might be useful, at that," I said, looking at Tom.

"That's great," Hank said. "Now what I figure is, first we'll—"

"Figure in the morning," Debbie interrupted. "Doc Parsons said you should get some rest. Now don't argue with me; just come quietly."

After a surprised look at her, Hank got meekly to his feet. He towered over her; but as she stood holding him firmly by the arm, her sleek black head barely reaching his shoulder, I had a feeling things were going to work out there, too.

He grinned at me and winked as she led him out. Tom and I sat in silence for a while. He was sprawled in a chair, his long legs stretched out and his eyes half closed as he stared at the flickering flames on the hearth.

"Have those two got something going?" he asked.

"Men are so unobservant," I said.

"Well, I don't know; I just thought he seemed moved when I told him how she went after Edna. I don't blame Edna for squealing on Jesse; I would have too, with a fury like Debbie shoving me around and screaming Indian curses."

"Edna would have cracked at almost any point the last few days," I said. "I saw how edgy she was and never made the connection. I could kick myself for being so obtuse."

"No damage was done, fortunately. She had enough guilt feelings to make sure Hank was taken care of physically, and Jesse stopped by now and then to give him another fistful of pills." Tom grinned. "I think Hank rather enjoyed that part of it. You know we found him in the cellar of one of those abandoned houses in the ghost town? Jesse moved him there, from a cave in the mountains, after we searched the place. Maybe it's just as well I did put the rat out of commission for a day. If he had moved Hank again, to a hiding place Edna didn't know about. . . ."

"He was probably getting disenchanted with Edna," I agreed. "What I don't understand is why you suspected Jesse in the first place."

Tom's eyes shifted in a manner I had seen once or twice before.

"It was obvious," he said, a little too glibly. "You kept saying that Joe and Edna had opportunity because they were strong enough to handle Hank, and knew the area well. The same was true of Jesse, only more so. And I had seen enough of that lad to know his treasure hunting was more than a hobby with him. It was a full-blown obsession. I know people commit crimes for a number of bizarre reasons, but there's nothing like cold hard cash to move a man to violence. I got to thinking, suppose Jesse really has found something out there. . . . After you got the dope in your drink, I searched the house—"

"You did what?"

"You must take me for a fool," Tom said indignantly. "Did you think I was just sitting around here wringing my hands and bleating futile warnings of disaster, like Cassandra? I couldn't report the incident to Hank or to the police without getting you in trouble, but I wasn't about to let some character wander around here with a pocketful of drugs. I've got the combination of that safe in Jesse's room, just as I have all the keys. As soon as I found his supply of drugs, I knew he was my boy. I took a few pills, thinking they might come in handy."

"Why didn't you tell Hank then?" I asked. "You said he hates drugs; he'd have kicked Jesse out, and. . . . Wait, let me figure it. You're just as bad as Hank! You hoped Jesse would try to steal the second magnetometer, so you could catch him in the act and beat him up. You were jealous, that was it."

"That's the most ridiculous thing I ever heard."

"Jealous, jealous, jealous," I said, savoring the word. "Let me tell you, my boy, you had good reason to be. Jesse was *nice* to me. You were insulting and rude. All those cracks about the way I eat. . . . But I forgive you. I even forgive you for being a classical scholar. But you'll have to change fields, officially, before we get married. That would give Dad too great an advantage. Mother would never get over it."

Tom sat up in his chair, his eyes wide.

"What do you mean, your mother would never. . . . No, don't tell me. I don't think I'm strong enough to find out about your crazy family yet. What makes you think we are going to get married?"

"Oh, I think we'd better. Leaving my mother out of it —which is probably a good idea—Hank is pretty conventional. He won't let me help him dig if I'm living in sin."

"Come here," Tom said.

I hesitated. Tom flopped back in the chair, and tried to look feeble.

"I'm a wounded man," he remarked. "I've had a long, hard day."

"*You've* had a hard day?" I said. But I went.

We were sitting there in the big chair when the door opened and Hank's head peered in.

"You're supposed to be in bed," I said, not moving.

"I sneaked out for a minute." Hank came tiptoeing into the room, glancing guiltily over his shoulder. "I just wanted to give you this, D.J. You don't have to be afraid to wear it now."

I took the bracelet and slipped it on my arm.

"Morenci," I said.

"Right."

274

"Thank you, Hank."

"Right."

He turned and tiptoed toward the door. Then he turned.

"No problems?"

"Not a problem in the world," I said.

AUSTIN MEMORIAL LIBRARY
220 S. Bonham
Cleveland, Texas 77327